THE LODGE

DAMIEN MARLOWE

BLACK SWAN
DIGITAL

First published in 2025
Created by Black Swan Digital. Developed by Annie Kenyon.

PROLOGUE

I am the breath in the walls. The whisper that slides beneath the crack of a door. The shadow that flickers in the corner of your eye, gone before you can turn. I am often silent, but I am never still. Always listening. Always watching. And I have been waiting for you.

Do you feel it yet? In the air, the cold that settles not on your skin but somewhere deeper—inside your chest, nestling in your ribs. You may call it unease. I call it a greeting. You are not the first to step inside me, nor will you be the last. I remember all who have come before, their secrets seeping into the marrow of my bones like blood into soil. I know what you've done. I know what you've hidden. I know the lies you tell yourself to keep the darkness at bay. But here, there is no hiding.

I take what you bring to me, and I feed on it. Your anger, your pain, your love turned rancid—I devour it all. And in return, my gift to you, I give you exactly what you fear most: the truth. Not the sanitized version you tell the world and your own reflection, but the blackened thing you bury deep down. The thing you cannot face. I will hold it up to you like a mirror, force you to look, and when you finally shatter under the toll of it, I will take what remains. The most valuable piece of you. I will take your soul.

You will fight me, of course. They always do. At first, you'll tell yourself it's nothing. Just the creak of old floorboards, the moan of the wind through the eaves, the house going to sleep. You'll laugh at the shadows, call them tricks of the light, blame your vivid imagination and too many scary movies when you were a kid. But soon, your laughter will hollow, your nerves will fray, your sleep will fracture, and the walls will begin to close in. That's when I'll show you my true face. The face you've hidden from yourself all this time.

You'll scream. They always scream. But no one will hear you —not here, in my embrace. By the time you realize it's not the house you're afraid of, but the things I've unearthed inside you, it will be too late. Because the truth is this. You didn't come to me by chance. You came because I called you. And you stayed because you belong to me now.

I have no beginning, and I will have no end. People rot and crumble like the walls they build, but I endure. For I am hunger. I am grief. I am the poison you carry within you, and I will never stop feeding on it. The snow may bury me, the winds may howl, but I remain, waiting for the next. And the next. And the next.

Come inside. Shut the door. Let the cold take hold.

You're home now.

1

HARPER

The clinking of crystal glass echoed like tiny screams in my ears. Somewhere near the head table, a woman let out a shrill laugh that cut through the low hum of conversation, and I winced. The room was suffocatingly warm, too crowded with faces I didn't recognize, faces I wasn't meant to recognize. This was Michael's side of the family—perfectly groomed, effortlessly charming, and unfailingly polite in that clipped, condescending way that made me itch under my skin.

The ballroom gleamed, a riot of gold and ivory, with every surface polished to a mirror shine. Light from the chandeliers shimmered across the floor like liquid diamonds, reflecting the swirl of satin gowns and tailored suits. The music was a lilting melody of strings and piano, soft enough to encourage murmured conversation but lively enough to keep the mood buoyant. It was the kind of wedding people described as "fairy tale" without a trace of irony—a perfectly curated celebration of love.

I stood at the edge of it all, gripping a champagne flute like it might steady me against the tide of joy that threatened to pull me under. The bride, resplendent in an off-shoulder dress that cascaded like a waterfall of silk, twirled in the arms of her new husband beneath the spotlight. Her laughter floated above the music, effortless and unrestrained. Happiness clung to her like a second skin, and the crowd absorbed it, reflecting it back at her in smiles and toasts and cheers.

And then there was Michael and me, a silent tableau of discontent amid all the exuberance. Michael looked impeccable as always. His tuxedo was a sharp, midnight black, tailored to perfection, the white of his shirt stark against his tan skin. His dark hair was neatly combed back, and the glasses he wore for certain occasions—part of his cultivated "intellectual" look—rested lightly on the bridge of his nose. His entire demeanor was a carefully constructed performance: Michael Holloway, the respected psychologist, the charming conversationalist, the man who had everything under control.

Except for me.

I could feel his disappointment like a chain around my neck, though his face betrayed none of it. His smile was polite, practiced, but the tension in his jaw, the subtle way his hand lingered on my back as he began guiding me as though I might veer off course, told the real story.

And me? I didn't belong here, not among these polished people with their easy laughter and glittering champagne flutes. My dress, a muted blue sheath that I'd told myself was sophisticated, now seemed out of place among the sequins and tulle. My dark blonde hair, hastily pinned into a low bun, felt like an afterthought compared to the glossy updos around me. Even my makeup was wrong—too subdued, as though I were trying not to be noticed.

As we wound our way through the throng, I sipped my champagne, enjoying the sensation of bubbles prickling the back of my throat while I glanced around the room. The table settings were absurdly elegant: crystal glasses, gold-edged plates, centerpieces of white roses and eucalyptus that seemed to grow out of the tablecloth itself. Everything gleamed, immaculate and perfect, and I hated it.

"This is exhausting," I murmured under my breath, though I wasn't sure if I meant the event or my own inability to inhabit it.

"Smile," Michael murmured, ignoring that I'd verbalized my distress, his voice like a handheld drill grinding its way into my brain. I could feel his fingers on the small of my back, guiding me toward a circle of his cousins. The same fingers that had typed out that devastating dismissal of my career just six months ago. The memory still burned, an ache I carried in my chest like a wound that refused to close.

To anyone else his one-word instruction might have sounded like encouragement. To me, it was a warning.

"I am smiling," I replied, forcing my lips into something that might pass as pleasant if you didn't look too closely.

His fingers tensed briefly against my back. "Not like that. I hope you're not going to make a scene tonight."

"I'm not," I said through clenched teeth. "This is my happy face."

Michael sighed, a barely audible exhalation that carried all the truth of his irritation. I knew exactly what he was thinking—that I was making this harder than it needed to be, that I couldn't just *behave* for one evening. His cousins, tall and sleek and beautiful, were already waiting for us, their champagne flutes catching the light as they gestured animatedly.

"Michael!" one of them called, her voice bright and warm as she opened her arms in welcome. Her name was Clara, I thought, though I couldn't be sure. She had the kind of beauty that didn't need a name—glossy chestnut hair swept into an intricate twist, lips painted a bold crimson, and a laugh that seemed to light up the room.

"We were just talking about your latest book," Clara said,

slipping seamlessly into conversation as we joined the circle. "Brilliant as always. You must tell me—how do you manage it all? The work, the travel, the lectures... and, of course, everything else?"

Her eyes slid to me as she said it, her smile holding just the faintest trace of condescension. Everything else. A polite euphemism for *your wife who's falling apart*.

Michael laughed softly, a practiced sound that seemed to say, *It's nothing, really*. But before he could answer, I stepped in.

"It's not easy," I said, my voice as sweet as I could make it. "But I manage. I imagine it's a bit like being married to a surgeon. You get used to being second place."

Clara's laughter was brittle, a crack in the polished surface of her poise, but Michael's reaction was more satisfying. His smile tightened, just enough for me to see it, though no one else seemed to notice.

"Excuse me," I said, stepping back before anyone could respond. I let the circle close around Michael, their conversation carrying on as though I'd never been there.

The windows at the far end of the room called to me, their tall frames draped in gold curtains that seemed to shimmer in the low light. On the other side, the world was covered in snow, a pristine white blanket that glowed faintly in the moonlight. I knew the cold night air would be pressing against the glass, a sharp contrast to the warmth of the room, and I found myself wishing I could place my cheek against a pane, craving the cool on my skin. Or step outside and into it, kick off my shoes and let the snow nip and bite through my stockings, numbing the layers of artifice and expectation in the room behind me.

No matter how fast I walked I could still hear Michael's voice, smooth and confident as he answered another question about his work. He always thrived in these settings, slipping from conversation to conversation like he belonged to everyone at once. I used to love that about him—his ability to charm, to make people feel seen. Now, it felt like a weapon. A mask he wore to keep the cracks hidden.

"Harper."

I turned, and there he was, standing just behind me, his expression carefully neutral. He always looked so composed, even when he was angry. Especially when he was angry.

"You walked away in the middle of a conversation," he said, his voice low. "Do you have any idea how that makes me look?"

"How it makes *you* look," I said, the champagne burning in my chest. "Of course. What was I thinking?"

"Don't do this here," he said, his tone softening just enough to sound reasonable. "This isn't the time or the place."

"It never is, is it?" I said, meeting his gaze. "Because there's no room for anything that doesn't fit your narrative. I shouldn't have come tonight. It was a mistake, a pantomime and I feel like I'm starring in it."

He opened his mouth to respond but stopped himself, his jaw tensing. And then, after a long moment, he exhaled, his voice shifting into something almost tender.

"You need to let this go, Harper," he said. "The article, the job—it's over. I was trying to help you see that. To help you move on."

"Move on?" My voice rose, and I caught a few heads turning before I lowered it again and hissed. "You destroyed me, Michael. You didn't just disagree with me—you humiliated me. And you did it for what? Your reputation?"

His silence was answer enough.

"I can't do this. Not when everyone here is laughing behind my back, pitying you for having to put up with me and pitying me for having a husband who betrayed her," I said, brushing past him. My head buzzed as I made my way toward the exit. I needed air. I needed to get away from him, from all of it.

"Harper." His voice halted me just before I reached the door. When I turned, his face was unreadable, his tone calm but edged with something I couldn't quite place. Desperation? His next words made me suspect I was right. "Let's get away for a while. Somewhere quiet. Somewhere we can... fix this, fix us."

"Fix this?" I laughed. Although the sound was hollow, mirthless. "There's nothing left to fix and especially not us. You well and truly broke us this time, Michael."

He stepped closer, lowering his voice. "Listen, please. There's a place—a lodge, up in the mountains. It's remote, private. We can start fresh. Take time to work things through together. I've been thinking about it for a while. Surely we owe each other one last shot."

I stared at him, searching for sincerity. But all I saw was the man who always knew how to get what he wanted.

"I'll think about it," I said, though I already knew I'd give in. I always did.

And maybe—just maybe—this time would be different.

2

PRINCETON

The house was quiet, the kind that felt deliberate, heavy. Outside, the wind rustled the brittle leaves that had clung stubbornly to the trees through the winter, whispering promises of more snow. Harper sat at the kitchen table; her hands wrapped around a mug of coffee that had long gone cold. She hadn't taken a sip in over an hour, too distracted by the blinking cursor on her laptop screen. The word count at the bottom of the document read "0."

Their house in Princeton was beautiful. There was no denying it but where it had once felt aspirational, it now felt sterile. It was one of those colonial-style homes with white siding and black shutters, set back from the road on a neatly manicured lawn that Michael insisted on maintaining himself. Everything about it was symmetrical, orderly, and carefully curated, from the wraparound porch to the polished brass knocker on the door. It belonged in a real estate catalog, the kind where everything looks perfect on the glossy page but once you step inside, it feels lifeless.

Harper hated it.

It had been a dream when they first bought it, a place to grow into as their careers soared. Harper had pictured herself writing her best work in the cozy study upstairs, a room with built-in shelves and a desk that overlooked the backyard. And for a while, it had worked. She'd written her first big exposé there, the one that won her the national award for investigative journalism. But that was years ago, before Michael started treating her victories like threats.

Descending the stairs, she glanced toward the living room, where he was sitting in his favorite leather armchair, a thick book open on his lap. His reading glasses perched low on his nose, and his lips moved slightly as he read, like he was silently rehearsing the words. He always looked so composed, so steady, even when everything was falling apart.

"How's the article coming?" he asked without looking up, his voice smooth and even.

Harper didn't answer right away. She thought of her laptop, the empty screen that seemed to mock her. "It's not," she said finally, her voice flat.

Michael sighed softly and closed his book, setting it on the side table next to a half-empty glass of scotch. "You need to stop putting so much pressure on yourself. Just... write something. Anything. You're overthinking it."

"Thanks for the advice," she said, a sharp edge creeping into her tone. "I hadn't thought of that." Deflated, Harper slumped onto the nearest chair, her arms folded defensively across her chest as a weariness settled into her body.

Michael's brow furrowed slightly, but he didn't rise to the bait. Instead, he leaned back in his chair, crossing one leg over the other in that casual, confident way of his. "I'm just saying, maybe if you approached it with a clearer head, you'd have an easier time."

"A clearer head," she repeated, letting out a bitter laugh. "Right. Because I've been *so* clear-headed since you torched my career."

"Harper," he said, his tone warning. "We've been through this."

"No, *you've* been through it. You've rationalized it. You've made your peace with it. But I'm still here, in this mess you created, trying to figure out how to put the pieces back together."

"I didn't create this mess," he said, his voice cooler now. "You did that all on your own when you decided to publish an article that wasn't properly vetted."

"It *was* vetted," she snapped, turning to face him fully. "You just didn't agree with it. And instead of supporting me, you wrote that op-ed and made me look like an idiot in front of the entire industry *and* your family."

"I didn't make you look like an idiot," he said calmly. "You did that when you based your story on a single source who turned out to be unreliable. I did what I had to do to protect my reputation."

There it was again—*my reputation*. Not *ours*. Not *yours*. Just *his*. Harper clenched her fists, her nails digging into her palms. "You could have talked to me. You could have told me how you felt instead of blindsiding me like that."

"I did what was necessary and I'd hoped that in doing so I'd be instrumental in salvaging your career, too," he said simply, as though that excused everything. "You were spiraling, Harper, struggling with the pressures of work and you took your eye off the ball, allowing passion to cloud your judgement. You still are. And if you don't see that my subtle references to your state of mind were intended to deflect your incompetence, then I don't know how to help you."

She stood abruptly, the chair scraping against the hardwood floor. "Incompetence. How dare you even use that word? And I don't need your help, Michael. I needed your support. There's a difference."

The room fell silent again, but this time, it wasn't the heavy, deliberate kind. It was the brittle, fragility of something stretched too thin, ready to snap. Harper turned away, her chest tight, and walked towards the kitchen, coming to rest at the window above the sink. Outside, the sun was setting, casting long shadows across the backyard. The trees stood bare and skeletal against the orange sky, their branches swaying in the wind like fingers reaching for something they couldn't grasp. Michael had followed and hovered by the island, the clink of his glass on marble alerting her to his presence and location.

"Do you ever think about how we got here?" she asked, her voice quieter now, almost wistful.

Michael didn't answer right away. She heard the faint clink of ice in his glass as he lifted it to his lips. "We were young," he said finally. "Ambitious. Maybe a little naïve."

Harper closed her eyes, letting the memories wash over her. They'd met at a journalism conference in Chicago, back when she was still freelancing for local papers, and he was presenting research on cognitive bias in media. She'd been drawn to his confidence, his intelligence, the way he seemed to command every room he entered. He'd told her he was impressed by her tenacity, her willingness to chase the truth no matter the cost. They'd fallen fast, their shared ambitions binding them together as much as their chemistry.

For years, it had worked. They'd celebrated each other's successes, supported each other through failures. But somewhere along the way, their ambitions stopped aligning. Michael's career in psychology flourished, with bestselling books and speaking engagements that made him a household name. Harper's career, once just as promising, began to falter under the pressure of deadlines and editorial compromises. And then there was the article—the one that should have been her moment but instead became her downfall.

"You remember the apartment we had in Boston?" she asked, her voice soft. "The one with the creaky floors and the terrible heating?"

Michael chuckled faintly. "I remember. You loved that place. I couldn't wait to get out of it."

"Of course you couldn't," she said, a small smile tugging at her lips despite herself. "It wasn't perfect enough for you."

"I just wanted something better for us," he said, his tone defensive but not unkind. "And we got it. This house, this life—it's everything we wanted."

"It's everything *you* wanted," she said, turning to face him. "But what about me, Michael? When was the last time you asked what I wanted?"

He opened his mouth to respond, but she didn't give him the chance.

"Never mind," she said, shaking her head. "It doesn't matter."

She left the kitchen, the sound of her footsteps fading as she climbed the stairs to the study. The room was dark, but she didn't bother turning on the light. Instead, she sat at the desk and stared out the window, at the horizon where the last traces of sunlight were disappearing into the night.

She'd been like that for over an hour, just sitting. The branches of the bare trees scratching against the last streaks of burnt orange. A crow landed on one of the branches, its black silhouette stark against the pale twilight. It cawed once, sharp and hollow, before flapping away into the growing night.

Harper heard Michael's footsteps on the stairs before she

saw him, slow and deliberate, as if he was carefully considering every step. He paused in the doorway of the study, leaning against the frame with his arms crossed. She could see him in the reflection of her blank screen so didn't turn to look at him, and kept her gaze fixed on the horizon.

"You didn't finish your coffee," he said after a moment.

"It's cold now," she replied, her voice as flat as the light in the room.

He sighed softly, stepping inside and flipping on the desk lamp. The warm glow spilled across the room, illuminating the shelves lined with books and awards that once made Harper feel proud. Now, they felt like relics of a life she barely recognized.

Michael sat in the chair opposite. His posture relaxed but his expression carefully measured. She knew this version of him well—the calm, composed psychologist, the one who always had a solution. He clasped his hands in his lap, his wedding ring catching the light as he leaned forward slightly.

"I've been thinking," he began, his tone gentle, almost coaxing. "About us. About everything."

Harper finally turned her head to look at him. His face was handsome in that classical, clean-cut way that seemed to age like fine wine. But it was the eyes that always struck her—sharp, intelligent, and, lately, so hard to read. She searched them now, trying to find the man she'd fallen in love with all those years ago. She wasn't sure if he was still there.

"You've been thinking?" she said, her voice edged with a faint bitterness. "That's new."

Michael ignored the jibe, his expression softening as he continued. "We can't keep going like this, Harper. This... tension, the constant fighting—it's not healthy for either of us. It's not who we are, or were and I hate it, it's exhausting."

"Isn't it?" she said, leaning back in her chair. "Because it feels like this is exactly who we are now."

He hesitated, his hands tightening briefly in his lap before he relaxed them again. “Maybe we need a change. A chance to get away from everything—the house, the work, the distractions. Somewhere quiet, where we can focus on us.”

Harper raised an eyebrow. “What are you suggesting? A vacation?”

“Not a vacation,” he said quickly, shaking his head. “Something... more intentional. A temporary relocation. Remember at the wedding I mentioned to you I’d been looking at a place in the mountains, Ravenscreek Lodge.”

She blinked. The name unfamiliar. “What’s that?”

“It’s a property up in the mountains,” he explained. “It’s remote, private. People use it as a retreat—to disconnect, reset. It’s beautiful, Harper. Peaceful. Exactly the kind of place we need right now. And I’ve always had a yearning to be a mountain man, take a break from life as we know it and step back in time. It’d be an adventure.”

She frowned. Her skepticism evident. “You want us to spend the winter in some isolated cabin in the woods? Would we need survival training and to hunt for our own food?”

“No, nothing like that. And it’s not a cabin,” he said, a faint smile tugging at the corner of his mouth. “It’s a lodge—fully equipped, comfortable, with everything we’d need. And it’s not about isolation. It’s about giving us some space to heal. To really work through everything without all the noise.”

Harper turned back to the window, watching as the last bit of light disappeared, leaving only the faint glow of the streetlamp below. The idea sounded ridiculous at first—running away to some mountain lodge as if changing the scenery would magically fix everything. But then again, what they were doing now wasn’t working. The house, their routines, their endless arguments—it all felt like quicksand, dragging them deeper with every step.

And there was something tempting about the thought of escaping, even if just for a while. Leaving behind the ghosts of her career, the stigma of their crumbling marriage, and the unrelenting feeling of failure. Maybe somewhere new, somewhere untouched by all the mess, she could find herself again. Or at least figure out if there was anything left to salvage.

"How long?" she asked finally, her voice quiet.

Michael straightened slightly, as if sensing her wavering. "A few months. Just the winter. We'd come back in the spring."

"And what happens if it doesn't work?" she said, turning to face him again. "What if we go up there and nothing changes? What if we're just prolonging the inevitable?"

Michael's jaw tightened for a moment, but he kept his voice steady. "Then at least we'll know we tried. That's all I'm asking, Harper. Just... try."

She held his gaze for a moment, searching for cracks in his resolve. But he looked earnest, sincere even, and she couldn't help but wonder if he truly believed this was the answer or if it was just another performance. Another way to control the narrative.

"Okay," she said finally, the word heavy on her tongue. "I'll go. But don't expect miracles, Michael. I'm not sure there's anything left to heal."

For the briefest moment, something flickered in his eyes—relief, perhaps, or maybe triumph. But it was gone as quickly as it appeared, replaced by his usual calm.

"That's all I'm asking," he said, standing and placing a hand on her shoulder. "We'll make this work, Harper. You'll see."

She didn't respond, watching as he left the room and disappeared down the stairs. Harper turned back to the window, her reflection faint in the glass. For a moment, she didn't recognize herself—the tight lines of her face, the hollowness in her eyes.

The thought of Ravenscreek Lodge loomed in her mind, both a promise and a threat. She wasn't sure what awaited them there, but deep down, she knew one thing: whatever happened in that lodge would either save them or destroy them completely.

3

THE ROAD TO RAVENSCREEK

The road stretched endlessly before them, a narrow ribbon of asphalt winding through barren winter trees. The sky was overcast, a pale, dreary gray that seemed to bleed into the snow-dusted landscape, smothering its life force. Harper stared out the passenger window, watching the skeletal branches blur past, their dark shapes fractured against the pale horizon.

Michael had insisted on driving. He always did, claiming he preferred being in control, though Harper suspected it was less about preference and more about maintaining the upper hand. The rental SUV was huge and smelled faintly of new leather. It was packed to the maximum with supplies, warm clothing, basic staples and groceries to fill the refrigerator and freezer enough for a long haul stay which, going by the weather forecast had been a smart move.

A front was moving in, and blizzard conditions were expected causing Harper to suggest they cancelled the trip or postpone until it passed. Michael was determined to carry on, reassuring her that they were ahead of the snow and would be settled in by the time it hit, if it hit, He had little faith in forecasters who he said got it wrong all the time. Harper didn't agree. The only thing that gave her real comfort were the photo's she'd seen online of the recently renovated lodge, which as Michael had said, looked charming. Telling herself they'd be cozy and well-fed, with all mod-cons to hand if they were snowed in for a few days, slightly dulled the tension that was making her bones ache.

"How much longer?" she asked, breaking the impasse that had hung over them for the last hour. Her voice sounded thin, unfamiliar, even to herself.

Michael glanced at the GPS mounted on the dashboard, his grip on the steering wheel steady. "About another forty-five minutes," he said. "It's further up the mountain."

"Great," she muttered, slumping back against her seat.

He glanced at her, his brow furrowing slightly. "You could try to be a little more positive, you know. This was your idea too."

She turned to him, incredulous. "My idea? Really? Because I don't remember suggesting we uproot our lives and spend the winter in the middle of nowhere."

He sighed, his jaw tightening as he returned his focus to the road. "You agreed to this, Harper. No one forced you."

"Yeah, well, agreeing and being excited about it are two different things," she shot back.

An awkward quiet fell between them again, thicker this time, the tension like a rope stretched too tight. Harper shifted in her seat, suddenly feeling claustrophobic despite the car's spacious interior. She adjusted the air vent, letting the cold air blast against her face, but it didn't help.

They hadn't seen a town for miles and the last one they passed through consisted of a few farm dwellings, a gas station and a closed-down diner. The trees grew denser as they climbed higher, the road narrowing and curving more sharply. Snow clung to the edges of the pavement, and the occasional patches of ice glinted ominously under the weak sunlight.

Harper couldn't shake the feeling that the trees were moving in on them, their twisted branches like claws reaching for the car.

"Do you remember when we used to take road trips?" Michael asked suddenly, his tone lighter, as if he were trying to pull them out of the pit they'd dug themselves into.

Harper glanced at him. "Barely."

"We used to have fun," he continued, his grip on the wheel relaxing slightly. "That trip to the Grand Canyon? You wouldn't stop singing that ridiculous song you made up about tumbleweeds."

She smirked despite herself. "Because you kept complaining about how boring the drive was. I had to entertain you somehow."

He chuckled softly, a sound that felt strangely foreign in the strained atmosphere of the car. "You did. God, that trip feels like a lifetime ago."

"Because it was," she said, her voice quieter now. "We're not those people anymore."

Michael didn't respond right away, and for a moment, the only sound was turning of the tires against the road. "Maybe we can be," he said finally, his tone measured. "That's why we're doing this, isn't it? To try."

Harper didn't answer. She wanted to believe him, wanted to believe that this trip could be a fresh start. But the cracks between them felt too wide, too deep to bridge, no matter how far they drove or how remote the lodge was.

The GPS chimed, announcing a turn onto a smaller, less-traveled road. Michael slowed the car, carefully navigating the sharp turn. The trees were thicker here, their branches arching over the road like a canopy, shutting out what little light filtered through the clouds. The snow was heavier, clinging to the trees and the ground in uneven patches.

"This must be it," Michael said, his voice tinged with something close to relief.

Harper peered ahead, her stomach tightening as the road grew even narrower. It felt more like a path than a road, the kind of place that didn't want to be found. The car bumped and jolted over uneven patches of ice and gravel, and Harper gripped the armrest to steady herself.

"You sure this is the right way?" she asked, her voice tinged with unease.

Michael tapped the GPS. "That's what it says. It should open up soon."

It didn't. The trees seemed to close in tighter, the snow now falling lightly, casting an eerie stillness over the road. Harper couldn't see anything beyond the trees—no signs, no clearings, nothing to suggest they were heading anywhere at all.

"Michael... I meant to ask, how far away is the next town, civilization?" she began, her voice hesitant.

"There it is," he said, ignoring her question and pointing ahead.

Harper leaned forward, squinting through the windshield. At first, she saw nothing but the dark shadows of the trees. Then, as they rounded a final curve, the lodge came into view.

It loomed at the end of the road like something out of a dream—or a nightmare. A massive, angular structure of dark wood and stone, its sharp lines and steep roof cutting into the pale sky. The windows were tall and narrow, their glass dark and reflective, giving the impression of unblinking eyes. A wide porch wrapped around the front, its wooden beams thick and weathered. The entire building seemed to radiate a cold, bleak atmosphere, as though it were watching them approach. This looked nothing like the grand lodge in the photos online but maybe... maybe in the morning it would.

Michael pulled the car into the small, snow-covered lot in

front of the lodge and cut the engine. The sudden loss of noise was deafening, broken only by the faint rustle of the wind through the trees.

"Here we are," he said, his tone light, as though they'd just arrived at a cozy bed-and-breakfast.

Harper stared at the building, her chest tightening. It was beautiful in a way, but not the kind of beauty that invited you in. It was the kind of beauty that warned you to keep your distance.

"Home sweet home," she muttered under her breath.

Michael turned to her, his expression unreadable. "It's going to be good for us, Harper. You'll see."

She didn't answer, opening her door and stepping out into the snow. The cold hit her immediately, sharp and biting, but she welcomed it. It was better than the tension in the car.

As she stood there, staring up at the lodge, a strange sensation washed over her. It wasn't fear, exactly, but something close—an unease that settled deep in her gut. She couldn't shake the feeling that they weren't alone, that the lodge itself was watching them, waiting. But that's what people said, wasn't it. That windows were like eyes. She was being silly, infantile, so had a word to self. *Grow up Harper.*

Michael came around to her side, placing a hand on her back. "Come on," he said softly. "Let's get inside."

Harper nodded, but her feet felt heavy as they trudged toward the front steps.

The wind howled around them as they stepped onto the porch, the sound high and keening, like a distant scream. Harper shivered, pulling her coat tighter around herself as her boots crunched against the snow-dusted planks.

Michael fumbled with the keys; his breath visible in short puffs as he tried each one. The lock resisted at first, groaning as he turned it, but eventually relented with a sharp click. He pushed the heavy wooden door open, revealing a yawning darkness beyond.

"Cozy," Harper muttered under her breath.

Michael shot her a look but didn't respond. Instead, he flicked on the lights, and the dim glow of an overhead chandelier spilled into the entryway. As described in the brochure, the great room that greeted them was vast, with high vaulted ceilings and thick wooden beams crisscrossing overhead. The walls were paneled in dark oak, the grain rough and uneven, and the floor was covered in a threadbare rug that looked like it had once been beautiful but had long since faded into muted tones of red and gold. A massive stone fireplace dominated one wall, its hearth blackened with soot, though there were no logs in sight.

This was not what Harper had been expecting. Yes, everything was exactly like the photos but where the interior had appeared vibrant and newly restored, this was a faded version. Like someone had edited out all the colour, sliding the bar to the left so that only a hint of what was before, remained.

The air was stale, too, carrying a faint scent of damp wood and something metallic, like rust. No beeswax furniture polish, a scented candle, lavender from a diffuser, all the sensory touches she'd been expecting.

It felt too still, too quiet, the kind of quiet that made her ears strain for a sound, any sound. As though the house had been smothered, absorbing all the weight of the snow-covered forest outside and was now pressing it inward, toward them.

"It's perfect," Michael said, his voice cutting through her thoughts as he set their bags down near the door. "Exactly what we need."

Harper didn't answer. She stepped further into the room, her eyes drifting to the tall, narrow windows that lined one side of the lodge. The glass was streaked with frost, distorting the view of the snow-covered grounds outside. In the dim light, she thought she saw something move—a flicker of shadow, quick and fleeting—but when she turned to look directly, there was nothing.

She hugged herself, her unease growing.

"Do you feel that?" she asked quietly, glancing at Michael. He was busy unpacking one of their bags, pulling out a folded blanket and tossing it onto the worn leather couch. He barely looked up.

"Feel what?" he said, his tone dismissive.

"The... atmosphere. It's heavy, like the air's pressing down on you."

Michael straightened, giving her an exasperated look. "Harper, it's an old lodge. What did you expect? It's probably just the altitude or the weather. And you're tired. You never travel well, always grouchy whenever we arrive. You've been tense since we set off so try to relax now."

"Relax," she repeated, her voice flat. "Sure. Easy."

While Michael headed upstairs like an eager kid on the first night of his vacation, she wandered further into the room, her boots skimming the worn rug whose intricate patterns were as muted as her feelings. Her eyes were drawn to the staircase, its wooden banister twisting upward like a spine. The steps creaked as she climbed, the sound unnervingly loud in the otherwise quiet lodge. The second floor was dimly lit, with a long hallway stretching out before her. The walls here were lined with faded photographs, their frames crooked. She paused in front of one, squinting at the image.

It was a black-and-white photo of a couple standing on the lodge's front steps. The woman's face was slightly blurred, her features indistinct, but the man's expression was clear: his smile too wide, his eyes too intense. Harper shivered and turned away and followed the sound of Michael's clomping boots as they investigated the rooms along the hall.

The bedroom Michael had chosen for them was at the end. It was large, with a king-sized bed framed by heavy, dark wood and draped in a quilt that looked hand-stitched but faded with age. A single window faced the back of the property, the forest encompassing the lodge. Harper let out a long breath, her shoulders slumping. She was tired—bone tired—and the sight of the bed, however uninviting, made her want to collapse.

Michael appeared in the doorway behind her, his expression softening slightly. "What do you think?"

"It's fine," she said, not meeting his eyes. "The whole place is fine."

"It's more than fine," he said, stepping inside. "This is exactly what we need. Time away from everything, just the two of us. You'll see. Once we settle in, you'll feel better."

She wanted to believe him, but the words felt hollow, like they were meant more for his benefit than hers. She turned to the window, gazing out at the forest. The trees were dark shapes against the snow, their branches twisting and interlocking like skeletal fingers. The light was fading fast, and as she stared, the shadows seemed to deepen, stretching across the ground like ink spreading through water.

"I don't know, Michael," she said finally, her voice quiet. "This place feels... wrong. It's not what I was expecting at all, and I don't think I want to stay."

He sighed, running a hand through his hair. "It's just your nerves, Harper. Look, let's see how you feel in the morning, after you've slept."

She didn't respond, her gaze still fixed on the window. A flicker of movement caught her eye again, this time closer, and her breath hitched. She could have sworn she saw something—a figure, maybe, slipping between the trees. But when she blinked, the space was empty, nothing but the swaying branches and the snow.

"I'm going to start unpacking, we need to get the food into the freezer and I'm hungry," Michael said, his tone clipped now, as though exasperated by her reticence. "Why don't you come down and help when you're ready? I'll make dinner."

He left without waiting for an answer, the sound of his footsteps fading as he descended the stairs. Harper remained where she was, her fingers brushing against the cold glass of the window. The lodge creaked around her, the sound low and groaning, as though the building itself were settling—or shifting.

She stepped away from the window, her heart pounding. Something about this place didn't feel right. The architecture was too imposing, the shadows too deep, the isolation too intense. And the way the forest pressed in so close, —it all made her chest tighten with unease.

Harper didn't believe in ghosts, but standing there in that dimly lit room, she couldn't shake the feeling that the lodge would be riddled with them, and they were there right now. Watching. Waiting.

4

HOME SWEET HOME

The snow became thicker with each passing day, muffling the world outside Ravenscreek Lodge. Harper had made the mistake of giving it a go and promised to stay one more night, doing as Michael asked which was to take it a day at a time. Then on day two, the snow buried the road they'd come in on, sealing them into the vast, cold isolation of the mountains.

The television stopped working on day three and the only other link to the outside world was an old radio they'd found in the kitchen that sometimes found a station but mostly, emitted white noise and strains of disembodied voices which Harper could do without. There was no landline, and she'd given up trying to get a signal on her cell. Resigned to waiting for the snow to stop and a chance to dig themselves out, something she swore she would do singlehandedly if necessary, Harper resigned herself to watching it from the window, her coffee cooling in her hands, the horizon swallowed by white.

Michael, on the other hand had settled comfortably into his new routine, spending most of his time in the study, which he had claimed within hours of their arrival. It was the only room in the lodge that felt remotely lived-in, with his books and notes sprawled across the old oak desk and the faint whir of his laptop cutting through the quiet. Harper rarely went in; she wasn't invited. When she passed by the half-closed door, she'd see him hunched over, his glasses catching the dim light of the desk lamp, his expression focused. She wondered, not for the first time, what he was working on so intently. But every time she asked, his answer was the same.

"Just reviewing some notes. Keeping my mind sharp."

There was no warmth in his tone when he said it, no inclination to invite her into the conversation. She didn't push. She knew better by now. So much for re-connecting. Walks in the snow, hand in hand, re-discovering themselves over dinner and a bottle of wine.

Her plans to lounge on the couch under a blanket, watching trash television crashed and burned so unable to settle into one of the paperbacks she'd brought along, the rest of the lodge was Harper's to roam, though it hardly felt like a privilege.

The main living area was vast and cold, with its cathedral ceiling and the enormous stone fireplace that never quite banished the chill no matter how close she huddled to it. The kitchen, though functional, was outdated, its faded countertops and warped cabinets adding to the feeling that time had stopped here decades ago. She tried cooking—a simple soup to take the edge off the biting cold and a casserole—but the stove sputtered to life reluctantly, the flames weak and inconsistent, as though the house itself resisted the effort or was determined to thwart her attempts at making it homely.

After that, she ate minimally—cereal, toast, fruit she'd brought with her from the city. Anything quick and easy that didn't require wrestling with the ancient appliances. Michael didn't seem to notice. When he emerged from the study, it was usually to grab a coffee or a sandwich and a handful of almonds before disappearing again, his mind firmly elsewhere.

The distance between them felt insurmountable, a chasm that grew wider with each passing hour. Harper flew into rages where she blamed Michael for not researching the lodge thoroughly or even reading the reviews for it and threatening to sue the owner for false advertising. After exhausting her vocabulary and herself, she then lapsed into sulky silence where she festered on scenarios of them being stuck there for months, dying of starvation or being eaten by equally hungry bears.

Consequently, they barely spoke, and when they did, the conversations felt clipped, transactional. Harper couldn't work out whether Michael was reacting to her mood swings and keeping out of her way, or this was what he'd planned all along. He was living his mountain man dream and had only brought her along so he could keep an eye on her. Not trusting her to stay home he'd duped her into agreeing to her own prison sentence on the pretense of saving their marriage. It made her mad as hell but the angrier she got, the more attuned she became to something so weird, something that was starting to freak her out.

The lodge seemed to be listening, enjoying the tension in the air, swallowing their words, gulping down her anger, gorging on the bitterness that bubbled inside. If they were quiet, studiously ignoring one another then it amplified the disparity between them, made it so loud she wanted to cover her ears so she couldn't hear the nothingness. And when she wanted to knock on the study door and say she was sorry, even though she wasn't, to reach out and ask for comfort, a hand to hold, a conversation even, her desperation and loneliness was reflected in the emptiness she felt inside. A void of black, blacker than the shadows she was sure had started to linger in the corners of every room.

. . .

At night, though, that's when Harper's unease grew. The lodge, so quiet during the day, seemed to shift and stir once the sun set. It was subtle at first—a faint creak in the floorboards, the whisper of wind against the windows—but as the days stretched on, the noises grew more persistent. A soft, rhythmic tapping at the edge of her hearing. A door open, just a crack, though she was certain she'd closed it. Footsteps, faint but deliberate, pacing the hallway outside her bedroom.

She lay awake for hours, staring at the ceiling, her body rigid beneath the heavy quilt. Her breath felt loud in the stillness, each exhale a reminder of how alone she was. She wanted to wake Michael, to tell him about the sounds, but she knew what he would say.

Instead, she told him in the morning, over coffee. He listened, his brow furrowed as she described the footsteps, the doors, the scratching sounds in the eaves, the way the lodge seemed to shift and breathe at night.

"Harper," he said finally, setting his mug down on the table. "It's an old house. It's going to make noises. Floorboards creak. Wind gets into the walls—it's all perfectly normal."

"It didn't sound normal," she insisted, her voice sharper than she intended. "It sounded like someone walking. Like someone was moving around upstairs. Our bedroom door opened by itself last night, just enough for someone to peep in."

"It's probably an animal," he said with a shrug. "Squirrels or raccoons, maybe. We're in the middle of the woods. It happens."

She stared at him, incredulous. "You think a squirrel opened the door to our room?"

Michael's expression shifted slightly, softening in that infuriating way he had when he thought she was overreacting. "No Harper, I meant that the sounds in the eaves that you hear are made by animals. Look, you've been stressed. This is a big change—being out here, away from everything. It's natural to feel unsettled at first. But I do understand, and I promise, there's nothing here."

"There is," she said, her voice quiet but firm. "I can feel it. Something's... off about this place."

He sighed, running a hand through his hair. "You're overthinking again and looking for excuses to leave as soon as the road is passable. Look, why don't you try writing? Distract yourself. That always helps, doesn't it? I've seen you, turning pages of your book but you're not reading the words, I can tell. So why not write some of your own."

She didn't respond, her fingers tightening around her mug. The suggestion felt like a dismissal, another way to brush off her concerns without really addressing them. But then, that was Michael's specialty, wasn't it? Subtle control, wrapped in a veneer of patience and reason. He didn't need to argue or shout. Not like she did. He just made her doubt herself until she gave up.

By the third night, the noises became impossible to ignore. Harper was sitting in the living room, the fire crackling in the hearth but still not managing to warm the room, when she heard it again—a faint thud, followed by the creak of a floorboard overhead. She froze, her breath catching in her throat. The sound came again, deliberate and slow, as though someone was walking from one end of the upstairs hall to the other.

She turned toward the staircase, her pulse quickening. "Michael?" she called, her voice trembling.

No response.

She stood slowly, the fire casting long, flickering shadows across the walls as she moved toward the stairs. Her hand tightened on the banister as she ascended, the wood cold and smooth beneath her palm. The hallway stretched before her, dimly lit by the single bulb in the sconce at the far end. The air felt heavy, oppressive, as though the house were holding its breath.

"Michael?" she said again, her voice barely above a whisper.

The door to their bedroom was ajar, the crack of darkness beyond it impossibly still. She reached out, her fingers trembling as she pushed it open. The room was empty. The bed was undisturbed, the quilt neatly folded where she'd left it.

But the sound came again, this time from behind her—closer now, a faint shuffle just at the edge of hearing. She spun around, her heart hammering in her chest, but the hallway was empty. For a moment, she felt dizzy, her vision swimming.

A hand touched her shoulder, and she gasped, spinning around to find Michael standing behind her, his face etched with concern.

"Harper," he said, his voice soft. "What's wrong?"

"There's someone here," she said, her words spilling out in a rush. "I heard footsteps. I thought it was you, then I called you but—"

"I was out back, taking the trash," he said gently, his hands resting on her shoulders. "You're scaring yourself. Come back downstairs."

She wanted to argue, to tell him he was wrong, but the touch of his hands, the calm in his voice, made her hesitate. She let him lead her back to the living room, her thoughts spinning. He stoked the fire, its warmth filling the space as he handed her a blanket.

"Try to relax," he said, his tone reassuring. "Everything's fine."

But it wasn't fine. Harper knew it wasn't fine. The lodge was shifting around them, shuffling closer for a better look at her misery. Its shadows lengthening, its veiled intent growing stronger with each passing night.

And Michael didn't see it. Or worse, he didn't want to.

5

THE CROW

Once again, the snow had blanketed everything overnight, leaving the grounds of Ravenscreek Lodge in eerie tranquility. The wind had died, and now the world was still, unnervingly so. Harper stood on the porch, wrapping her coat tightly around her as she surveyed the untouched expanse of white. It was too quiet—no birdsong, no rustling leaves, just the crushing hush of winter. The forest loomed on all sides, its trees dark and bare, their branches stretching out like brittle veins against the pale sky.

She descended the porch steps, the snow crunching beneath her boots. The pleasure she would once have taken from making fresh footsteps a distant memory. The air was sharp, every breath burning her lungs, but she welcomed it. Anything was better than the being inside the lodge, where Michael sat barricaded in his study, oblivious to the tension that burrowed further into her chest with each passing day.

The lodge grounds were expansive, but unkempt, as though they had once been meticulously maintained but had long since been abandoned to nature. There was a garden off to the side of the house, or at least what had once been a garden. The skeletal remains of rose bushes jutted out from the snow, their thorny branches like deformed claws. A rusted bench sat beneath an ancient oak tree. Harper paused there, brushing snow from the seat before sitting down. She let her gaze wander over the grounds, taking in the dilapidated greenhouse in the distance, its glass panels cracked and frosted over. Beyond that, the forest rose like a wall, dense and impenetrable.

A thought flickered across her mind, that Prince Charming would see them as a challenge, hacking through them one by one to get to Sleeping Beauty. Oh, the irony. Because there were no princes in the vicinity who would step up and save this princess and that was a fact.

She then remembered how Michael had described this place when he first brought it up—a peaceful retreat, he'd called it, somewhere they could heal. But standing here now, with the cold biting at her cheeks and the army of the trees pressing in, it felt less like a retreat and more like a graveyard. Shaking that unhelpful image away, Harper's thoughts drifted further as she sat there, fingers growing numb inside her gloves. Back to the first time she had seen Michael.

He'd been so confident, so effortlessly charming, standing at the podium during his keynote speech. The room had been packed, every seat filled with journalists and academics, all of them hanging on his every word. Harper had sat near the back, furiously scribbling notes as he spoke about cognitive bias in media. She remembered the way his voice had carried, deep and steady, with just enough humor to keep the audience engaged.

Afterward, she had approached him, nervous but determined. She had introduced herself, mentioning her work as a freelance journalist, and to her surprise, he had smiled warmly, genuinely.

"Harper Sinclair," he had said, repeating her name like he was testing how it felt on his tongue. "I read your piece on the zoning corruption case last year. Impressive work."

The compliment had floored her. No one ever noticed her bylines back then, let alone someone as respected as Michael Holloway. They had talked for hours that night, first at the conference and later at a nearby bar, where he had leaned across the table and told her, "You're going to change the world someday, Harper. I can tell."

That version of Michael felt like a stranger now. She couldn't remember the last time he had looked at her like that, with admiration and warmth. These days, his gaze was distant, clinical, as though he were studying her rather than loving her. Preparing a report about his very own lab rat. The one he'd captured and transported to a faraway place in a wilderness where only the wildlife that lurked out of sight, would hear her scream.

That clear but troubling image freaked Harper out so much that she stood abruptly, brushing snow off her coat and in an attempt to leave it behind on the bench, continued walking. She noticed immediately that the air was colder here, near the edge of the forest, like a barrier of invisible ice that repelled strangers, and the trees crowded together like sentinels. Harper hesitated for a moment, staring into the dark spaces between the trunks. Did she dare. Yes she damn well did because she was sick to the back teeth of being penned inside that house and penned inside of Michael's covert control.

In one step, it felt like she'd broken through the ice barrier, stepping into another world. The forest was dense, the ground uneven beneath the snow. Harper ducked under low-hanging branches, her boots slipping on patches of ice hidden beneath the white powder. She followed no particular path, letting her feet carry her deeper into the woods, until the lodge was just a dark shape in the distance. Common sense told her not to lose sight of it because the last thing she wanted was to become disorientated, and if the gentle flakes of snow covered her footprints she'd have no trail to follow, yet she was enjoying pushing a boundary so chanced a few steps more.

That was when she heard it—a sharp caw that echoed through the trees. Harper stopped, her breath hitching. She scanned the branches overhead, searching for the source of the sound. It came again, louder this time, closer. Her eyes finally landed on the crow.

It was perched on a branch just above her, its feathers black and glossy, its beady eyes fixed on her with an intensity that made her skin crawl. She felt a strange unease ripple through her, as though the bird were staring not at her but into her, seeing something she didn't understand.

The crow cawed again, its cry sharp and grating, and Harper took a step back. The bird tilted its head, its gaze following her every move. She tried to shake the feeling of being watched, of being judged. *Get out of my forest, go on, get out. You don't belong here.*

"You're just a bird," she said aloud, though her voice wavered. "You can't tell me what to do."

But the crow didn't move. It stayed rooted to the branch, its claws gripping the bark like talons, its head cocked at an unnatural angle. Harper faltered, took a step back, her heart pounding. The bird's caw cut through the air again, louder this time, almost angry. Then, without warning, it launched itself from the branch.

Harper stumbled, falling into the snow as the crow swooped low, its wings beating the air inches from her face. She threw her hands up instinctively, shielding herself as the bird circled her once, twice, before landing on another branch a few feet away. Its caw was sharp and mocking, and Harper could swear its eyes glinted with something malicious, something far too intelligent for an animal.

She scrambled to her feet, her hands shaking, her breath coming in short, ragged gasps. The crow stayed where it was, watching her, its head tilting side to side, as though amused by her fear. Then it swooped again, this time skimming her head so close she felt its claws catch on her hair, causing her to frantically bat it away. Once again it landed on a branch and took up position from where it watched her, locking its eyes on hers.

"Leave me alone," she muttered, her voice barely audible. She turned and hurried back toward the lodge, her boots slipping on the snow. She didn't dare look back, but she could feel the crow's gaze on her, heavy and unrelenting and as though the touch of its claws had left their stain on her scalp.

By the time she reached the lodge, her legs were trembling, and her cheeks stung from the cold. She raced up the steps and once inside, slammed the door behind her, leaning against it as she tried to steady her breathing. The lodge as always was quiet, the only sound the faint crackle of the fire in the living room.

Michael's study door was closed, a faint strip of light visible beneath it. Harper didn't bother knocking. She knew he wouldn't understand—he never did. Instead, she made her way upstairs, her steps slow and heavy.

In the hallway, she passed the mirror again. Her reflection was pale, her hair disheveled, her eyes wide with fear. She paused, staring at herself, and for a moment, she thought her reflection moved—just a fraction of a second too late, like it was lagging behind real time. Her stomach twisted, and she quickly looked away, hurrying into the bedroom.

After kicking off her boots and throwing her coat onto the

chair she crawled under the quilt, her body curling into itself as she tried to block out the memory of the crow, of the forest, of her vivid imagination that was starting to feel like an unhelpful friend when what she really needed was an ally. But no matter how tightly she closed her eyes, she couldn't shake the feeling that something was watching her. Had the crow followed her back to the house. Was it on the windowsill right now, peering in, a feathered voyeur.

The answer came swiftly, as though someone, it was reading her mind when from outside, in the forest, the crow cawed again, its cry faint but deliberate, like a warning.

6

THE LODGE

After the crow, Harper had descended into a hole she dug herself. Refusing to communicate with Michael because what was the point? Two more days passed. The ritual of existing was wearing her down, barely eating, never sleeping. She'd taken to carrying the radio with her wherever she went and to preserve the batteries, would religiously turn it on every thirty-minutes, desperate to hear another human voice. When the batteries finally died, she felt like a piece of her did too.

The lodge, however, seemed more alive than ever and the sense of being watched was almost tangible. There was a presence, and it was wrapping itself around her like a thick fog. The dark wood walls seemed to close in when she wasn't looking, the shadows creeping further into the corners. It wasn't just the way the house moved and shifted—it was the way it seemed to breathe. The faint creaks and groans of the old timbers no longer felt random; they were deliberate, like whispers exchanged in secret.

Everywhere she went, the lodge felt distorted, the living room downstairs, dubbed the great room, seemed smaller than it should, as the hallways stretched out infinitely when she wasn't looking. She'd turn a corner expecting to find a wall or a room, only to be met with a hallway she swore hadn't been there before.

She found herself avoiding certain parts of the house—the storage attic filled her heart with dread just knowing it was there; the far end of the second-floor hall made her avert her eyes—there were places where the air was oppressive. In the end Harper resolved to stick to one room during the day, and the bedroom at night because at least there she had Michael for company if only in physical form.

Where possible she kept her eyes cast downwards, fixed on the floor and her feet, so that as she moved the lodge couldn't taunt and play tricks. Like when she noticed the carving on the newel post, a strange angular shape, the size of a watch face, that hadn't been there before and when she went back later, had disappeared causing her think she'd imagined it. Until one appeared on the wooden lintel above the range in the kitchen, and another on the doorframe to Michael's study. It was as though she was playing a game of peek-a-boo because once she'd seen one, it would disappear. She hadn't told Michael yet, not until she was sure she wasn't dreaming them.

In her periphery she noticed that the light bulbs flickered more often now, casting fleeting shadows across the walls. Harper had tried replacing one of them in the living room, but no matter how tightly she screwed in the new bulb, the light refused to hold steady. When she sat on the couch in the evenings, watching the fire sputter and dim, the flickering shadows seemed to stretch unnaturally, growing longer and darker, like reaching fingers.

Her reflection in the windows unnerved her. At night, when the glass became a dark mirror, she tried not to look. But sometimes she caught glimpses anyway, and the shapes she saw didn't feel like her own. She started leaving the curtains drawn, shutting out the encroaching darkness that pressed against the windows. And then she'd open them again when the paisley pattern morphed into a host of spiteful faces, watching her intently.

Harper's sleep had become more fragmented, her nights filled with fitful tossing and waking up gasping in the dark. Every time she drifted off, she would wake minutes later, certain she'd heard a sound—footsteps, whispers, the faint creak of a door opening. But when she sat up and listened, there was nothing.

The lack of rest was starting to take its toll. Her head ached constantly, a dull throb that refused to fade. Her limbs felt heavy, her movements sluggish, like she was wading through molasses. She couldn't concentrate long enough to read or write, and every time she tried to piece together her thoughts, they scattered like leaves in the wind.

Her reflection in the bathroom mirror told her the truth she didn't want to face. She was unraveling. Her cheeks were pale and hollow, her eyes bloodshot with dark circles smudged beneath them. She barely recognized herself anymore, and that scared her more than anything else.

Michael didn't notice, or maybe he chose not to. He was so absorbed in his work that he barely seemed to register Harper's presence most days. When she emerged from her self-enforced vow of silence, she tried bringing up the noises and the moving objects again, but he'd shut her down with the same patronizing calm.

"Harper, you're exhausted," he'd said, not looking up from his notes. "But I'm glad we're communicating again, that's a start. Perhaps you could make some lunch, raid the freezer and prepare something wholesome because it looks like you're losing weight, and maybe take a shower, wash your hair. Take a bit of pride in your appearance."

The faint smirk and condescension stung, and although she desperately wanted to reject his suggestions partly out of pride, the rest sheer stubbornness, she acquiesced on one condition. "Will you wait in the bedroom while I take a shower? Please Michael. I don't want to be alone upstairs."

After a sigh and dropping his pen onto the desk before rubbing his eyes, Michael agreed, albeit it begrudgingly. "Okay, if it pulls you out of your mood but seriously Harper, you're behaving like a child and I can't babysit you every minute of the day, I have work to do. Come along then. Let's hope this makes you feel better."

But afterwards, despite feeling clean and half-human again, forcing herself to make them pasta and enduring a stilted conversation about the weather whilst they ate, Harper didn't feel better. Anything but.

The lodge was taking hold of her, and she couldn't escape it. Even when she went outside to walk the grounds, the cold air biting at her cheeks, it loomed behind her, its dark-eyed windows following her every move. She avoided the forest after her encounter with the crow; the memory of its sharp, intelligent gaze still haunted her. Skirting the woods, taking a route through the gardens that was becoming a ritual that gave her solace. And bizarrely she felt safest when she could see the house, even though the sight of it filled her with dread.

Having no concept of how many days they'd been at the lodge and no desire to try to work it out, a day had once again merged into night and with Michael snoring by her side, the bottle of red he'd consumed with his cold supper aiding his slumber, Harper lay staring at the ceiling. Drifting in and out of fitful sleep, wishing her one glass of Bordeaux would tranquilize her into oblivion, she prayed for happy dreams, some respite from her daily nightmare.

Minutes, maybe an hour later her eyes opened, wide and frightened. Footsteps. They started faintly, somewhere above her, the slow, deliberate creak of someone—or something—moving across the floor. She sat up, holding her breath, her pulse hammering in her chest.

The sound grew louder, closer, as though it were descending the stairs. Harper clutched the quilt tightly, her knuckles white as she strained to hear. The footsteps stopped abruptly, and the hush that followed was deafening.

Then came the whisper.

It was soft, so faint she wasn't even sure she'd heard it. But the sound was unmistakable. Words spoken in a low, raspy voice, unintelligible yet deeply unsettling. Harper froze, her entire body tense, her ears straining to catch the sound again.

"Michael," she whispered, her voice trembling.

But he didn't respond. She turned her head, realizing he wasn't there. He must have crept downstairs once he knew she was asleep. He'd be ensconced in his study. She was alone.

Summoning what little courage she had, Harper swung her legs over the side of the bed and stood, her bare feet sinking into the cold wooden floor. She crept toward the door, every step agonizingly slow, her heart pounding in her ears. The hallway was dark, the faint glow of the firelight from downstairs casting flickering shadows along the walls.

She leaned over the banister, peering down at the living room. It was empty. The fire had burned low, its embers glowing faintly, and the flickering shadows seemed to dance unnaturally, reaching up toward the ceiling.

"Michael?" she called again, her voice shaking.

The study door creaked open, and Michael stepped out,

squinting at her. His shirt was rumpled, and his glasses were slightly askew. "What is it, Harper?" he asked, his tone weary.

"Why did you leave me? I heard... something," she said, her voice faltering. "Footsteps. And... whispers. Did you hear them?"

Michael sighed, rubbing the bridge of his nose. "Harper, I was working. I waited until you nodded off and we've talked about this. It's an old house. It creaks. You're overtired and imagining things and I'm tired of telling you. Maybe sleeping pills might help. I have some with me, you know that."

Harper knew only too well that Michael would have brought his stash of medications with him, antidepressants, relaxants, sleepers and as she'd told him time and time again, even when they were at home, that she would not succumb to drugs, he persisted. After all, a spaced-out wife would be even more malleable than she was now. She ignored his suggestion and focused on the noises.

"I'm not imagining it," she insisted, her frustration bubbling to the surface. "I know what I heard, Michael. Something is wrong with this place."

He stepped closer, his expression softening, though his tone remained calm and measured. "Imagine if this was someone else, and you had to placate them, what would you say, Harper? Go on, swap places and logic it through. You'd tell them that they're not sleeping, which is making them anxious, and a new, isolated place temporarily cut off from the outside world is... unsettling. They're letting stress get the better of them. But there's nothing here, it's a quirky old house and maybe they watched too many X-rated films when they were a teenager."

His words felt like a slap, cutting through her fear with cold precision. Condescending and patronizing in the extreme. Harper glared at him; her hands clenched at her sides. "You always do this," she said, her voice trembling. "You make me feel like I'm crazy, like I can't trust myself and stop talking to me like I'm a kid who had a bad dream."

"That's not what I'm doing," he said, his voice firm. "I'm trying to help you."

"No, you're trying to control me, my thoughts, my will, " she snapped. "Just like you always do."

Michael's jaw tightened, and for a moment, she thought he might argue. But instead, he sighed, his shoulders slumping slightly. "Go back to bed, Harper," he said quietly. "We'll talk about this in the morning."

She stared at him, her chest heaving, but he didn't meet her gaze. Instead, he turned and walked back into the study, closing the door behind him.

Harper stood there for a moment, the shadows of the lodge closing around her. The walls seemed closer now, the air cloying. No way was she going back upstairs so instead she turned and walked over to the couch, her movements stiff and mechanical. As she crawled under the throw, her body trembling, she felt her fears settle over her like a shroud.

The whispers didn't come again that night, but Harper didn't sleep. She lay awake, listening out, hearing the odd cough from Michael who remained in his study, the tick of the mantle clock and the slide and thud of a log as it cooled and shifted in the flameless grate. Staring into the darkness, Harper knew the house was doing the same. Watching her. Waiting.

7

CUTTING WOOD

The sharp sound of the axe splitting wood echoed through the icy air, each strike precise and deliberate. From the kitchen window, through the giant flakes of snow, I watched Michael in the yard, his breath fogging in the cold as he worked. He moved with a steady rhythm, his jacket flecked with white flakes, his movements calm and purposeful, like this was just another day, like everything between us hadn't already cracked wide open.

There was something maddening about his composure, the way nothing ever seemed to touch him. He could just go on, steady and unbothered, while I felt like I was drowning. I turned away from the window, my coffee mug warm but untouched in my hands, and let my restless feet carry me through the house.

The fire in the living room was down to embers, its faint heat barely enough to cut through the chill that seemed to seep from the walls. I hated being alone in here, but unless it was while we slept, I hated being around Michael. Unable to sit still my feet eventually took me toward the study.

His study. He'd claimed it as soon as we arrived, filling it with his books and notes, his laptop center stage on the desk. I hadn't been inside since then. It felt like his domain, the one place in the lodge where I was undeniably unwelcome. But now, as I stood in the doorway, the faint scent of leather and coffee drifting out, something pulled me in.

The door was slightly ajar, an invitation or a warning, I wasn't sure. I pushed it open and stepped inside.

The study felt different from the rest of the lodge. Perhaps because a small electric heater warmed the room. The walls were paneled in dark wood, much like the rest of the house and a tall bookcase lined one wall, its shelves packed with old, leather-bound volumes that looked like they hadn't been touched in decades. The air carried a faint, metallic tang, like the smell of rust, and something else—something musty and organic, like damp earth.

Michael's desk sat in the center of the room, a hulking piece of furniture that seemed almost too large for the space. Its surface was cluttered but carefully organized, with his laptop positioned just so, his books and papers stacked in neat piles. A green banker's lamp cast a pale glow over the desk, its light too weak to reach the far corners of the room, which remained steeped in shadow.

Once again I had the unsettling feeling that the room was watching me. The way the shadows shifted as I moved, the way the books seemed to lean forward ever so slightly, as if straining to hear—it all made my skin crawl. The lodge had felt oppressive from the moment we arrived, but this room was different. It felt alive, like it was holding its breath, waiting.

Not for the first time I wondered if I was hallucinating. And not for the first time did I forbid myself from uttering those words to my husband.

I hesitated, my hand resting on the edge of the desk. My reflection in the darkened screen of Michael's laptop caught my eye, warped and distorted by the curve of the glass. Once again it looked like it was moving just a fraction of a second behind me, but when I turned my head, it was gone.

The notebook lying in the center of the desk drew my attention like a magnet. It looked worn, scuffed from use, the edges of the pages slightly frayed. My heart began to pound as I reached for it, my fingers trembling slightly. I shouldn't. I knew I shouldn't. But the thought of walking away now felt impossible.

The pages crackled faintly as I opened it, his neat, looping handwriting immediately familiar. At first, the words seemed like harmless observations about the lodge, notes on the weather, musings about the isolation. But as I flipped through the pages, my stomach sank.

Harper seems agitated again. She keeps mentioning noises at night, though I've heard nothing myself. Tried to reassure her, but she becomes defensive when challenged. This isn't new—she's always been resistant to hearing difficult truths.

Harper's paranoia is escalating. She's convinced the house is 'watching' her. It's clear she's struggling with the isolation, but she won't admit it. I've tried to approach her gently, but she lashes out.

Her fixation on the lodge is concerning. She spent hours wandering the grounds today, muttering to herself. She has formed an attachment with the transistor radio and caries around like a pet. When I suggested she write in order to focus her thoughts, she accused me of trying to control her. Classic projection.

The words blurred as I read, the sharp edges of them cutting through me. He'd been documenting me. My every move, my every word, twisted into evidence of instability. My hands shook as I turned the pages, anger rising in my chest like a flood I couldn't stop.

The further I read, the more I felt the room closing in around me. The faint click of the heater grew louder, almost deafening, like a swarm of insects buzzing in my ears. My breaths came shallow and quick as the entries painted a picture of me that I didn't recognize—a paranoid, unstable woman spiraling out of control.

Harper seems more detached than ever. She barely speaks to me anymore, and when she does, it's laced with hostility. I suspect she's retreating into herself, as she's done before. I need to tread carefully—too much pressure will only push her further.

I've offered medication which she refuses. She is sleep deprived, has no interest in food and is losing weight and has no regard for her personal hygiene and appearance. She cannot focus, stares at the television screen as if willing it to work and only abandoned the radio when the batteries stopped working.

I'm worried about her mental state. She's growing more erratic, more combative. I know this isn't her fault; she's overwhelmed, and the stress is manifesting as paranoia. She needs help, but I don't think she's ready to accept that yet. For now, I'll keep documenting—this is for her own good.

"For her own good?" I whispered, my voice trembling with fury. The air in the room felt too thick to breathe, and the notebook seemed to burn in my hands. He wasn't helping me. He was dissecting me. He was turning me into a case study, an experiment.

The shadows shifted again, darker now, as though the room itself were reacting to my anger. I slammed the notebook shut and stumbled out of the study, the sound of my heartbeat roaring in my ears.

Michael was stacking wood on the porch when I found him, the axe propped against the railing. Snow clung to his hair and jacket, but his face was calm as always, a picture of patience that only fueled my rage.

"What the hell is this?" I demanded, holding up the

notebook. My voice was louder than I intended, echoing off the porch beams.

His brow furrowed, and he took a step closer, his breath visible in the icy air. "Harper, where did you— have you been snooping? I know you've been going in there."

"Don't," I snapped, cutting him off. "Don't act like I'm the one in the wrong here. You've been writing about me, keeping track of everything I say and do like I'm some kind of... of case study. And how dare you accuse me of snooping. I haven't been in there once because you make it clear it's your domain and I'm not welcome."

His expression softened, his voice lowering in that maddeningly calm way he always used when I was upset. "Harper, you're overreacting. It's not what you think."

8

THE STORM

The storm had rolled in overnight, sealing us further into the isolation of Ravenscreek Lodge. The snow was relentless now, a thick, unbroken sheet stretching as far as the eye could see. The road, if it could even still be called that, had disappeared completely. The house groaned in the wind, the faint creaks and whispers of its old bones audible even through the study door.

I sat at the desk, staring at the phone sitting on the corner. It was an ugly thing, outdated and bulky, the kind of landline you only saw in places like this. When we'd first arrived, I'd picked up the receiver to test it, expecting nothing. But to my surprise, it worked—a thin, crackling connection, but a connection, nonetheless. I hadn't told Harper right away. The line died on the first full day, so I hadn't thought about it since. I only picked it up just now to check and that action surprised me, and I then had to admit if only to myself that I'd hoped to hear that familiar crackle. One that connected me to the outside world because even though I'd never mention it to Harper, the isolation and her behavior is starting to rattle me, too.

I thought she'd been in here the moment I stepped inside that morning. It was subtle—but the small things gave it away.

The chair had been shifted slightly, just an inch to the left. A pen was missing from its place on the desk, its absence creating a void I couldn't unsee. The notebook I'd left in the exact center of the desk was slightly off-kilter, the leather cover closed in a way I wouldn't have left it.

I closed my eyes for a moment, letting out a long breath. She thought she was being stealthy, but I knew her too well. Harper always left traces, even when she didn't mean to. I imagined her in here, rifling through my things, her fingers flipping through the pages of my notebook, her anger building with every word. I could almost hear her sharp intake of breath, the way her hands would tremble when she realized what she was reading.

She must have been furious. I'd seen it in her eyes last night, the fire barely contained as she confronted me on the porch. I'd told myself I was ready for that conversation, that I could handle it, but the raw anger in her voice had shaken something loose in me. She didn't understand, couldn't understand, that everything I was doing was for her. For us.

Then the denial. That annoyed me so much. Saying she'd never snooped before and the first time she had, came across the notebook. That's a blatant lie and worries me.

But, if I'm honest with myself, it's not the first time Harper's lies and anger have left me shaken. And I know exactly when it started—when everything between us began to crack.

The article. God, the article. Even now, the memory of it feels like a stone lodged in my chest.

Harper had been so proud of that piece. She'd spent months researching it, chasing down leads, conducting interviews, building her case. It was about corruption in the pharmaceutical industry—specific companies manipulating clinical trial data to push unsafe drugs onto the market. She'd uncovered damning evidence, pieced together a story that was bold and damning.

She was relentless, the way she always was when she believed in something.

And for a while, I'd been proud of her too. Her passion, her determination—it was one of the things that had drawn me to her in the first place. But the deeper she got into the story, the more reckless she became. She started taking shortcuts, leaning on sources that weren't as solid as they should have been, making leaps in logic that she couldn't back up. I tried to warn her, tried to make her see that she was risking everything, but she wouldn't listen. She never listened.

And then the article was published.

At first, the response was electric—headlines, interviews, a wave of public outrage. But it didn't take long for the cracks to show. One of her key sources backed out, claiming they'd been misquoted. A critical piece of evidence turned out to be weaker than she'd claimed. The pharmaceutical companies hit back hard, discrediting her in the press, threatening lawsuits. Her credibility unraveled in real time, and she couldn't stop it.

Neither could I.

I remember sitting in my office at the university, watching the fallout play out on the news. Colleagues started asking questions, making comments, wondering how a journalist married to a respected psychologist could make such basic errors in judgment. And I felt it then, that gnawing sense of fear—not for Harper, but for myself. For my reputation.

So, I made a choice. A necessary one.

I went on record—just once, just enough to protect myself. I gave a carefully worded statement to a reporter I trusted, distancing myself from Harper's work, emphasizing the importance of rigorous standards in investigative journalism. It wasn't an attack, not directly, but it was enough. Enough to plant doubt. Enough to make it clear that I wasn't complicit.

I told myself I was doing it for us, for our future. But the look on Harper's face when she found out—it gutted me. She never said it outright, but I knew she saw it as a betrayal. And maybe it was. Maybe I betrayed her to save myself.

There is no doubt the article destroyed her career. She hasn't written anything substantial since, hasn't tried. And though we never talk about it, I know it's always there, sitting between us like a ghost. She doesn't trust me the way she used to, and I don't blame her. But what else could I have done?

That choice—necessary, rational—had opened a chasm between us that I didn't know how to close. Harper had pulled away after that, her bright, sharp energy dimming into something quieter, more brittle. She stopped talking about her ideas, stopped fighting for the things she believed in. And I've tried, over and over, to reach her, to help her rebuild. But she doesn't want my help. She wants the version of me that she fell in love with, the one who admired her without question, who believed in her no matter what.

I don't know if I can be that person anymore.

The heater in the corner struggled to keep the room warm against the bitter cold that pressed in from the windows. I stared out at the snow, watching as the wind swirled it into eddies and drifts. Harper was in the living room, or at least she had been when I'd last checked. She'd wrapped herself in a blanket and curled up on the couch, staring into the fire as though the answers to all her questions lay somewhere in the flames.

I knew I needed to approach her carefully. Harper was a storm in her own right—volatile, unpredictable. I'd learned over the years that pressing her too hard, too fast, was a mistake. She needed to feel like she was in control, even if she wasn't.

I reached for the notebook, flipping through the pages absently. The entries were clinical, objective, or at least that's what I'd told myself when I'd started writing them. They were observations, a way to document the patterns I'd seen emerging in her behavior, a way to understand her. But now, as I read over them, I realized how they might look through her eyes. Cold. Detached. Condescending.

I set the notebook down, rubbing a hand over my face. She was already on edge, and the notebook had only made things worse. I'd seen the way she'd looked at me after finding it, as though I'd betrayed her in some fundamental way.

She didn't understand. I wasn't the enemy. I was trying to help her, trying to make sense of the woman I loved unraveling before my eyes. But she couldn't see that. Not yet.

9

THE PHONE

The lodge tensed its shoulder and bore the brunt of the storm, the sound it made as it stood firm was low and hollow, like a deep exhale from an ancient beast. I sat in the living room, attempting to counteract my husbands' observations, pretending to read one of the dusty novels I'd found on the bookshelf. The words on the page blurred and swam in front of my eyes, meaningless shapes that couldn't distract me from the gravity of my situation.

Michael was in the study again, the soft click of his keyboard the only evidence of his presence. He hadn't said much to me all day, just a few neutral, polite comments about the weather and the dwindling firewood. I didn't push. Pushing him never went well.

But the phone was in there. The only link to the outside world, tucked away on the corner of his desk like some relic of a time when communication wasn't fleeting and fragile. Now, as the snow piled higher and higher, cutting us off entirely, the thought of that phone sitting in his study, out of reach, gnawed at me. I needed to know if it worked. Maybe, on the other side, an engineer had braved the storm and fixed the line. It was possible and the idea gave me hope.

If it did work, it would also confirm my suspicions. That Michael was holding me here on purpose and that he had an ulterior motive for bringing me to this hideous place.

I waited until the lodge settled into its late-night quiet, when even Michael's relentless typing had stopped, and the only sound was the crackle of the fire slowly dying in the hearth. He'd said he was taking a bath, needed to unwind so I'd grunted a response and once I heard him ascending the stairs, peered over the edge of the couch and watched his weary climb.

My heart pounded as I crept down the hallway, the wooden floorboards cold and unyielding beneath my bare feet. The door to the study was closed, but a faint strip of light still seeped through the crack beneath it.

I stood there for a long moment, listening for any sign that he was on his way back downstairs. The house creaked softly around me, the wind rattling the windows in their frames. Slowly, carefully, I eased the door open, just enough to slip inside.

The shadows in the corners seemed to stretch and shift as I moved, so I tried not to look at them too closely. My focus was on the desk, on the phone sitting there like a beacon. I picked it up, my fingers trembling slightly as I pressed it to my ear.

Nothing. No dial tone, no faint crackle of a connection.

I stared at the receiver, my stomach twisting. It had worked before—I knew it had. Michael had made a call to check on the weather report when we first arrived. Unless...

My breath caught in my throat as the thought formed, unbidden. *Unless he sabotaged it.*

I shook my head, trying to push the thought away. It was absurd, paranoid. Michael was controlling, yes, but he wouldn't do something stupid like this. Would he?

I replaced the receiver carefully, my hands shaking. As I turned to leave, I froze.

A whisper. Soft, faint, like a breath against my ear.

"I know."

I whipped around, my heart pounding, but the room was empty. The shadows in the corners seemed to pulse and shift, but there was no one there. I took a step back, my legs unsteady beneath me, and the whisper came again, faint and taunting.

"Lying... always lying..."

I clapped my hands over my ears, squeezing my eyes shut.

"You're a fake and I know."

"No," I whispered, my voice trembling. "I'm not—I'm not lying."

The sound grew louder, filling the room, a cacophony of whispers overlapping and intertwining. "I know. I know. I know."

I stumbled out of the study, slamming the door behind me, the whispers cutting off abruptly. My chest heaved as I pressed my back against the door, my hands still clamped over my ears. The hallway was dark, the only light coming from the faint glow of the dying fire in the living room.

The house seemed to settle around me, the creaks and groans of the old wood almost soothing now compared to the whispers. I lowered my hands slowly, my fingers trembling as I let out a shaky breath. It wasn't real. It couldn't be real.

I stumbled back into the living room, collapsing onto the couch. The fire had burned down to embers, casting faint, flickering shadows across the walls. I pulled the blanket around me, trying to steady my breathing, but the whispers still echoed in my mind, taunting and cruel.

. . .

I didn't tell Michael what happened. What would I even say? That the house was whispering to me, accusing me of things. He would dismiss it, the way he always did. He'd look at me with that calm, patient expression that made me want to scream, and he'd tell me I was tired, that I was imagining things.

"You've been under a lot of stress," he'd say, his voice soft and measured. "It's natural to feel unsettled."

He'd always been good at that—at making me question myself, at planting just enough doubt to keep me off balance. And maybe he was right. Maybe I was imagining things. Maybe the lodge wasn't alive, reacting to our emotions, twisting them into something unrecognizable.

But maybe it was. And maybe it did know something. Maybe somehow it knew my secret.

The next morning, Michael found me still curled up on the couch, the blanket pulled tight around me. His brow furrowed as he looked down at me, his expression unreadable.

The snow was relentless, a heavy curtain of white that pressed against the lodge, wrapping it in quietude so profound it felt unnatural. The isolation gnawed at me. Even the fire in the hearth, the only source of vibrant colour in the whole house seemed dimmer, as though the lodge was swallowing its light before it could reach the shadows.

I couldn't stop thinking about the phone. Michael had mentioned it casually on our first day here, claiming it was the only working connection to the outside world. At the time, I'd accepted it without question. But now, with each passing day, it felt like that single link had become another leash in Michael's hand.

I found myself pacing more often, my mind spiraling,

riddled with paranoia as I tried to piece together the fragments of my thoughts. Michael was always in his study, the door closed, the tap of his laptop keys muffled behind the thick wood. I rarely saw him except at meals, and even then, the tension between us sat heavy and unspoken.

That afternoon, while he was outside stacking wood again, I decided to make my move. My pulse raced as I crept toward the study, every creak of the floorboards underfoot making me wince. I glanced out the window as I passed, spotting Michael in the yard, his back turned to the house. He was moving slowly, methodically, the axe in his hand catching the pale light. I hurried on, slipping into the study and closing the door behind me.

The atmosphere in the study was more unsettling than before, colder. The dark wood paneling seemed to absorb what little light the green desk lamp cast, leaving the corners steeped in shadow. I couldn't help but glance at the notebook on the desk, the one that had sparked our fight. It lay closed now, its leather cover gleaming faintly. I ignored the landline and searched for Michael's cellphone, rummaging in the drawers until I saw it. He'd told me he had no signal, just like mine but what if...

My hands shook as I pressed to switch on the screen and immediately my heart sank. No signal and one per cent battery. And then a thought pinged into my head but before I could action it and check his messages and calls, the screen went black. Nausea curled in my stomach. The landline had worked when we arrived. I'd seen Michael test it myself, heard the faint crackle of the connection. I'd believed him when he said it was fragile but at least it was there for emergencies. So why didn't he keep his cell charged, just in case? Now, with both options dead, a dark suspicion began to take deeper root.

Did Michael have some other plan? The thought felt paranoid, ridiculous even, but it stuck, refusing to let go. Was it really such a stretch to think he'd take things further?

My breath came fast and shallow, my chest tightening as the walls of the room seemed to press closer. I leaned against the desk, gripping its edge to steady myself, but the panic didn't relent.

And then I heard it.

A whisper, faint and fleeting, just at the edge of my hearing. I froze, my head snapping up as I scanned the room. The shadows in the corners seemed to deepen, stretching toward me like black tendrils. The whisper came again, louder this time, though I couldn't make out the words. It sounded like the same voice as before, low and raspy, as though the speaker's throat was raw.

"I know," it hissed.

I flinched, my pulse spiking. "Who's there?" I demanded, my voice trembling.

Silence.

The whisper didn't come again, but the air in the room felt electric, charged with something I couldn't name. I backed away from the desk, my eyes darting to the door. The feeling of being watched, of something unseen lingering just out of sight, terrified me. I needed to get out of that room.

I found Michael in the kitchen, chopping vegetables with the same unnervingly steady rhythm he used with the wood outside. He looked up as I entered, his expression calm and unreadable.

"I'm using up anything that's about to rot," he said, his tone casual.

I hesitated, holding onto the edge of the counter. "The phone's still dead," I said finally, watching his face closely.

He didn't miss a beat. "I know. They mustn't have repaired the cables yet. It's not surprising, given how remote we are."

I waited for more, for some sign of guilt or unease, but he just returned to his chopping, his movements unhurried. "Have you tried your cell?" I said, my voice sharper than I intended.

He glanced at me, raising an eyebrow. "Of course. I tried it earlier. Still no signal."

"Did you?" I asked, folding my arms. "Or don't you care we're stuck out here in this living hell?"

He set the knife down and turned to face me fully, his expression softening in that maddening way he always used when he thought I was overreacting. "Harper, why would I be glad when it's clearly making you unhappy being here? And it's not like I can control the weather."

His condescension lit a fire in my chest. "Because you control everything else," I snapped. "The phone. The notebook. Every time I try to talk to you about what's going on, you brush me off like I'm some... some hysterical child."

"Harper," he said, his voice calm but firm, "that's not fair. I've been trying to help you, but you won't let me. You resist medical intervention and logic, so what the hell am I supposed to do?"

"Help me?" I laughed bitterly, shaking my head. "You're not helping me, Michael. You're controlling me. There's a difference."

He sighed, rubbing a hand over his face. "You're tired," he said quietly. "You're stressed, and you're letting this place get to you. I know it's hard, but you need to trust me."

The words hit me like a slap, leaving me breathless with anger. "Trust you?" I said, my voice trembling. "How am I supposed to trust you when you keep me in the dark? When you make decisions for me, about me, without even asking? I bet you knew this place was really a decrepit pile of crap before we even set off."

"For one, I truly believed that the photos we saw were recent and I was as disappointed as you when I saw that wasn't the case but rather than add to your mood, I tried to jolly you along and make the best of a bad job. Second. I am trying to protect you," he said, his voice rising slightly. "Because you won't protect yourself."

"From what?" I demanded. "From this place? From myself? Or from you?"

He didn't answer. Instead, he turned back to the cutting board, picking up the knife with a calmness that made my skin crawl. "We'll talk about this later, when you've calmed down," he said, his tone clipped.

I stared at him, my chest heaving, but I knew I wouldn't get anything more out of him. He always had the last word.

That night, the whispers came again.

I lay in bed, staring at the ceiling, my body tense beneath the heavy quilt. The room was dark, the only light coming from the faint glow of the fire in the corner. At first, I thought it was the wind, a soft rustling that seemed to move through the walls. But then the whispers started—low and fragmented, like a conversation I wasn't meant to hear.

"Liar," they hissed again, the word clearer this time, cutting through the air like a knife.

I sat up, my breath catching in my throat. "Michael?" I whispered, but he just grunted and turned on his side. The whisky he was drinking like water had anesthetized him.

My heart pounded in my ears. I closed my eyes, willing the whispers to stop, but they didn't.

"I know your secret," they repeated, over and over, until the word felt like a hands pressing down on my chest.

I didn't sleep that night.

And for the first time, I wasn't sure if the lodge was feeding on my fears—or creating them.

10

THE LABYRINTH

The storm hadn't let up for days now, the wind howling through the surrounding forest and battering against the walls of the lodge. It was as if the world outside had ceased to exist, leaving just the two of us trapped in this isolated void. For most people, this kind of solitude would be unbearable, but for me, it had become a strange kind of refuge. Here, I could focus on Harper —on understanding her, on piecing together the threads of what was happening to her.

But Harper was making it more difficult than I'd anticipated. She was restless, agitated. I'd catch her pacing the grounds, her footsteps uneven, her movements erratic. Her gaze would linger on the windows, as though she was searching for something just out of reach. Inside the house she'd flinch at shadows, her breath catching in her throat at sounds I couldn't hear.

Her paranoia was growing.

And I couldn't risk letting it spiral further.

But there was something else bothering me and as much as I tried to focus on my wife, I couldn't ignore that it wasn't just Harper who was changing. I'd felt it too, though I didn't dare admit it. The lodge seemed to pull at the edges of my mind. I found myself spending more time in the study, where the small green lamp cast a pool of light that felt almost protective. The rest of the house seemed darker somehow, its air thicker, harder to breathe.

Then came the shadows, that moved differently. I noticed it in the corners of my vision—the way they seemed to ripple and shift, reaching out toward me when I wasn't looking. It was subtle, easy to dismiss if I focused hard enough on something else. But the moments of unease were growing. Still, I pushed the thoughts aside. I couldn't afford to get lost in them. Harper needed me to stay grounded.

I decided I needed to watch her more closely and although I got the impression that she didn't want to be around me, I now sensed she craved my company and if I'm honest I was sick and tired of being locked away. First, though, I moved the phone, locking it in the desk drawer. It wasn't as if the line worked anymore, the storm had taken care of that—but even the sight of it seemed to unsettle her. She'd stand in the doorway of the study, glancing at it too often, her eyes narrowing, her fingers twitching as though she were resisting the urge to pick it up and test it again. Removing it was a kindness, I told myself. It would ease her mind.

I also began subtly reorganizing the living spaces. The great room became our joint domain, the fireplace crackling as I worked at the small desk I'd dragged in from the hallway. I stacked my books and notes there, turning the space into something that felt purposefully occupied, a clear signal that I was close by. Harper didn't say anything, but I noticed how she avoided me, her movements skirting around it like it had become hostile territory.

She gravitated more toward the couch, as though it were an island, a safe place so I brought down extra blankets, rearranged the furniture to make it cozier, left her favorite mug on the side table. It wasn't much, but I hoped to ease her growing unease.

But the rest of the lodge—the labyrinth of halls, the forgotten rooms—I claimed as my own. While she slept or stared at the pages of a book or into the flames, I tested my scientific mind, pushing the boundaries of logic and a measure of fear.

It was during one of my wanderings that I discovered the locked door.

It was tucked away at the opposite end of the narrow hallway furthest away from our bedroom, almost hidden in the shadows. It crossed my mind that it hadn't been there before but that was impossible. The wood was dark and warped with age, the brass doorknob tarnished and uninviting. When I tried it, the knob wouldn't budge, the lock refusing to give even a fraction of an inch.

For a moment, I considered forcing it open. But something about the door gave me pause. It felt... wrong, as though it didn't want to be opened. The air around it was colder, sharper, biting at the exposed skin of my hands like a warning. I couldn't explain it, but the thought of what might lie beyond it sent a shiver down my spine.

I left it alone for the time being, returning to the study and jotting down a note about it in my journal. It wasn't until later that I realized Harper had found it too. She called me upstairs early one morning, a hint of panic in her voice.

"Have you seen this? I didn't notice it before. Do you think it's a store cupboard or an actual room?"

My first thought was to lie. "Yes, of course... I think it's a box room, now come away because it's locked anyway."

Harper glanced at me, "why do you think it's locked?" Then when she looked back to the door, her voice trembled as she spoke, "and it wasn't there before, I know it wasn't. It just appeared."

She became fixated on the door almost immediately. I saw her gaze drift towards it during her restless pacing along the hallway during the day, the way her steps slowed as she neared. Soon her movements became more deliberate, her fingers brushing the wood as she passed. She began lingering there, staring at the door for long stretches of time, her brow furrowed in concentration.

And when she finally brought it up, her voice was quiet, hesitant. "Have you noticed anything about the door upstairs?" she asked over dinner one evening, her fork picking absently at the food on her plate. "The one that's locked?"

I set down my glass, keeping my expression neutral. "What about it?" I said carefully

"Why would it be locked? What's behind it?" She pressed, her gaze sharpening

"It's an old house, Harper," I said, keeping my tone light. "There are probably lots of locked doors. Maybe it's really just a storage room."

Her eyes narrowed slightly, suspicion flickering across her face. "Then why would it be locked? What are they storing that needs to be kept shut away?"

I sighed, leaning back in my chair. "You're overthinking it. It's just a door. There's no reason to make it into something it's not."

Her lips tightened, and I could see the frustration bubbling beneath the surface. "You're dismissing me again," she muttered, her voice barely audible.

"I'm not dismissing you," I said, forcing a note of patience into my voice. "It's just a door, Harper. That's all."

But even as I said it, I felt the faintest flicker of doubt. The lodge was really getting to me. It had crept in quietly at first—a lingering sense of unease, a hesitation in the dark hallways—but now its presence was undeniable. And there really was something about that door...

No. I shook the thought away. Harper didn't need me feeding into her paranoia.

That night, the house shifted.

I don't mean it creaked or groaned like it always did—I mean it *moved*. I'd been lying in bed, staring at the ceiling, when I felt it. A faint tremor beneath me, as though the lodge itself was breathing. The walls seemed to swell and contract, the floorboards groaning in protest.

Harper stirred beside me, her breath hitching as she muttered something I couldn't quite make out. I turned to her, my hand resting lightly on her shoulder. "Harper?" I whispered.

Her eyes fluttered open, wide and glassy. "It's watching," she murmured, her voice distant. "It knows. It knows about me. It told me."

"Harper, you were dreaming," I said, though my own voice wavered. "Go back to sleep."

But as I lay there, staring into the darkness, I couldn't shake the feeling that she was right, and I felt compelled to return to my journal. Creeping from the room, determined not to be spooked, I made my way to the study.

The lodge feels different. I'm not sure if it's my imagination or if something is truly shifting here. Harper's fixation on the locked door continues to grow. She's begun speaking about it with more urgency, as though she thinks that whatever lies behind it is calling to her. I don't know if I should intervene or let her work through it. Could I cross the line and administer some medication without her knowledge? My gut tells me I shouldn't, but my brain assures me I should have done it days ago.

I had the strangest thought earlier. That the lodge could be feeding on our emotions—on Harper's paranoia, on my own frustration. It twists them, reflects them back at us. I've noticed myself growing more irritable, more controlling. I tell myself it's out of necessity, but I wonder if that's entirely true.

I set the pen down, staring at the words I'd written. Was the lodge working its way into us, pulling at the frayed edges of who we were. But I couldn't let it win. I couldn't let Harper spiral further.

I wouldn't lose her.

11

THE ARGUMENT

The lodge watched.

From the deepest shadows, from the spaces between breaths and beneath the groaning of its old bones, it observed. The tension between Michael and Harper was a living thing now, feeding the unseen, stirring the dormant. The man and the woman—it had known many like them, but these two were different. They burned brighter, their cracks deeper, and their emotions richer, rawer.

They were unraveling, and the lodge soaked it in like dry earth drinking rain.

Harper's pacing had become erratic, her footsteps uneven as she roamed the halls, muttering under her breath. She lingered near the locked door, her fingers resting on its surface as though it might whisper its secrets to her. She moved with the energy of someone teetering on the edge, her desperation palpable. But there was something else. She was becoming bolder since accepting what the lodge was doing. It was fascinating.

And while on the surface Michael remained composed, he was weakening. His meticulous order, his calculated movements —it was all a veneer. Beneath it, a growing uncertainty about the things his academic and scientific mind accepted versus his imagination and frustration. They simmered like soup on the hob. He watched Harper with a clinical eye, making notes, observing her like a specimen under a microscope. He thought this grounded him and he was in control. He wasn't. He was scared.

They were becoming combustible. Their myriad emotions colliding and sparking like flint and steel.

That night, the spark ignited.

It began in the kitchen, Harper standing by the sink, her hands gripping the counter as Michael's voice droned on behind her. He was calm, measured, each word deliberate and careful, but it was a thin thread stretched too tight. It snapped when she spun around, her voice cutting through his like a knife.

"I'm not a child, Michael!" she shouted, her hands trembling. "Stop treating me like I'm incapable of making my own decisions."

"I'm not treating you like a child," Michael replied, his voice cool but carrying the edge of frustration. "I'm trying to help you, Harper. You don't see what's happening to you."

"What's happening to me?" she snapped, her laugh bitter and sharp. "The only thing happening to me is *you.* You and your control, your constant need to tell me what to think, how to feel."

"That's not what this is," Michael said, stepping closer, his tone firming. "You're spiraling, Harper. You don't see it, but I do. I'm trying to protect you."

"Protect me from what?" she yelled, her voice rising. "From myself? Or from you?"

Michael flinched, his composure faltering for the first time. His voice sharpened. "This isn't about me, Harper. It's about you.

Look at yourself. You're pacing the halls like a ghost, muttering about shadows and doors. Do you even hear yourself?"

Her eyes widened, her face twisting in anger. "You think I'm crazy," she said, her voice trembling. "You've thought it all along, haven't you? That I'm some kind of unstable project for you to fix."

"Don't put words in my mouth," Michael shot back. "You're twisting everything I say because you can't face what's happening."

"Twisting everything you say?" she repeated, her laugh turning into a bitter bark. "That's rich coming from you. You've been controlling me since the day we got here. The phone, the notebook, the way you rearrange the house to suit you. You're suffocating me, Michael!"

"I'm *suffocating* you?" he snapped, his voice rising now, louder than it had been in years. "Do you have any idea how hard I've been trying to keep this together? To keep you together? You won't even admit that you need help!"

"I don't need *your* help!" Harper screamed, her voice cracking. "I need you to stop. Stop hovering over me, stop twisting everything into some goddamn therapy session. I need you to leave me alone!"

Michael's hands balled into fists at his sides, the tension in his body spilling out in sharp, erratic movements. "Fine!" he roared, grabbing the glass tumbler from the counter and hurling it at the wall.

The sound of shattering glass tore through the kitchen, pieces scattering across the floor in jagged shards. Harper froze, her breath catching in her throat as the glass glittered at her feet, some fragments no more than a foot away from where she stood.

For a moment, neither of them moved. Michael's chest heaved, his face flushed with anger and something else. Regret, maybe, or fear. Harper's eyes darted between him and the broken glass, her hands still gripping the counter behind her.

"Get out of my way," she said, her voice low and dangerous.

"Harper—" he began, his tone softening.

"Get out of my way!" she screamed, pushing past him and storming toward the hallway. The sound of her footsteps echoed through the lodge, heavy and uneven, before the slam of a door reverberated through the house, shaking the walls.

In the quiet that followed, the lodge exhaled.

The air shifted, thickening. The fire in the hearth sputtered, the shadows it cast stretching and twisting unnaturally. The walls seemed to close in, the ceiling pressing down, and settling heavily on Michael's shoulders. He didn't notice, not fully. He felt it in his bones, in the quickening of his pulse, but he dismissed it as adrenaline, as exhaustion.

He stood there in the kitchen, staring at the shattered glass, his fists still clenched. His mind raced with everything he wanted to say, everything he couldn't say. He told himself it wasn't his fault—that she'd pushed him, that she'd been irrational. But the truth gnawed at him, sharp and insistent.

This wasn't who he was. He didn't lose control. He didn't throw things. That wasn't him. It wasn't.

And yet, the evidence was right there, gleaming on the floor.

Harper didn't sleep that night. She lay awake in the darkness, her body tense beneath the heavy quilt, her mind racing with the echoes of their argument. Michael's words looped in her head, twisting and warping until they were no longer his but something else entirely.

When she couldn't bear it any longer, she rose, her feet cold against the wooden floor. The house was silent, but it wasn't empty. Shadows seemed to shift and ripple at the edges of her vision. She told herself it was her imagination, but the house knew better.

She wandered into the bathroom, her steps slow and deliberate. The light above the mirror flickered as she entered, casting the room in a sickly yellow glow. She stared at her reflection, her face pale, her eyes hollow. She looked like a stranger.

And then the stranger moved.

It was subtle at first—a flicker, a delay in the movement of her reflection as she raised her hand to her face. She froze, her breath catching in her throat. Her reflection froze too, staring back at her with wide, unblinking eyes.

Then, slowly, it smiled.

Her hand flew to her mouth, a strangled gasp escaping her as the reflection twisted further. Its features blurred and darkened, crimson streaks spreading across its face like blood dripping from invisible wounds. It raised its hands, palms up, red and glistening as though it had bathed them in gore.

Harper stumbled back, her heel catching on the edge of the rug as she fell against the doorframe. The impact jarred her, and she blinked, her breath coming in short, ragged bursts. When she looked back at the mirror, the reflection was normal again. Her pale face stared back at her, wide-eyed and trembling, but unchanged.

She pressed her back against the wall, her chest heaving as she tried to steady her breathing. The house was silent again, the air heavy with the kind of stillness that comes just before a thunderstorm.

The lodge watched. It was patient. It waited.

12

THE VOYEUR

The lodge had become a maze of unease, its stillness punctuated by the creaks and groans of its old frame. I barely spoke to Michael after our fight, avoiding his calculated calm like the plague it was. The shards of glass he'd thrown still lingered in my mind, lethal, sharp, just like the fracture between us. I didn't clean them up. It was his mess to sort out.

The shadows in the lodge seemed to stretch toward me, and to my own surprise I no longer shook or cowered, instead I waited for them to make their move because after all, what could I do? There was nowhere to run or hide. I was trapped in the eye of the inevitable, whatever that was. And anyway, I'd realised there were worse things than the shadows. The feeling that something was wrong, that Michael had an agenda, that the thoughts in my own head meant I was losing my mind—that could be the true enemy.

Was I losing it?

I couldn't shake the question. It lingered, gnawing at the edges of my sanity like a relentless insect I couldn't swat away.

Upstairs there was a small lounge, tucked under the sloping roof with a tiny window overlooking the forest. Now I was resigned to some unknown fate at the hands of an unseen enemy and Michael was in situ in the great room, I preferred to be in the lounge. It was the only place that felt remotely mine. The thick, dusty air clung to the walls, and the faded floral wallpaper peeled at the corners, revealing patches of splintered wood beneath. The furniture smelled faintly of mildew, and the lone armchair near the window had lost much of its cushioning. Yet, it was a space I could retreat to, away from Michael's endless scrutiny.

I was rearranging the few books on the shelves, moving them pointlessly from one spot to another, when I noticed it. A glint of light, faint but insistent, caught my eye. I paused, my fingers hovering over a book spine, and squinted toward the corner near the window. At first, I thought it was just a nail poking out of the paneling, but as I moved closer, I realized what it was.

A camera.

Small, sleek, and expertly hidden, its black lens stared back at me like an unblinking eye. My heart stopped, then restarted at a furious pace. I reached up, my fingers brushing against the cool metal as I carefully dislodged it from its perch. A thin wire trailed behind it, snaking into a crack in the wall. I didn't dare pull it free. Holding the camera in my hand, I felt a chill ripple through me.

My stomach turned, bile rising in my throat. How long had it been there? How many others were there? My skin crawled at the thought of being surveilled, every movement recorded, every private moment violated. There was only one person who could have done this.

Michael.

I stormed downstairs, not bothering to put socks or slippers on regardless of the cold, my bare feet slapping against the wooden floors. My breathing was shallow, my pulse pounding in my ears by the time I got downstairs and pushed open the study door.

Michael was at his desk, as always, hunched over his notebook with his glasses perched on the bridge of his nose. The room smelled of coffee and old paper, the dark wood paneling absorbing the faint glow of the green desk lamp. He looked up when I entered, his pale face and tired eyes appeared shocked by my abrupt arrival.

"What the hell is this?" I demanded, throwing the camera onto his desk. It rolled slightly before coming to a stop near his hand.

Michael glanced at it. His expression was unreadable. "What is what?"

"This," I snapped, jabbing my finger toward it. "I found it upstairs in the lounge. Were you planning to tell me you've been spying on me, or were you hoping I wouldn't notice?"

He leaned back in his chair, his gaze moving from the camera to me. "Spying on you?" he repeated, his tone calm but laced with a defensive edge. "Harper, I don't know what you're talking about."

"Don't you dare lie to me," I hissed, stepping closer. "You've been watching me, haven't you? Monitoring me like some kind of experiment."

Michael exhaled slowly, removing his glasses and setting them on the desk. "Harper, listen to yourself. Why would I plant a camera? What would I even do with it?"

"To control me!" I yelled, my voice breaking. "To track my every move and prove I'm the problem, just like you always do."

He stood, his full height looming over me as he crossed his arms. "This is insane," he said sharply. "I didn't plant the camera. I have no idea how it got there."

"Oh, please," I spat, my hands trembling. "You're the only

one in this house who's obsessive enough to do something like this."

"You think I did this?" he asked, his voice rising. "Do you even hear yourself? This paranoia, this constant suspicion—it's exactly what I've been trying to help you with!"

"Help me?" I laughed bitterly, my chest heaving. "You're not helping me, Michael. You're plotting against me. Admit it."

His jaw tightened, his hands clenching into fists. "Harper, I'm truly not," he said, his tone hardening. "You've been forgetting things, losing track of time. It's not your fault, but this... this camera? Maybe the owners put it there to keep an eye on the guests which I'm not too thrilled about, but I swear it wasn't me."

The words hit me like a punch to the gut. "Oh."

"Think about it," he said, his voice softening slightly. "You've been under so much stress. People do strange things when they're overwhelmed and as I'm the only one here I make the perfect scapegoat."

"Stop trying to confuse me... I know that's what you're doing. I'm not stupid so go on, tell me, what are you really up to?" I asked, my voice trembling with a mix of rage and disbelief.

"I'm not up to anything, Harper. I'm just trying to make sense of this," he said, stepping closer. "You've been—"

"Don't you dare finish that sentence," I interrupted, taking a step back. "You're gaslighting me, Michael. You're trying to make me think I'm losing my mind."

"That's not what I'm doing," he said, his voice rising again. "I'm trying to get you to see what's happening to you. This isn't just about the lodge—it's about you. You need help, Harper, you have done for a while, but you won't let me in."

I stared at him, my chest tight, my vision blurring with tears I refused to let fall. "You're destroying me," I whispered. "Don't you see that?"

He opened his mouth to respond, but I didn't give him the chance. I turned on my heel and stormed out of the study, slamming the door behind me so hard that the sound echoed through the house.

The hallway did it's psychedelic thing as I stomped, the walls undulating, the patterns on the cushions writhing like snakes so I looked down, silently told them to fuck off as I clutched my arms, my fingers bruising my skin as my thoughts spiraled.

What is Michael up to? What is he trying to prove?

The question burrowed into my mind like a splinter while all of Michael's words stuck like treacle to my brain, their poison spreading through me.

I paused at the foot of the staircase, glancing over my shoulder. The shadows seemed darker now, shifting in ways that didn't feel natural. I thought I heard something—a faint hum, like static—but when I turned, the hallway was empty.

I climbed the stairs slowly, the wood creaking under my feet. My hands trembled as I reached the lounge where I sank into the armchair, burying my face in my hands.

Think. Focus. You must stay strong. Work it out.

All I could come up with was that the lodge was alive. I was sure of it. But I couldn't tell if it was feeding on my fear—or creating it. There was a malevolent energy I couldn't ignore, and I could feel it getting stronger by the hour.

13

MEMORIES

The fire crackled low in the hearth, casting long, flickering shadows across the study. The light of the green desk lamp doing little to dispel the gloom I was experiencing. I sat at my desk, staring at the notebook in front of me. The lines on the new page were blank, but my mind wasn't. My thoughts tumbled over one another in disjointed patterns, each one sharp enough to cut.

I gripped the pen tightly, the metal cool against my palm, but I couldn't bring myself to write. What was the point? I'd documented everything—Harper's restlessness, her outbursts, her fixation on the locked door, and now the damn camera. But no matter how much I wrote, how carefully I observed, it wasn't enough. Harper was slipping further away, and I was starting to wonder if I could stop it.

Or if I even wanted to.

My mother always said that control was the only thing separating us from chaos. She'd told me that over and over, drilling it into me as though the very world depended on my ability to manage every moving piece. She was a woman who made rules for everything—when to wake, when to eat, when to speak, when to be silent. There was never any gray area in her house. Either you followed the rules, or you didn't, and if you didn't, you paid the price.

I was the eldest of three boys, the one she relied on to set an example. When my brothers cried or misbehaved, it was my fault for not keeping them in line. When things went wrong, it was my responsibility to fix them. Even now, I can still hear her voice, sharp and cutting, laced with disappointment. *"Don't let things fall apart, Michael. You're better than that."*

And I was. At least, I tried to be.

It wasn't until I was older, until I went to college, that I realized how much of her voice had taken root in me. I wasn't just organized I was obsessive. I couldn't stand loose ends, couldn't tolerate chaos. My roommates hated me for it, but I didn't care. Order was how I survived, how I thrived. It was what led me to psychology. I wanted to understand people, to decode them, to figure out why they did the things they did. And once I figured it out, I wanted to fix them.

I was good at it too. My professors praised me, my peers envied me, and my clients trusted me. I built my career piece by piece, carefully, meticulously, never letting a single detail slip through the cracks. By the time I was thirty, I had a reputation as one of the most promising psychologists in the field. People came to me because they believed I had answers. They weren't wrong.

But Harper... Harper was different.

When I married her, I thought I understood her. Even though her past was a blank page, a no-go area, refusing to discuss her childhood and her dead parents and sister, I found it appealing because I saw our marriage as a new beginning, the future a white unblemished canvas that we would paint together. I didn't care where she came from and I was relieved that unlike others, she hadn't let a tragedy define her. After all I had patients to fix and didn't want a wife than required my expertise. My family, however, were not so understanding or liberal and remain so to this day. Perhaps they were right, after all.

In the beginning Harper was relentless, driven in a way that was both intoxicating and exhausting. She had this fire inside her, this unshakable determination to carve out a space in the world where she could shine. It was what drew me to her in the first place. She didn't just challenge me; she pushed me, forced me to be better, sharper. I admired her for it. Loved her for it.

But admiration has its limits.

Her career became everything—her obsession with chasing the next story, the next scandal to uncover. It wasn't just a job to her; it was a crusade. She threw herself into it with a single-minded intensity that left little room for anything else. For me. For us.

I told myself I was okay with it. That I understood. But there was always this voice in the back of my head, whispering that I wasn't enough for her. That I would never be enough. That I would never be in control where she was concerned.

Then came the article.

I knew it would be a disaster before she even finished writing it. She was reckless, ignoring the gaps in her evidence, taking shortcuts, she wouldn't have dared to take in her earlier work. I tried to warn her, to get her to slow down, but she wouldn't listen. She never listened. And when it all came crashing down, she acted like it was my fault for not supporting her enough.

I did what I had to do. Distancing myself wasn't just about protecting my career—it was about protecting us. Or at least, that's what I told myself at the time. But the truth? The truth was that part of me wanted her to fail. I wanted her to see what happened when she didn't listen to me, when she let her pride and stubbornness drive her into a brick wall. I wanted her to admit that I was right.

She never did. And now she's paying the price.

I leaned back in my chair, staring at the ceiling. The shadows there seemed to writhe like smoke trapped under glass. My chest felt tight, the air in the room too thick, too heavy. I loosened my tie, my fingers trembling slightly.

The lodge was getting to me. I could feel it. Even the light felt wrong—dimmer, colder, as though the lodge was swallowing it before it could reach the edges of the room and have a chance to shine. I rubbed my temples, trying to push back the creeping unease.

Harper wasn't the only one unraveling. I could feel it happening to me too, slow and insidious. But I couldn't let it show. Not in front of her. She needed me to be strong, to be stable. Even if she hated me for it.

I picked up the pen again, tapping it against the edge of the desk. The sound was sharp, rhythmic, grounding. I needed to write, to make sense of everything, to keep my mind from wandering further.

Harper's paranoia has escalated. The camera incident has only fueled her distrust of me. She's convinced I planted it, despite my repeated denials. I've tried to reason with her, to help her see that her suspicions are unfounded, but she refuses to listen.

I paused, the pen hovering above the page. My hand ached from how tightly I was gripping it. I forced myself to relax, shaking out my fingers before continuing.

I know she thinks I'm controlling her. That I'm trying to manipulate her. But what choice do I have? Someone must maintain order, to keep us grounded. Harper has always been... impulsive.

Emotional. She doesn't see the bigger picture the way I do. She never has. It's not her fault. It's just how she is.

My breath hitched, and I set the pen down, my hands trembling. The words on the page blurred, twisting and shifting as though the lodge itself was mocking me. I clenched my jaw, closing the notebook with a sharp snap.

She didn't understand. She never would.

I stood, pacing the study. I sensed a presence pressing against my skin like a cold, damp cloth. But I couldn't let it win. I had to stay in control. For Harper's sake. For mine.

The fire crackled weakly, the flames barely visible beneath the heavy layer of ash. I stared at it, my mind racing. Harper was my wife, my partner. I loved her. I did. But loving her felt like holding a live wire—thrilling and dangerous, the current always threatening to burn me alive.

I wasn't trying to control her. But some part of me, the part I didn't like to examine too closely, wondered if I was doing it for her—or for me. Because if I didn't keep her in check, if I didn't hold the pieces together, what would be left?

Nothing. That's what.

14

IN THE AIR

I had spent most of the morning wandering aimlessly through the halls, avoiding Michael, avoiding my thoughts. My mind felt like a tangled web, every strand sticky with doubt and fear. Every step I took seemed to echo louder than it should, the sound reverberating off the walls in a way that made my skin crawl.

The sunlight, when it managed to penetrate the snow-covered windows, seemed weak, almost afraid to touch the lodge. I wasn't sure how long I had been walking when I found myself in the hallway near the locked door again. I hadn't meant to end up here, but my feet seemed to have a mind of their own. The door loomed at the end of the corridor, its dark wood warped with age, the brass knob tarnished and uninviting. It seemed to breathe, the air around it colder than the rest of the lodge.

I wanted to turn back, to walk away, but something held me there. The door pulled at me. Its presence magnetic, oppressive. My hand hovered over the knob, trembling slightly.

Then I heard it—a whisper, low and guttural, coming from somewhere behind me. I spun around, my heart leaping into my throat, but the hallway was empty. Just the same endless stretch of shadows and silence. I told myself it was my imagination, but my feet carried me away from the door all the same, moving faster now, almost frantic.

I ended up in one of the guest rooms on the second floor, a small, sparsely furnished space with the same drab décor that dragged the house into another decade. A single window overlooking the snow-covered grounds. I didn't remember choosing this room, but somehow, I was here, standing in the center of it, my breathing shallow and erratic. The room itself looked like it was decaying. The furniture was sparse—an old wooden chair, a narrow bed with a lumpy mattress, and a wardrobe whose doors hung slightly ajar, revealing nothing but darkness inside.

The door swung shut behind me with a soft click.

I turned, my hand reaching for the knob, but it wouldn't budge. I twisted it harder, panic rising in my chest as I realized it was locked. "Michael?" I called. My voice shook. "Michael, are you there?"

No answer.

The walls felt closer now, the room somehow smaller, tighter. The single window offered no relief—just an endless expanse of white snow, as always the trees in the distance standing like skeletal sentinels. I pressed my hands against the door, pounding on it with all the strength I could muster. "Michael!" I screamed, my voice breaking. "Let me out!"

The room didn't respond. It just watched.

Then the first drop fell.

It landed on the floor near my foot, a deep, red stain that spread slowly across the wood. I stared at it, my breath catching in my throat. Another drop fell, and then another, until it wasn't drops anymore but a steady stream, thick and viscous, pouring down the walls.

I stumbled back, my hands flying to my mouth as the blood spread, coating every inch of the room in a slick, glistening sheen. The metallic smell hit me next, sharp and repugnant, filling my nostrils and making my stomach churn. It wasn't just blood—it was warm, steaming in the cold air, as though the walls themselves were alive, bleeding out in slow, deliberate agony.

It dripped from the ceiling in long, crimson rivulets, pooling around my feet, soaking into the hem of my pants. The sound was deafening, a relentless splatter that drowned out the frantic pounding of my heart.

"No," I whispered, shaking my head. "This isn't real. This can't be real."

The wardrobe creaked.

I froze, my eyes snapping to the partially open doors. They moved slowly, agonizingly slow, the hinges groaning as the darkness inside seemed to spill out, crawling across the floor like a living thing. I backed away, my chest heaving, but there was nowhere to go. The blood was everywhere, the walls pulsing as though the room itself had a heartbeat.

And then I saw them—hands, pale and skeletal, reaching out from the darkness of the wardrobe. They clawed at the edges of the door, their fingers long and impossibly thin, their nails cracked and blackened. A face followed, its features shrouded in shadow, but the eyes... the eyes burned. Not with light, but with absence, two hollow voids that sucked the air from the room.

It crawled forward, its movements jerky and unnatural, like a marionette pulled by invisible strings. Its mouth opened, too wide, impossibly wide, and from it came the sound I'd heard earlier—the low, guttural whisper that seemed to vibrate through my very bones.

"Liar," it hissed, the word stretching and distorting as it filled the room. "I know what you did. You're lying to yourself."

"No," I gasped, shaking my head violently. "Get away from me! Leave me alone!"

The blood rose higher, reaching my ankles, then my knees, its warmth scalding against my skin. The creature moved closer, its hollow eyes locked on mine, its mouth splitting into a grotesque grin.

I don't remember screaming, but I must have. The next thing I knew, I was in the hallway, my back pressed against the opposite wall, my breath coming in short, ragged gasps. The door to the room was wide open, the inside clean and dry. The blood, the creature, the whispers—it was all gone, as though it had never been there at all.

But I could still feel it. The warmth of the blood against my skin, the unbearable pressure of those hollow eyes. I stumbled down the hall, my legs shaking, barely able to keep myself upright.

I found Michael in the kitchen, standing at the counter with his back to me. He was chopping potatoes—but the sound of the knife against the cutting board was too sharp, too loud. It grated against my ears, setting my teeth on edge.

"Michael," I said, my voice barely above a whisper.

He turned, his expression calm, almost bored. "Harper. Are you okay? You look pale."

"I—" My words faltered. The memory of the blood still fresh in my mind. "The room... upstairs. Something happened."

Michael set the knife down, his brow furrowing slightly. "What do you mean? What happened? Here, sit" he pulled out a chair from the kitchen table and guided me to it and for a second, his concern and act of kindness not only made me want to weep but it opened a space for me to notice him and how dreadful he looked. Sallow skin, dark rings under his bloodshot eyes. This gave way to a swell of compassion I thought was beyond me but before I could react, he broke the spell with a question.

"Now, tell me what happened."

Back in the room, the desire for self-preservation at the fore, I tried to explain. "I got locked in," I said, my voice trembling. "And then... there was blood. It was everywhere. On the walls, the ceiling, the floor. I couldn't—" I stopped, my breath hitching.

Michael stared at me for a long moment, his expression unreadable. Then he sighed, crossing his arms over his chest. "Harper," he said, his tone carefully measured, "are you sure that's what happened? Or is it possible that you... imagined it?"

I blinked, the words hitting me like a slap. "Imagined it?" I repeated, my voice rising. "You think I'm making this up?"

"I'm not saying that" he said, though his tone suggested otherwise. "But you've been under a lot of stress lately. Sometimes, when people are overwhelmed, their minds can—"

"Don't," I snapped, cutting him off. "Don't do that. Don't try to make me think I'm crazy."

"I'm not trying to make you think anything," he said, his voice calm but firm. "I'm just pointing out that you've been having... episodes for a while now, even at home and you can't deny that your default setting is to bury things rather than confront them. And there was that fight we had—"

He stopped himself, but I knew exactly what he was referring to.

The memory surfaced, vivid and sharp. It had been last year, in the middle of one of our worst fights. I'd shoved him, my anger spilling over in a way I couldn't control. It hadn't been hard, but the look on his face afterward had stopped me cold. Disappointment. Shock.

"You punched me," Michael said now, his voice soft but pointed. "Do you remember that? And the scratches, the kicking?"

"Yes," I whispered. "But that was—"

"You were angry," he interrupted. "You lost control. It happens. But don't you see how that might be happening again now?"

I stared at him, my chest tightening as the doubt crept in. Was he right? Had I imagined it? The blood, the locked door, the whispers—they felt so real, but so had the anger that night. So had the shove.

"I don't know," I whispered, my voice cracking. "I don't know what's real anymore."

Michael stepped closer, his hand resting lightly on my shoulder. "It's okay," he said softly. "We'll get through this. You just have to trust me."

But as I stood there, his hand warm against my shoulder, trust was the last thing on my mind.

15

UNRAVELLING

The walls of the lodge breathed, contracting, expanding with each passing second, as though they were waiting. Harper and Michael moved within its halls like moths circling a flame, unaware that they were feeding it, that their fear, their anger, their confusion was seeping into the wood and mortar. The house was growing, and with it came whispers.

They began softly, almost imperceptibly—so quiet that Harper thought it might be the wind slipping through the cracks in the windows. But it wasn't the wind. The whispers had a rhythm, a cadence, and, worst of all, a voice.

Her voice.

It started that morning as Harper stood in the upstairs lounge, staring out the tiny, narrow window at the snow-covered grounds. The forest beyond the lodge loomed dark and unwelcoming, its emaciated branches clawing at the pale sky. The glass was cold beneath her fingertips, and she pressed her forehead against it, her breath fogging the surface.

The whisper came from behind her, soft and low, a distorted echo of her own voice.

"You'll never escape," it said, dragging out the last syllable like a taunt.

Harper froze, her blood turning to ice. Her heart raced as she spun around, her eyes darting across the room, but it was empty. Just the same faded floral wallpaper peeling at the edges, the old armchair by the window, and the warped floorboards murmuring faintly beneath her.

"Michael?" she called, her voice trembling and too loud. No answer. The lodge swallowed the sound whole.

She clutched her arms, trying to steady her breathing. It had to be in her head. It had to be. But as she turned back to the window, her reflection in the glass made her stop. It didn't look right. The face staring back at her was hers, but the expression was wrong—darker, more twisted. The reflection's eyes glittered with something cruel and knowing, something that didn't belong to her.

And then it moved, tilting its head slightly, its lips a faint, mocking smile. Harper stood frozen, her hand trembling against the cold glass.

"You'll never escape," the reflection whispered again, though its mouth didn't move.

Harper stumbled back, her hand flying to her mouth to stifle the scream rising in her throat. She turned and ran, her footsteps echoing loudly down the hallway, but the whisper followed her, growing louder, closer, until it wasn't one voice but many, all of them her own, distorted and accusatory.

Michael sat in the study, scribbling furiously in his notebook. The desk lamp cast a weak pool of light over the cluttered surface, barely cutting through the shadows that seemed to pool around him. His pen scratched against the paper, the sound sharp and grating on his nerves. He wasn't even sure what he was writing anymore or if it made sense, but it was as though he was purging his brain, spewing words, phrases from textbooks he read at college, passages from the bible, sentences from keynote speeches, scenes from his childhood, committing memories onto page after page of paper.

The lodge had felt different for days now, as though the air was thick with something he couldn't name. He told himself it was Harper—that her paranoia, her negativity, was seeping into the walls, poisoning the atmosphere. But deep down, he suspected he was playing his part.

The first sound came from the far corner of the room, a faint creak like someone shifting their weight. Michael's hand froze, the pen hovering above the page. He glanced toward the corner, his breath catching slightly, but it was empty. Just the same dark wood paneling and the bookshelf lined with old, dust-covered volumes.

He exhaled sharply, shaking his head. He was letting her get to him. That was all it was. Her fear was contagious, spreading like a virus. He returned to his writing, his grip on the pen tightening.

Harper's behavior is escalating. She claims to hear voices now, to see things that aren't there. I've tried to reason with her, but she refuses to listen. She's infecting this place with her hysteria, and it's becoming harder to separate her delusions from reality...

The whisper interrupted him.

At first, he thought it was Harper, standing just behind him. The voice was quiet, barely audible, but unmistakably hers.

"Why did you bring me here?" it asked, soft and accusatory.

Michael turned sharply, his chair scraping against the floor. The room was empty. His breath caught in his throat as he scanned the shadows, the corners of the room where the light didn't quite reach. "Harper?" he called, his voice rough, his throat dry. "Is that you?"

There was no answer.

He ran a hand through his hair, exhaling slowly. It was the

stress. The endless tension. It was making him imagine things. He stood and crossed the room to the door, opening it slightly to peer into the hallway. "Harper?" he called again, louder this time.

Still nothing.

But as he turned to go back inside, the whisper came again, closer now, just by his ear.

"You can't fix her."

Michael stumbled back, his chest tightening as the words sank into him like claws.

"Maybe you'd be better off without her... imagine that."

The door slammed shut of its own accord, the echo reverberating through the room. He leaned against the desk, his breath coming in shallow bursts. He stared at the notebook lying open, the words on the page swimming as his vision blurred.

The lodge felt alive, creepy, its noiselessness no longer comforting but menacing. He sank into his chair, his hands trembling as he gripped the edge of the desk. Harper wasn't the only one losing control. He could feel it too, creeping into his thoughts, twisting them into something dark and unfamiliar.

Harper had retreated to the bedroom by the time the repetitive whispers subsided. Telling her the same thing, that she was a liar, and they knew her secret but the whisper that struck pure terror into her heart was the answer to a question. The one she'd asked Michael many times.

"I know why he brought you here... to send you mad... so he can finally be rid of you."

It all made sense now. Her nerves were frayed, her mind a storm of doubt and fear. She sat on the edge of the bed, her hands gripping the blankets as she tried to steady herself. The walls seemed to buzz faintly, a low, throbbing vibration that made her teeth ache.

The lodge *was* alive. She was sure of it now. It wasn't just her imagination—it couldn't be. The whispers, the reflection in the glass, the way the shadows seemed to stretch and twist in impossible ways. The house was feeding on her, on them, and there was nothing she could do to stop it.

Her mind drifted to Michael. She hated him for bringing her here, for trapping her in this place that felt like a living nightmare. But she hated herself more for doubting her own sanity, for wondering if maybe—just maybe—he was right. What if it was all in her head? What if she was the one poisoning the lodge, infecting it with her fear? He wanted her to crumble, then he could send her away, to one of his clinics or worse, send her over the edge. Then she'd be gone forever, and he would be free to play the devastated widower who'd tried hard to save his wretched wife. How had she not seen it sooner?

The door creaked open, and Michael stepped inside, his face pale and drawn. He looked at her, his expression a mix of concern and something darker, something accusing.

"Harper," he said quietly, his voice strained. "Are you hearing them?"

"Hearing what?" she asked, her voice shaking.

"The voices," he said, stepping closer. "I heard them too. I thought it was you at first, but..."

She stared at him, her chest tightening. "You're hearing them too?"

Michael nodded, running a hand through his hair. "It's you, Harper," he said, his voice low. "It's your fear, your negativity. You're making this happen."

Her breath hitched, her hands clenching into fists. "You're blaming me for this?"

"I'm not blaming you," he said, though his tone suggested

otherwise. "I'm just saying... it started with you, didn't it? The whispers, the shadows. They weren't here before. It's like you've brought it with you."

Tears burned in her eyes as she stared at him, his words slamming into her like a physical force. "You think I'm doing this?" she whispered, her voice trembling. "You think I'm making this happen?"

"I don't know what to think anymore," Michael said, his voice breaking. "But whatever this is... We need to figure out how to stop it..."

He didn't finish the sentence. He didn't have to.

The lodge watched from the shadows, its whispers fading into the dark. It had them now, trapped in its grasp, their fear feeding its hunger, their unraveling drawing it closer to what it wanted most.

It always wanted more.

16

RESEARCH

Even though there were no sounds, it wasn't peaceful or still inside the lodge—it was alive, heavy, every negative emotion pressing down on me like an overcoat I couldn't shrug off. I could hear the ticking of the clock in the study echoing faintly down the hallway, a sound so small yet impossible to ignore. Michael was outside chopping wood, taking whatever was eating at him out on the tree trunks that were piled out back, leaving me alone with the shadows and the whispers that never seemed to stop.

After he'd told me about the voices we'd sat at the table and I for one felt too stunned to speak but I did observe. And I saw just how ill Michael looks. He reminds me of someone bereaved, shattered and diminished by the loss of a person they loved deeply, and it was as I thought it, I realised who had died or more to the point, what. Michael has lost the things he holds dear. Logic, the existence of cold hard facts, the stuff his scientific brain relies on. Last but by no means least, he's lost control. This place has turned everything that brings order to his life on its head because whatever is happening here can't be explained. There are no case studies in a reference book. There is only us.

I'd considered, just for a split second, giving him a taste of his own medicine and denying that I'd ever heard voices but to finally have him experience what I do, was for a brief period a great relief. Until he ruined it by trying to throw it all back in me.

I can hear him now, the thud of the axe as he brings it down on the trunk, and if I strain I can hear the spilt of wood as he cracks it open just like he's cracked our marriage wide by bringing us here. Which is why I'll allow him his macho moment because I can see him now, clearly.

He is weak and despite his bluster and front, probably always has been and that's why he controls me. Why he dragged me here. To dispose of me. I'm not too sure of how he plans to do it, but I'd bet money he has two options in mind, and I need to find out which one. Even this revelation, gifted to me by the whispering ones, makes me stronger and wiser than him and I must use those weapons wisely.

I also had to make the most of his absence and it wasn't like I wanted to go into the study, but I knew I had to. I'd told myself I wouldn't go back in, that it wasn't worth it, that I'd find nothing but frustration. But the urge wouldn't leave me. Something about that room—it called to me, as though the lodge itself wanted me to step inside, wanted me to find something.

I told myself it was just curiosity. That was all.

The door creaked as I pushed it open, the sound too loud, magnified and painful to my ears. The study was just as I remembered it, no hallucinations or shape shifting wallpaper, just the dark wood paneling absorbing what little light the single window let in. Michael's desk was cluttered but in his usual organized way, the papers and notebooks arranged in neat piles that practically begged me not to touch them.

But I didn't care what he'd think if he found out. Not anymore.

The hairs on the back of my neck stood on end as I crossed to the desk. My fingers hovered over the papers for a moment before I began to sift through them.

There was one notebook that surprised me because rather than the usual dull, clinical notes written in Michael's neat, precise handwriting, there were pages of illegible scribbles and symbols, like a child pretending to write, deep grooves and crossings out. Confused, I moved on and found the original notebook containing observations about the lodge, about me. My heart clenched as I skimmed the words:

Harper continues to display signs of paranoia. Claims of hearing whispers in the walls and seeing distorted reflections. Likely stress-induced hallucinations. Suggested distraction through routine activities, but resistance to that and medication persists.

Further evidence of irrational behavior. Obsession with locked door escalating. Denies any possibility of stress as a contributing factor. Appears to be fixating on me as a scapegoat.

I gritted my teeth, anger bubbling up as I read his cold, detached assessments of me, as though I were a lab rat instead of his wife. But I kept reading, flipping through the pages with increasing urgency, searching for something—anything—that would give me answers. And then I found it.

It was a photocopy of an email, tucked between the pages of one of his other notebooks. The words on the page made my stomach churn.

Thank you for the documents. I'll ensure they reach the right hands. Anonymous sources are always welcome here.

The signature at the bottom was from one of the editors at the newspaper that had published the hit piece on me, the article that had destroyed my career. My hands shook as I read it again, and again, my mind struggling to process what I was seeing.

The documents. The fabricated documents.

Michael had always denied having anything to do with it, had sworn up and down that he had no idea how the papers had been leaked. But this... this was proof. He'd given them to the editor, knowing full well what it would do to me. Knowing it would ruin me.

"No," I whispered, shaking my head as tears blurred my vision. "No, this can't be..."

But there was more.

I flipped through the notebook, the pages filled with notes and correspondence. Michael had been meticulous, documenting every step of his plan as though it were just another research project. There were emails, letters, even drafts of anonymous tips he'd sent to other journalists, all of them designed to discredit me, to paint me as reckless, irresponsible, and untrustworthy.

The timeline was clear: he'd started sabotaging me months before the article was published. Long before we'd ever discussed my "stress" or the supposed cracks in our marriage. He hadn't just sabotaged my career—he'd engineered my downfall.

My breathing quickened, the room spinning around me as the realization sank in. He hadn't just lied to me. He'd betrayed me on a level I couldn't even comprehend.

Rage coursed through me, hot and wild, drowning out the fear and doubt that had consumed me for weeks. For the first time in a long time, I felt clear. Focused.

All this was Michael. He was messing with my mind, probably popping something into my food since we arrived or even on the road trip. Hallucinogens' most likely.

As I looked at the damning information on the desk before

me, a surge of pure unadulterated hate washed over me and I vowed one thing. Michael would pay for this.

The sound of the back door closing jolted me out of my haze, my hands freezing mid-page. My heart raced as I scrambled to put the papers back where I'd found them, my fingers fumbling with the edges. The email slipped from my grasp, fluttering to the floor, and I bent to pick it up just as I heard his footsteps in the hallway.

"Harper?" Michael's voice called, muffled but close.

I shoved the papers into the notebook and slammed it shut, my hands trembling as I turned toward the door. My breath came in short, shallow bursts, the sound loud in my ears as I tried to calm myself.

The door opened, and there he was, his face flushed from the cold, his eyes narrowing slightly as he took in the scene. "What are you doing in here?"

"Nothing," I said quickly, my voice too high, too sharp. "I was just... looking for a pen."

Michael frowned, stepping further into the room. "You were looking for a pen in my private notes?"

"I wasn't reading them," I lied, crossing my arms over my chest. "I just needed something to write with. That's all."

He didn't respond, his gaze flicking to the desk, to the notebook sitting slightly askew on the surface. His jaw tightened, and for a moment, I thought he might press the issue. But then the air shifted.

The room grew colder, the shadows in the corners deepening. The faint metallic tang I'd noticed before became stronger, filling my nostrils with the sharp, unmistakable scent of blood. Michael froze, his eyes darting around the room as though he'd sensed it too.

"Did you hear that?" he asked, his voice low.

"Hear what?" I shot back; my anger momentarily replaced by a rising dread.

The clock on the wall began to tick louder, each second stretching out like an eternity. The shadows moved, slithering across the floor and up the walls, twisting into shapes that didn't make sense. The sound of my own heartbeat pounded in my ears.

"Michael," I whispered, my voice trembling. "What's happening?"

The desk lamp flickered, its weak green glow sputtering out entirely. The room was plunged into darkness, save for the faint, eerie light filtering through the window. And then the whisper came.

It wasn't my voice this time. It wasn't even human.

"Liars," it hissed, the word stretching and twisting, echoing from every corner of the room. "You're both liars."

Michael's head snapped toward me, his face pale. "What did you do?" he demanded, his voice rising.

"Me?" I shot back, my fear boiling over into anger. "This is your fault, Michael! All of it!"

The shadows surged toward us, their shapes shifting, forming something that almost looked like hands reaching out. The desk groaned under the weight of something unseen, the wood splintering as the temperature in the room dropped further.

"Harper, we need to get out of here," Michael said, his voice shaky.

But I didn't move. I stood my ground, my eyes locked on his, my rage burning through the fear. "You ruined me," I said, my voice low but steady. "You destroyed everything I worked for, and now you expect me to just walk away, with you?"

"Harper, this isn't the time—"

"Why, Michael?" I shouted, my voice cutting through the chaos. "Why did you do it?"

And then, just as quickly as it started, it stopped. The room was still again, the shadows retreating to their corners, the light returning to its dim, sickly glow. Like me, was it waiting for an answer?

Michael stared at me, his face pale, his eyes wide with something that looked like fear—but not of the lodge. Of me.

"You're losing it," he said, his voice barely above a whisper.

"No," I said, my hands trembling at my sides. "I've never been clearer." And then with all the bravado I could muster I pushed past him and headed for the door.

17

THE BEDROOM

The lodge had me. I didn't want to admit it, but deep down, I knew. I couldn't breathe freely anymore. The air in every room felt like I was wading through water. Every creak of the floorboards, every groan of the walls, felt deliberate, as though the lodge was tipping me off balance.

But I couldn't let it win. I couldn't let Harper win either.

The study had been my sanctuary, and she had invaded it. My notebook lay open on the desk as I tried to write it all down, to make sense of it, but the words felt meaningless, hollow. They slipped through my fingers like sand.

Harper has accused me of gaslighting her, manipulating her, sabotaging her career. She's convinced I'm the enemy, but I know it's the lodge feeding these thoughts. She's spiraling, and if I don't take control, I fear what she might do—to herself, or to me.

I stared at the words, my hand trembling as I wrote them. The ink smudged slightly under my fingers, the black lines bleeding into the page.. My chest felt tighter, my breath shallow. I told myself it was the stress, the tension of being trapped here with Harper and her endless accusations. But it was more than that.

The lodge was inside me now. I could feel it, crawling under my skin, whispering in my ears, twisting my thoughts into something dark and unfamiliar.

The fight earlier had left me shaken, though I tried not to show it. Harper's words had cut deep, her accusations slicing into me like knives. She called me manipulative, controlling, abusive. And maybe—just maybe—there was some truth to that. But I didn't have a choice.

When she mentioned the career scandal, I felt my stomach drop. I thought I'd buried that deep enough that it would never resurface, that she'd never connect the dots. But Harper was smarter than I gave her credit for, and now, it was clear she suspected something. Earlier, as she reached the door she looked back at me, her eyes burning with a mix of anger and betrayal, her voice shaking as she hurled accusation after accusation at me.

"You destroyed me," she'd said, her voice cracking with emotion. "You ruined everything I worked for, and for what? To make yourself feel superior?"

Her words echoed in my mind, sharp and relentless. I tried to push them away, to drown them out with the sound of my own voice, my own rationalizations. But they lingered, gnawing at the edges of my thoughts.

I was surprised when she went upstairs to our bedroom because she'd been afraid to stay there alone. Was even more surprised when from the dark hallway I watched as she lay on the bed, pulled the quilt over her shoulders. It was as though she was charging her battery, like a warrior before battle and this thought innerved me.

She was dangerous, her anger bubbling just beneath the surface, threatening to spill over at any moment. Her silence was unnerving in its intensity. And then she spoke. Her eyes stayed focused on the hallway the entire time, cold and unyielding, and I could feel her hatred radiating from every pore.

"I know you're there, Michael. I know you're trying to get rid of me, but you should know I won't go quietly. I won't let you control me. Not this time." Then she closed her eyes and appeared to sleep.

I waited in the darkness until I could hear a faint snore before creeping forward and pulling the door shut. Gently I turned the key in the lock, tensing as it clicked into place, and for a moment, I stood there, my hand lingering on the brass knob. A wave of guilt washed over me, but I shoved it down, buried it beneath layers of rationalization and necessity. This was for her own good. She'd thank me later. She had to.

But as I walked away, the whispers started again.

The hallway seemed longer than usual. My footsteps echoed loudly, unnaturally, the sound bouncing back at me as though the lodge was mocking my every move. The air grew frigid, my breath fogging in front of me as I made my way back to the study.

The first whisper was faint, barely audible over the creaking floorboards.

"You can't save her. I won't let you," it said, the words dragging out in a low, guttural tone.

I froze, my heart pounding in my chest. My eyes darted around the hallway, but it was empty. Just the same dark wood paneling, the same dim light from the sconces on the walls. I told myself it was my imagination, that the stress was playing tricks on me. But the whispers didn't stop.

"You're not in control," they said, louder this time, echoing around me like a chorus. "You never were."

I forced myself to move forward. The study was just ahead, its door slightly ajar, the green glow of the desk lamp spilling into the hallway. I stepped inside, closing the door firmly behind me, as though that would keep the whispers out.

But they followed me, growing louder, more insistent.

"Do you think she'll forgive you?" they asked, their tone mocking, almost amused. "Do you think she'll understand?"

"Shut up," I muttered under my breath, sinking into the chair behind the desk. My hands shook as I picked up the pen, trying to focus on the notebook in front of me. But the whispers wouldn't let me.

"You're losing her," one said, then another, voices overlapping in a chaotic, dissonant harmony. "You've already lost her."

"Enough!" I shouted. The room fell silent, the whispers cutting off abruptly as though they'd never been there at all. But their words lingered, settling on me like a swarm of ants that wanted to burrow under my skin.

I buried my face in my hands, my thoughts crashing out of control. The lodge was winning. It was turning me against her, her against me, me against myself and I didn't know how to make it stop.

While Michael sobs in the study, I watch Harper as she sits on the edge of the bed, her hands folded neatly in her lap, her face calm and composed. But beneath the surface, her mind is racing, every thought sharper and more focused than it has been in weeks.

She is going to let me think I've won. Let me believe she is compliant, that she is broken, that I have the upper hand. But she isn't broken. Not yet. And she isn't going to let me trap her here, in this house, in this nightmare. Or that's what she'd like to think.

But I am one step ahead. I am inside her head already.

The lock on the door is old, the brass tarnished and worn. It wouldn't take much to force it open if she could find the right tool. A hairpin, maybe. Or the small screwdriver in the drawer of the bedside table.

Go ahead Harper, give it your best shot.

She glances at the window, at the snow-covered grounds beyond. The lodge seems to stretch endlessly in all directions, its vastness disorientating and isolating. But there has to be a way out. There must be.

There isn't.

The whispers in the walls are quieter now, almost soothing in their persistence. They aren't accusing her anymore. They are encouraging her. Just like I told them too.

"Outsmart him," they whisper. "Outmaneuver him."

Harper's lips curl into a faint, determined smile. She isn't going to let Michael win. Not this time.

But it isn't Michael you have to defeat, Harper.

It's me.

And I'm not done with you yet.

18

THE PICTURE

The bedroom was colder than it should have been. I wrapped the blanket tighter around my shoulders, sitting stiffly on the edge of the bed, my eyes fixed on the door. Michael had locked me in. He thought I didn't know what he was doing—controlling me, silencing me, shutting me away like I was a problem to solve instead of his wife. But I wouldn't give him the satisfaction of breaking me. Not yet.

The lock on the door was old, the brass dull and pitted. I'd already tested it when the house creaked, masking the sound of my hand on the knob. If I could find something small enough to fit into the mechanism—a hairpin, maybe, or a screwdriver—I could get out. But for now, I stayed where I was, pretending to comply, letting him think he was in control.

The stillness stretched on, heavy and stifling, the only sound my own breathing and the faint ticking of the clock on the wall. The single window let in a pale, gray light, and beyond it, the snow continued to fall.

It was the walls that moved first.

I didn't notice it right away, too lost in my thoughts, too

preoccupied with the sound of the whispers still faintly lingering in the back of my mind. But when I glanced up, I saw it—the edges of the room weren't where they should have been. The corners seemed to breathe, stretching outward, then pulling back, like the room itself was alive. I blinked, telling myself it was a trick of the light, that my eyes were playing games with me in the dimness.

But it wasn't a trick.

The walls rippled again, the lines of the wallpaper shifting like water disturbed by an unseen hand. My breath caught, and I stood slowly, the blanket sliding off my shoulders to pool at my feet. I took a tentative step forward, my gaze locked on the far wall. It pulsed faintly, the floral pattern twisting and distorting, forming shapes that shouldn't have been there.

And then I saw them—more faces in the curtains.

Their features stretched and warped; their mouths open in silent screams. The floral patterns seemed to bleed into their skin, their hollow eyes following me as I backed away, my heart pounding in my chest. One face stood out—a woman, her hair a tangled mess, her lips cracked and bloodied. Her eyes locked on mine, and for a moment, I thought I heard her whisper my name.

"Harper."

I stumbled back, tripping over the edge of the bed and falling onto the mattress. My hands flew to my mouth to stifle the scream rising in my throat. The faces were multiplying now, dozens of them pressing against the walls, their features grotesque, their mouths opening wider and wider until I couldn't see anything else.

"No," I whispered, shaking my head. "This isn't real. This can't be real."

The walls didn't care. They moved closer, the faces grimacing, twisting, like they were trying to break free, their mouths forming words I couldn't hear. My chest tightened, the air growing colder, sharper, until every breath burned.

Then I saw the picture.

It had been there the whole time, hanging above the dresser opposite the bed—a small, framed painting of a graveyard at dusk. I'd barely paid it any attention before, but now it seemed to pulse with an energy of its own, the colors growing darker, deeper, more vivid. The trees in the painting swayed as though caught in a breeze, their branches clawing at the twilight sky.

At first, it was subtle. A flicker in the corner of my eye, a sense of movement where there should have been none. The graveyard was a small, unassuming scene—rows of crooked tombstones lined up beneath a gray, turbulent sky. A wrought-iron fence circled the plot, its spiked bars twisted with age. Beyond it, barren trees stretched their skeletal branches upward, as if clawing for some unreachable salvation.

But as I stared, transfixed, the painting came to life.

The shadows lengthened first, spilling out from between the tombstones like liquid ink. They grew darker, deeper, spreading across the painted ground until the grass was consumed, swallowed whole by the creeping black. The iron fence rattled faintly, the sound sharp and metallic, as though it existed in the room with me.

The wind picked up, rustling the branches of the trees, and the clouds overhead churned, moving unnaturally fast across the painted sky. Lightning flashed, illuminating the scene for a brief, blinding moment. In that instant, I saw them—figures moving between the graves, their forms vague and indistinct, but undeniably human.

They weren't walking. They were dragging themselves forward, their movements jerky and unnatural, as though pulled by invisible strings. The shadows clung to them, swirling around their feet like smoke, and as they came closer, I saw their faces—

or what was left of them. Hollow eyes, gaping mouths, skin stretched taut over bone. They moved with a single-minded purpose, their heads turning in unison to face me.

My breath caught in my throat as their hollow gazes locked on mine. It wasn't just a painting anymore—it was a window, a portal to something dark and alive, and it was looking back at me.

And then the bat appeared.

It started as a small, dark shape flitting through the graveyard, darting between the tombstones with erratic, frantic movements. At first, it seemed like a harmless addition to the scene, a detail I'd missed before. But as it grew closer, I realized it wasn't part of the painting at all. Its wings beat against the painted air, sending ripples through the clouds, and its screeches pierced the stillness, sharp and grating.

The bat wasn't content to stay in the painting.

It reached the edge of the frame and hesitated for only a moment before it burst free, shattering the glass with a deafening crack. The force sent the frame tumbling to the floor, its wood splintering against the ground. I screamed as the bat soared into the room, its wings impossibly large, its body casting an enormous, distorted shadow across the walls.

Its eyes glowed a sickly yellow, and its screeches filled the room, reverberating off the walls in a maddening echo. It circled above me, its wings brushing the ceiling, sending loose flakes of paint drifting down like ash. The smell of decay filled the air—earthy and sour, like something that had been buried too long.

I ducked, covering my head as it dove toward me, its claws extended, glinting in the dim light. It missed me by inches, the wind from its wings whipping through my hair, and I stumbled back, tripping over the edge of the bed.

"Help me!" I screamed. My voice hoarse. "Michael, help!"

Michael's voice came from the hallway, sharp and urgent.

"Harper!" I could hear his footsteps pounding toward the bedroom, the sound like thunder in the quiet. "Harper, what's going on?"

"Help!" I shouted again, my voice cracking. "It's in here!"

The doorknob rattled violently, the sound cutting through the chaos. "Harper, unlock the door!" Michael yelled.

"I can't!" I cried. "It's locked!"

I heard the key as Michael fumbled with the lock, the scrape of metal against metal. The bat screeched again, swooping low, its claws grazing my arm, leaving behind a burning sting. The door finally burst open, Michael stumbling into the room just as the bat dove toward him.

He flinched, throwing his hands up as the creature flew past his head, its wings beating furiously. It disappeared into the hallway, its screeches echoing as it vanished into the shadows. Michael staggered back, nearly falling as he caught himself against the doorframe.

"What the hell was that?" he demanded, his eyes wide and wild.

I sat on the floor, clutching my arm, my chest heaving as I tried to catch my breath. The room was silent again, the painting on the floor face-down, the walls still and unyielding. The faces were gone, the wallpaper lifeless and dull. The curtains bland and still.

Michael stepped closer, his gaze darting around the room. "Harper," he said, his voice softer now. "What happened?"

I looked up at him, my body trembling, my voice barely above a whisper. "The painting... the bat... it came out of the painting."

19

NIGHTMARES

The lodge eats time the way it eats light, dimming slowly and then snuffing it out until it's impossible to tell how long I've been sitting here, staring at the same four walls. I glance at the clock on the desk, its faint ticking a constant reminder that time hasn't stopped entirely. But the numbers blur when I try to focus, as if the lodge won't even let me have that much clarity.

I sit here for hours, pen in hand, trying to write, to document what's happening, to make sense of the madness that seems to seep from the walls. But the pages stay mostly blank, my words slipping away before I can pin them down. The only thing that remains is the sound of the whispers, invisible commentators who congregate in the corners of the room, just loud enough to make me flinch but too quiet to understand.

I haven't eaten since... yesterday? No, the day before, I think. I told myself I'd grab something from the kitchen, but every time I get close to leaving this room, I feel the lodge's grip tighten. It's like the house doesn't want me to leave, doesn't want me to distract myself from its influence. And honestly, I don't want to leave either. The thought of seeing Harper again, of facing her anger, her accusations, her damn *eyes*—it's too much. She's plotting something. I know she is.

Since she imagined that a bat flew out of a painting, she has reverted to her mute state, refusing to look at me, behaving like I don't exist. I know why. She thinks I've betrayed her again by not believing her, but the irony is, I don't know what to believe anymore. In this state of purgatory, for I pray we haven't descended the depths of hell just yet, the lines between exhaustion, mania, paranoia and fear have become blurred. The only thing I do know is that there is absolutely no point in trying to soothe or appease her. She rejects logic and now she has fully rejected me.

I haven't showered in days. My hair is dirty and my scalp itches like I have lice, my skin is clammy, the pungent smell of sweat clings to my clothes like an accusation. My beard has grown in uneven patches, scratching against my collar when I shift in the chair. I hate the feeling of it, but I can't bring myself to care enough to do anything about it. The mirror in the bathroom feels like a trap, like it's waiting to show me something I don't want to see. So, I avoid it, avoid everything, and sink deeper into the chair, the room, the lodge.

The whispers are louder today. They slither through the air like smoke, gliding around my ears, wrapping themselves around my thoughts. They're similar to Harper's voice, not distorted, twisted, like someone trying to mimic her but getting it just wrong enough to make my stomach churn.

"He knows," they say. "He's starting to figure it out."

Figure what out? I want to shout at them, demand answers, but I'm afraid of what they might say. The whispers never tell me anything useful, only enough to plant seeds of doubt, to feed the paranoia that's already growing like a cancer in my mind.

"She's planning something," they hiss. "She's waiting for the right moment."

I slam my hands down on the desk, the sound loud and jarring in the stillness. "Shut up!" I shout, my voice echoing in the small room. But the whispers don't stop. They never stop.

"She'll destroy you," they say. "Just like you destroyed her."

I don't remember falling asleep. One moment I'm sitting at the desk, my head in my hands, and the next I'm back in our bedroom, the bed cold and unfamiliar beneath me. I turn my head, and there she is. Harper. She's standing over me, her face calm, almost serene, but her eyes burn with something dark, something hateful. She's holding a knife, the blade long and gleaming, and I can see my own reflection in its polished surface. I try to move, to speak, but my body won't respond. I'm frozen, trapped, as she raises the knife higher.

"You deserve this," she says, her voice soft, almost tender. "You know you do."

"Harper," I whisper, my voice barely audible. "Don't—"

But she doesn't hesitate. The knife plunges into my chest, the pain sharp and blinding, and I gasp as the air is ripped from my lungs. She's smiling now, her teeth white and perfect, her expression one of triumph as she twists the blade. I can feel the blood pouring out of me, warm and sticky, soaking into the sheets beneath me.

"You brought this on yourself," she says, her voice echoing in my ears. "You should have left me alone."

I wake with a start, my heart pounding, my chest heaving as I claw at the air. The study is dark. My chest aches as though the dream were real, and I press a hand against it, half-expecting to feel the slick warmth of blood beneath my fingers.

There's nothing there. It was just a dream. But it doesn't feel like *just* a dream. It feels like a warning.

I glance toward the door, half-expecting her to appear, to

burst in with that same cold smile, the knife hidden behind her back. I leave my desk, slowly and as silently as possible I ease open the door and peer out. The hallway is silent, the only sound the faint creak of the floorboards as the lodge shifts around me.

The whispers return, softer this time, almost soothing.

"She's waiting," they say. "She's always waiting."

My hands tremble as I pick up the pen, forcing myself to write, to document, to do *something* other than sit here and listen to my own thoughts. I need to protect myself, leave evidence in case she... The thought I dare not think petrifies me. But the words don't come. All I can think about is the dream, the way her eyes glowed in the darkness, the way her smile felt more real than anything else I've seen in weeks.

I know she's plotting something. The whispers wouldn't lie. They've been right about everything else. Harper is dangerous. I brought her here to help her, to heal her, but now I see the truth. The lodge isn't breaking her—it's revealing her. She's always been like this, hasn't she? Manipulative, vindictive, waiting for the perfect moment to strike.

Or maybe it's me. Maybe I'm the one unraveling.

I don't know anymore. I don't trust her, but I don't trust myself either. The lodge has me in its grip, and it won't let go.

The shadows deepen, in the corners of the room like silent spectators, and I swear I see movement just out of the corner of my eye. A flicker of light, a shape that disappears the moment I turn my head. I think I can hear her footsteps in the hallway, coming closer.

But when I open the door, the hallway is empty.

I snap my eyes awake. I don't know what time it is. The clock on the desk ticks, but I've stopped looking at it. It doesn't matter.

Time in this house is meaningless. It's the whispers that guide me now—theirs is the rhythm I follow, the cadence that dictates when I write, when I stop, when I stare into the shadows until they stare back. I rub my stiff neck that must have been leaning at an awkward angle while I slept when exhaustion claimed me. I suppose I should be grateful for the respite but in truth the thought of sleeping, being unguarded, terrifies me.

I look down at the desk which is littered with notebooks, loose pages, and scraps of thoughts that don't quite fit together. My handwriting has become erratic, the once-neat lines now sprawling and chaotic, as though the pen has a mind of its own.

I was writing about Harper. Now, whatever is on the page could have been written by a madman.

I am determined to write something legible. Concentrate, focus, block out the whispers long enough to get it all down on paper. So that if she comes for me, if someone finds me, they will be in no doubt what happened here.

Harper believes a painting in our bedroom came alive and she was attacked by a bat. Now, she is hiding somewhere in this house. She is watching and waiting for me to leave this room which has become my refuge. I fear for my safety owing to her state of mind. She is angry, erratic, paranoid and delusional and refuses to accept she needs help.

The pen presses harder against the page as I write, the ink bleeding through to the sheet below. My hand aches, but I don't stop. I can't stop.

She's dangerous. Her anger is directed at me now, and I can see it in her eyes—the hatred, the blame. She wants to hurt me. I don't know how much longer I can keep her under control. I have to stay ahead of her. I have to understand her before it's too late.

I sit back, my chest heaving as I drop the pen onto the desk. The words stare back at me, stark and unrelenting. They don't feel like mine anymore, as though someone else wrote them. But they're true. I know they are.

I glance toward the door, half-expecting her to burst in, to catch me in the act. But she's locked in the bedroom. She can't hurt me now. But the whispers say otherwise.

"She might escape," they hiss. "She knows what you're doing. She wants to stop you."

I shake my head, trying to block them out, but they persist, growing louder, overlapping until they're a deafening cacophony.

"She's watching you," they say. "She'll destroy you."

"No," I mutter under my breath, my hands clenching into fists. "Not this time."

I reach for the notebook again, flipping to a blank page, the pen trembling in my grip as I begin to write. My mind is sharp now, focused, every word coming faster, clearer, as though the whispers themselves are guiding me.

Hypothesis: Harper's behavior is not entirely her own. The lodge is influencing her, feeding on her fear, amplifying her emotions. It's using her as a conduit, a vessel for its malice. But why? What does it want?

The question lingers in the air, heavy and unanswered. I pause, my hand hovering above the page as my thoughts spiral. The lodge is alive—I'm sure of it now. It's not just affecting Harper. It's affecting me too. Twisting my thoughts, warping my perception, making me see things that can't be real.

Or maybe they are real.

The desk lamp flickers, its faint green glow sputtering like a dying flame. I glance at it, my breath hitching as the shadows in the room seem to shift, slithering toward me like tendrils. The air grows colder, the anxiety that wracks all of my body makes my chest hurt. My eyes dart to the far corner of the study, where the light doesn't quite reach, and for a moment, I think I see something move.

A figure. Tall, dark, indistinct, but unmistakably human.

"Harper?" I say, my voice barely above a whisper.

The figure doesn't respond. It lingers in the shadows, its head tilted slightly, as though it's watching me. My pulse quickens, my hands gripping the edges of my chair.

"You're not real," I say, louder this time, the words meant for myself as much as for whatever is standing there. "You're not real."

But the figure doesn't move. It doesn't vanish. It just stands there, silent and still, its presence pressing against my mind like a vice.

The whispers return, softer now, almost soothing.

"She's always watching," they say. "You'll never escape her."

I close my eyes, taking a deep, shaky breath. When I open them again, the figure is gone, the shadows in the corner still and lifeless. The pain in my chest remains and for a second I wonder if I'm about to have a heart attack. In the next second I wish it to be so and then this torture would end.

I turn back to the notebook, my pen moving faster now, the words pouring out of me in a frantic rush.

Conclusion: Harper is the key. The lodge is using her, manipulating her, but why? Is it trying to break her? Or is it trying to break me? I need to study her further, to understand her completely. Only then will I understand the lodge. Only then will I survive.

The pen drops from my hand, the ink smearing slightly as it rolls across the page. My chest heaves, my body trembling as I stare at the door. I need to find courage. I need to find Harper and face whatever demons possess her, possess this house and if I'm not careful, will possess me.

20

THE SHIFT

The lodge shifted.

It was subtle at first—small changes that might have gone unnoticed if Harper hadn't already been on edge, pacing the bedroom. She paused mid-step, her arms wrapped tightly around herself and stared at the walls. Something felt... off.

The room seemed smaller than it had just moments ago, and the furniture had shrunk causing her to feel like a giant in a picture book from her childhood. Harper shook her head, telling herself it was nothing—just her mind playing tricks again, the same way it had with the bat, the whispers, the faces in the wallpaper. But as she turned toward the doorway, her breath caught in her throat.

The door was gone.

In its place was a blank stretch of wall, the same faded wood paneling as the rest of the room, as though the door had never existed. Harper's chest tightened, her pulse quickening as she stumbled back a step. Her eyes darted to where the window should have been. But it wasn't there either.

"What the hell..." she whispered, her voice trembling.

She turned in a slow circle, her gaze sweeping over the walls, the furniture, the flickering firelight. The room was the same, yet entirely different. The walls seemed even closer now, pressing inward with an almost imperceptible motion, their edges soft and blurred as though they were melting into the floor.

Harper reached out a hand, her fingers brushing against the nearest wall. The wood felt warm, pulsing faintly beneath her palm, as though it had a heartbeat of its own. She yanked her hand back, a shiver running down her spine.

"Michael!" she called, her voice rising. "Michael, where are you?"

Since refusing to speak, the sound of her own voice was a shock. It echoed strangely, the sound bouncing back at her in warped, distorted fragments. She took a step toward where the door had been, her hand pressing against the wall, searching for some hidden seam, some clue that it was still there. But the wall was smooth and solid, unyielding beneath her touch.

Harper's breath came in short, shallow gasps as she frantically searched for an escape route, running her hands over the walls, tapping the panels with her knuckles.

"Let me out!" she screamed, slamming her fists against the nearest wall. "Michael! Help me!"

But there was no answer. Just the hush, broken only by the faint, rhythmic creak of the floorboards beneath her feet.

And then she heard it—a sound like distant screaming, faint at first but growing louder, more distinct. It wasn't her voice. It was deeper, rougher, filled with pain and desperation.

It was Michael.

Harper froze, her hands pressed against the wall, her heart pounding in her chest. The screams were coming from everywhere and nowhere, echoing through the room like the whispers that had haunted her before. She turned in a slow circle, her eyes searching the shifting shadows, but there was no sign of him.

"Michael?" she called, her voice cracking. "Where are you?"

The room pulsed, the walls bending and warping as though they were alive, and Harper stumbled back, her legs trembling beneath her. The floor beneath her feet rippled like water, the wood soft and pliable, and she struggled to keep her balance, reminded of the fun house at the fair, where nothing was as it seemed.

And then the vision came.

It started in the corner of the room, where the shadows were darkest, pooling like ink in a still glass. The air shimmered. A heatwave distortion that spread outward until it filled the entire space. Harper blinked, her breath hitching as the room around her seemed to dissolve, replaced by a different scene entirely.

She was standing in the study. Michael's study. The desk was cluttered with papers, the faint green glow of the desk lamp casting long shadows across the walls. But something was wrong. The room was unbearably cold—like stepping into an ice box—and the shadows seemed darker, deeper, more menacing.

Michael was there, sitting at the desk, his face pale and drawn, his hands gripping the edges of his chair so tightly his knuckles were white. He looked terrified, his eyes darting toward the door, toward the corners of the room, as though he were being hunted.

"Help me!" he shouted, his voice hoarse and desperate. "Harper, help me!"

Harper shivered, her feet were numb, but she forced them to take a step forward, her hand outstretched, but her voice caught in her throat. She couldn't move any closer, couldn't speak, couldn't do anything but watch as Michael's terror grew.

The shadows in the room began to shift, writhing like living things, stretching toward him with unnatural speed. Michael screamed, his chair toppling backward as he scrambled to his feet, his hands clawing at the air as though trying to fend off the invisible threat.

"Please!" he cried, his voice breaking. "Don't let it take me!"

Harper's heart ached, her body trembling as she tried to move, tried to reach him, but the vision held her in place, forcing her to watch as the shadows engulfed him, pulling him into their depths.

His screams faded, swallowed by the darkness, and the ice-cold room became warm.

Harper collapsed to her knees, her chest heaving, her hands shaking as she pressed them against the floor. The room was silent again, the walls still, the shadows retreating to their corners. But the memory of the vision lingered, sharp and vivid, burning itself into her mind.

She looked up and what she saw made her gasp. The bedroom. She was back where she started. Alone on the floor. Michael was downstairs and safe.

It wasn't real. It couldn't have been real. But it felt real. Too real.

The lodge had shown her something—something it wanted her to see.

A warning. A threat. An invitation?

By watching it take Michael, by not intervening, had she become its ally, or was she next?

21

TEST SUBJECT

The bedroom appeared as it used to be so, seizing my opportunity before it morphed into another nightmare scene, I lunged for the door, yanked it open and ran downstairs, the sense that a thousand invisible feet followed me hastened my descent.

My pulse quickened as I approached the study. The door was ajar, and the faint green glow of his desk lamp spilled out into the hallway, pooling on the floor like stagnant water.

I pushed the door open without knocking. The movement was deliberate, sharp, a declaration of war.

Michael, seated at his desk, flinched at the sound, his eyes wide and startled, like a child caught doing something they knew they shouldn't. He looked terrible. His hair was a greasy, matted mess, sticking up in places as though he'd been running his hands through it compulsively. The beginnings of a beard shadowed his jawline, uneven and patchy, and dark circles hung beneath his bloodshot eyes, making him look older than he was.

"Harper," he said, his voice carefully measured, though his expression betrayed his unease. "What are you doing?"

The study was a mess. Papers were scattered across the desk

and floor, the once-neat stacks of books now leaning precariously or toppled over completely.

I stepped into the room, closing the door behind me with a quiet, deliberate click. The sound echoed unnaturally. Michael stared, his brow furrowing, but he didn't speak.

I took the initiative and positioned myself in front of his desk and pointed at the detritus strewn across it.

"What's this? Your masterpiece," I said, my voice trembling despite my effort to keep it steady. "Your research. Your little experiment. On me."

His jaw tightened, his hands making fists on the desk. The muscles in his neck tensed, the veins standing out against his pale skin. "Harper, you don't understand—"

"Don't tell me I don't understand! Not one more time, do you hear me." I snapped, the anger bubbling up and spilling over before I could stop it. "I've read every word, Michael. Every observation, every hypothesis, every damn note about how 'unstable' I've become. You've been studying me like I'm one of your cases. Like I'm some... some lab rat!"

"That's not what this is," he said quickly, his voice rising slightly. "It's not like that."

"Then what is it?" I demanded, my hands slamming down on the desk, making the papers flutter and his chair squeak as he flinched. "Tell me, Michael. Explain to me why you've been documenting my every move, my every thought, like I'm a subject in one of your damn papers."

His eyes flicked toward the notes, then back to me. For a moment, he looked as though he might deny everything, might try to spin some story to make himself the victim. But then he sighed, his shoulders slumping as though the weight of the lodge itself had finally bore him down.

"I was trying to help you," he said quietly, his voice almost a whisper. "I thought if I could understand what was happening to you, I could fix it."

"Fix it?" I repeated, the words bitter on my tongue. "You thought you could *fix* me by betraying me? By treating me like an experiment?"

"I didn't know what else to do!" he shouted, his voice breaking like a glass shattering in a silent room. "You were falling apart, Harper. Even at home you were becoming depressed, irritable, combative. Everyone was noticing, and they expected me to step up and help you. It's my job and you are my responsibility."

"Everyone. Tell me, who is everyone? Ah, I get it. Your precious perfect family and your well-to-do friends and esteemed colleagues no doubt." Harper knew she was correct without hearing his answer, or denial. It could go either way.

Instead, Michael deflected. "And once we arrived here you began seeing things, hearing things, and I didn't know how to help you. So yes, I took notes. I made observations. I thought if I could make sense of it, I could save you."

The fire in the corner of the study sputtered, its weak flames casting a flickering light that seemed to deepen the shadows rather than banish them. The room smelled faintly of smoke and something older, something damp and earthy, like a graveyard after the rain. I stared at Michael, my chest heaving.

"Save me? How very noble." I said, my voice trembling. "You're not trying to save me, Michael. You're trying to save yourself. From the guilt, from the shame, from whatever it is you're afraid of admitting."

"That's not true," he said, but his voice was weaker now, less certain. His hands were shaking as they rested on the desk. He ran a hand through his hair, his movements jerky and frantic, like a man on the verge of breaking. "This place... it's doing something to us, Harper. To both of us. I thought if I could figure it out, I could stop it."

"And what have you figured out?" I demanded, my voice rising again. "What great revelations have you come to after all your *research*? What does your precious science tell you about the walls that move, the whispers in the dark, the things we see that can't possibly be real?"

He didn't answer. His eyes darted to the shadows in the corners of the room, as if he expected them to move. As if he feared they already had.

For a moment, the room was silent except for the faint crackle of the fire and the slow, deliberate creak of the floorboards beneath us. Michael looked at me, his face gaunt, his eyes hollow and bloodshot. He looked like a ghost of himself, worn down by something I couldn't see but could feel all around us.

"I don't know," he said finally, his voice so quiet I almost didn't hear it. "I don't know what's happening here. I don't know what this place is, or what it wants, or why it's doing this to us."

The words hung in the air like a fog. I wanted to scream at him, to throw the folder in his face, to make him feel the same betrayal, the same anger, the same helplessness that I felt. But instead, I just stared at him, my hands trembling as they clenched into fists at my sides.

"You brought us here," I said quietly, my voice shaking with barely contained fury. "You brought me to this place, knowing what it would do to me. To us."

"I didn't know," he said, his voice cracking. "I swear to you, Harper, I didn't know it would be like this. I thought... I thought it was just a house. A quiet place where we could fix things, where we could... heal."

I laughed bitterly, the sound harsh and hollow. "Heal? This place isn't healing anything, Michael. It's tearing us apart."

"I know that now," he said, his voice trembling. "But I don't know how to stop it. I don't know how to make it let us go."

And then, from some buried corner of her still sane and functioning mind, Harper remembered something, a realization she'd since buried through fatigue and probably fear.

"Have you been drugging me?"

The simple question caught Michael by surprise.

"Dear God, no... I wouldn't. I swear Harper I wouldn't disrespect you like that. Please believe me."

Harper huffed. "Well at least that shows us one thing, if you're telling the truth that is."

"And what's that? And yes, I am." Michael sounded sincere.

"That I'm not hallucinating as a result of medication which means the things I've seen and heard are real. And that, dear husband means we are well and truly fucked."

Michael gasped, and then said, "I'm sorry, Harper. For bringing you here, for all of it and I'm going to try to save you, if I can. I promise with all my heart I will try."

There was something about the way he said it, that reminded Harper of a man she once knew, one she trusted and married and for that reason alone she decided to retreat and give herself time to think. Without another word she turned and left the study, the sound of Michael's apology and promise following her like a shadow.

22

HAPPIER TIMES

The lodge's grip tightened around them both, suffocating and insidious. Neither Harper nor Michael spoke much after their confrontation. The house had settled into an unnerving quiet, the kind that wasn't peace but preparation—as though it were holding its breath before the plunge. As though it were angry with them for calling a truce. Having the audacity to communicate and air their grievances like a couple in therapy when all it wanted was for them to tear each other's throats out.

Outside, the snow continued to fall, smothering the world in its icy grip, isolating them further from reality. But inside, the air vibrated with tension, heavy and electric. The walls of the lodge seemed to pulse faintly, a low, rhythmic sound that neither of them acknowledged but both felt. It was in this mood-altering atmosphere, with the fire in the hearth crackling weakly, that the visions came.

It started in the dining room. They had sat opposite each other at the long, dark table, the flickering flames of the candelabras casting distorted shadows on their faces. Michael had poured himself a glass of whiskey, the amber liquid catching the light as he swirled it absently. After insisting he tipped the contents of every single bottle of pills down the sink, Harper agreed to eat and drink in his presence. She sat stiffly, her fork scraping against her plate as she pushed food around without eating. The gap between them was now a chasm.

Harper couldn't bear it any longer so stepped into the void. "I've had an idea."

Michael paused, mid sip and listened.

"Tomorrow, we're going to be pro-active. We can't wait any longer for the snow to stop so we need to attract attention, and we can do that by writing SOS in the snow. I bet there are search and rescue teams out and about and that means helicopters. At first light we're going to go outside and use whatever we can find, even furniture from in here, to make the letters. Then we'll build a fire and keep it going day and night. We can use the logs out back, or this fucking table if need be but I'm not sitting here one more day while this house eats us alive. So, are you in?" Just saying the words had given Harper hope, made her feel real again so she prayed Michael would too. She didn't have to wait long for an answer.

"I'm in. In fact, maybe we should start a fire tonight. Why wait? Eat up and then we can get cracking." Michael raised his glass and was rewarded with a faint smile which he returned immediately.

And then the room shifted.

The air grew thicker, the shadows darker, inside the walls there was a low, resonant thrum. Harper looked up sharply, her fork clattering against the porcelain plate. Michael froze, his glass halfway to his lips. Their eyes met, both wide with sudden, shared awareness.

"Do you hear that?" Harper whispered, her voice trembling.

Michael nodded slowly, his grip tightening on the glass.

"I think we've made it angry." Michael looked terrified.

The sound grew louder, vibrating through the floorboards,

through the table, through their very bones. The walls seemed to shimmer, the wood grain rippling like water, and the room grew colder, the warmth of the fire all but vanishing.

And then the dining room dissolved.

They were standing in a church. The shift was so sudden, so jarring, that neither of them could move for a moment. The air smelled of roses and candle wax, the faint echo of a choir humming softly in the background. Harper's breath caught in her throat as she looked down at herself, at the white gown she hadn't worn in years. Her hands trembled as she lifted the fabric, the lace delicate and familiar.

Michael was at the altar, his dark suit pressed and pristine, a rose pinned to his lapel. He looked younger, less worn, the lines on his face softer, but his expression was unreadable. His hands were clasped in front of him, his body tense as though bracing for something.

"This isn't real," Harper whispered to herself, her voice shaking. "This can't be real."

But it felt real. The smell of the flowers, the cold stone beneath her feet, the faint rustle of her dress as she took a hesitant step forward—all of it was so vivid, so sharp, that it cut through her disbelief like glass.

Michael turned his head toward her as she walked down the aisle, his eyes locking on hers. For a moment, she thought she saw relief flicker across his face. But then he smiled.

It wasn't the soft, tender smile she remembered from their wedding day. It was cruel, mocking in a way that made her stomach twist. The closer she got, the more twisted his expression became, his eyes glittering with something dark and malicious.

"Harper," he said, his voice low and dripping with condescension. "You look... perfect."

Her steps faltered, her heart pounding as she froze in the middle of the aisle. "Michael?" she whispered, her voice barely audible.

He laughed. The sound was sharp and cutting, echoing off the stone walls of the church. It wasn't his laugh—it couldn't be. It was too cold, too hollow, like the lodge itself had stolen his voice and warped it into something unrecognizable.

"Go on," he said, gesturing toward the altar. "Say your vows. Tell me how much you love me."

Harper's throat tightened, her breath coming in short, shallow gasps. The walls of the church shrank, the stained-glass windows darkening, the once-brilliant colors fading to gray. The choir grew louder, discordant, the melody unraveling into a cacophony of whispers.

And then she saw herself.

At the same moment, Michael's vision fractured.

He was standing at the altar, his hands clammy and trembling as he watched Harper walking toward him. She was beautiful, radiant, the way she had been on their wedding day. But there was something wrong. Her steps were slow, hesitant, her eyes downcast as though she couldn't bear to look at him.

"Harper," he said, his voice cracking. "What's wrong?"

She didn't answer. She kept walking, her head bowed, the train of her dress trailing behind her like a shroud. The air grew colder, the faint scent of roses turning sour, and Michael's chest tightened with an unnamed dread.

When she reached him, she didn't stop. She kept walking past him, her face turned away, her movements mechanical and unfeeling. Michael reached out, his hand brushing against the sleeve of her dress, and she flinched as though his touch burned her.

"Harper, wait!" he shouted, turning to follow her. "Don't go!"

But she didn't look back. She walked down the aisle, her steps growing faster, more determined, until she reached the doors of the church. They swung open with a deafening crash, revealing nothing but darkness beyond. Harper stepped into the void without hesitation, her figure swallowed whole by the shadows.

Michael's breath became erratic, his chest heaving as he stared at the empty doorway. The whispers in the air grew louder, swirling around him, and when he turned back toward the altar, his blood ran cold.

She was standing there, in his place.

Harper stood at the altar, her wedding gown pristine and white, her head bowed as though in prayer. When she lifted her face, her eyes locked on his, and he saw nothing but emptiness. Her lips twisted into a cruel smile, and she held out her hands, her palms slick with blood.

"You let me go," she whispered, her voice echoing in the silent church. "Now it's your turn."

The visions collapsed in on themselves, the church dissolving into darkness as the lodge reasserted its presence. Harper and Michael found themselves back in the dining room, the fire in the hearth burning low, the shadows on the walls deeper and more menacing than before.

Harper sat slumped in her chair, her chest heaving, her hands trembling as she gripped the edge of the table. Michael stood frozen, his face pale, his eyes wide with terror. They didn't speak, didn't look at each other.

Somewhere in the distance, the faint sound of laughter echoed through the walls.

23

THE BATHROOM

Our newfound state of solidarity had crashed and burned. We were no longer unified because Michael was too traumatized to be of assistance, too terrified to show any outward signs of solidarity. After the vision, he collapsed into a heap, a jabbering wreck who was now convinced that we'd angered the lodge and to even attempt escape would hasten whatever punishment it had planned for us. His logic infuriated me and any respect I'd had for him, that had somehow endured the trials of recent months, had been snuffed out.

He'd spent the evening self-medicating, scrunched into a ball on the couch in the great room, drinking whisky, begging me to stay close but not speak of rebellion and SOS signs. There had been nothing left for me. All he cared about was self-preservation and his earlier valiant promises of protection had evaporated, swallowed by this vile, evil house.

As I watched him weep and shake, slurp and dribble and wipe snot from his nose something occurred to me. That the lodge was sucking the life from him and there was a very good chance it would eventually bend Michael to its will. He had always been weak and now there was very little left of him, so I had to rely on myself.

Poor Michael... he wasn't just complicit anymore. He was part of it. Or maybe he was as much a victim as I was. I couldn't tell where his manipulation ended, and the lodges began. Maybe they were the same thing now.

I also wondered if the house could read my mind and if it could, that meant I had to show it that I would not bend to its will regardless of what psychedelic sorcery it threw at me. And at the same time, God forgive me, if necessary I would throw Michael to the lions. The house could have him, but if it meant playing dirty and fighting to the bitter end, it wasn't going to have me.

I knew one thing, a platform on which to build a plan. I couldn't survive this if I stayed in his shadow and allowed him to drain my reserves. He needed to believe I was gone. If he thought the lodge had taken me, he'd stop watching me, stop trying to control me. Maybe then I could find a way out.

I sat there all night, waiting for the first light of dawn and as soon the sun broke through the clouds I left Michael comatose on the couch and made my way outside. I needed fresh air and a space to think about how to handle my husband and the lodge and while I walked, I'd start collecting things for my SOS signal. It was a solid plan which gave me hope, purpose and strength.

The plan came to me the moment I saw the animal in the trap.

The cold air bit at my skin as I trudged through the snow that blanketed the earth, its pristine surface broken only by a faint trail of tracks that led me to the trap. It was old and rusted, hidden beneath a thin layer of snow, its cruel metal teeth clamped around the leg of a small fox. The creature was barely alive, its breath coming in short, sharp gasps, its body trembling with exhaustion and pain.

I knelt beside it, my heart pounding in my chest as I stared into its wide, frightened eyes. It tried to move, but the trap held it fast, its sharp edges biting deeper into the fox's flesh with every struggle. Blood stained the snow around it, dark and vivid, and the sight of it made my stomach churn.

"I'm sorry," I whispered, my voice trembling. "I'm so sorry."

I didn't want to do it. But I knew I had to. The lodge had taught me that survival required sacrifice, and if I was going to survive, I needed the blood. It was the only way to make it believable.

I found a large rock nearby, its surface rough and cold beneath my fingers. The fox whimpered as I raised it above my head, its eyes locking on mine one last time. My breath halted, my hands shaking as I hesitated.

"I'm sorry," I said again, tears blurring my vision as I brought the rock down.

Back in the house, scurrying past the sleeping waste of space, I headed upstairs to the bathroom. Closing the door behind me I stared at the lifeless body of the fox, its blood soaking into the scarf I'd wrapped it in to carry it inside. My hands were stained crimson, the smell of copper and fur clinging to me like a second skin. I could still hear the faint crunch of bone, the pitiful whimper that had escaped its throat before the end. My stomach turned, but I swallowed the nausea, forcing myself to focus.

The bathroom was small and cramped, the pale-yellow tiles stained with years of neglect. The flickering overhead light made the room feel even more claustrophobic, the shadows it cast dancing across the cracked ceiling. The mirror was speckled with black spots of corrosion, its surface warped just enough to make my reflection look unfamiliar. A stranger stared back at me, her wide eyes rimmed with red, her hair limp and matted against her forehead. I didn't look like myself anymore. Maybe I wasn't.

The knife was already laid out on the edge of the sink, its blade gleaming under the faint light. I dipped my hands into the fox's blood, the thick, warm liquid clinging to my skin as I smeared it across my arms, my neck, letting it drip down onto my shirt. The fabric clung to me, sticky and damp, the smell of iron filling my nostrils.

The sink was my canvas. I smeared the blood across the porcelain, letting it streak and pool as though I'd collapsed there, bleeding out. My hands trembled as I worked, leaving handprints on the edge of the basin, on the cracked mirror, on the tiles. I splattered some of the blood onto the floor, creating a trail that led to the bathtub. The sight of it made my stomach churn, but I forced myself to keep going.

The knife came next. I dipped its blade into the remaining blood, coating it thickly before laying it on the edge of the tub. It looked deliberate, intentional, like it had been dropped in a final, desperate act. My hands shook as I adjusted it, the metal cold and unyielding beneath my fingers.

I wrapped the carcass in the scarf and after apologizing one more time, I stuffed it under the clothes in the laundry basket. I climbed into the tub, my legs folding awkwardly beneath me, my back pressed against the cold porcelain. The tub groaned faintly under my weight, the sound loud in the otherwise silent room. I let my head loll to the side, my body slack, my eyes half-closed. I didn't have to play dead for long—Michael would come looking eventually. He always did.

The minutes stretched on. The silence thick, gluey. I could hear the faint creak of the floorboards outside the bathroom, the muffled grumbling of the lodge settling around me. Every sound felt amplified, each crack and groan a jolt to my frayed nerves. My breaths came slow and shallow, my chest rising and falling just enough to keep me conscious.

Then, the footsteps came.

They were hesitant at first, soft and uneven, as though he were unsure of what he was hearing. The closer they got, the louder they became, until they stopped just outside the bathroom door. I could feel his presence on the other side, his hesitation, the way his hand must have hovered just above the doorknob.

"Harper?" Michael's voice was tentative, edged with unease. "Are you in there?"

I didn't respond. My fingers curled against the slick surface of the tub; my nails daubed red against the porcelain.

The doorknob turned slowly, the hinges groaning as the door crept open. Michael stepped inside, his breath catching in his throat as he took in the scene. I could hear it—the sharp inhale, imagined the sound of the blood draining from his face.

"Harper," he whispered, the word trembling. "Oh my God."

I heard the shuffle of his feet as he moved closer, the faint creak of the floor beneath his shoes. He stopped just short of the tub, his breath coming in ragged gasps, his body casting a long shadow across me.

"Harper," he said again, his voice cracking. "No... no, no, no."

I risked a glance, my eyes opening just enough to see him. His face was pale, his eyes wide and glistening with unshed tears. He looked lost, hollow, as though the sight of me had drained him of whatever fight he had left. He reached out a trembling hand toward me, but stopped short, his fingers becoming a fist.

"This isn't real," he muttered to himself, his voice shaking. "This can't be real."

He backed away, his hands raking through his hair, his movements frantic and disjointed. "The lodge... it's the lodge. It took her. It's—it's not my fault. I didn't... I didn't do this."

He turned away from me, his breath hitching as he stumbled toward the door. I stayed still, my heart pounding in my chest, every muscle in my body tense as I waited for him to leave.

Michael stopped in the doorway, his hand gripping the frame so tightly his knuckles turned white. He looked back at me, his face contorted with a mix of grief and fear.

"I didn't do this," he said again, his voice barely above a whisper. "The lodge did."

Then he was gone, the sound of his footsteps fading down the hall. I waited until I could no longer hear him, my body trembling as I slowly sat up in the tub. The room spun around me, the air thick and stifling, the faint smell of blood making my stomach turn.

I'd done it. He believed it. But as I climbed out of the tub, my feet slipping on the slick floor, a strange sense of unease settled over me.

The lodge wasn't done with either of us. And I wasn't sure how much longer I could keep playing this game.

24

A HAUNTING

The lodge is a living thing.

I can feel it in my bones, in the air, in the creaking floorboards beneath my feet. It breathes, a slow and deliberate rhythm that matches the pounding in my chest. The walls seem to ripple in my peripheral vision, as though they're alive, flexing and contracting like muscle and sinew. The faint hum that used to be barely noticeable has grown louder, more insistent, until it feels like the entire house is vibrating with it. The fire in the hearth flickers weakly, its embers casting dull, feeble light. The cold has crept into my skin, into my very soul, and the oppressiveness of the shadows threatens to pull me under.

The shadows are the worst. They have mass now, a tangible presence that fills every corner of the lodge. They've grown darker, thicker, pooling in spaces that used to be safe. Sometimes I catch movement in them—just the barest flicker of something humanoid, something that shouldn't be there. Other times, they stretch toward me, long and sinuous, like fingers reaching to wrap around my throat.

I tell myself it's the lodge. It's *only* the lodge. But the doubt creeps in, whispering at the edges of my mind. Is it the lodge? Or is it Harper?

I haven't slept in what feels like days. Every time I close my eyes, I hear her voice, soft and mocking, weaving through the walls like smoke. Sometimes I see her too—not the Harper I knew, but something twisted, something wrong. Her eyes are darker, her smile too wide, her movements too smooth, like she's gliding instead of walking. I know it isn't real, but it doesn't matter. My pulse races all the same, and I can't shake the feeling that she's watching me, waiting for me to falter.

The whispers have started to change. They used to be indistinct, unintelligible that I could ignore if I tried hard enough. Now they have words, sentences, meaning. They curl around me, seeping into my thoughts, planting seeds of doubt and paranoia.

"She's not gone," they say. "She'll never leave you."

I'm starting to believe them.

This morning, I found my coffee laced with salt. I didn't notice at first, not until I took a sip and nearly choked on the bitter, acrid taste. I spat it out into the sink, staring down at the dark liquid swirling down the drain. My hands trembled as I rinsed the cup, my mind racing.

It wasn't me. I didn't put the salt there.

But it couldn't have been Harper. She's gone. I saw the blood. I saw the tub. She's gone.

And yet, the thought lingers, gnawing at the edges of my sanity. What if she isn't? What if she's still here, somewhere in the shadows, watching me, tormenting me? I can't go in there, to the bathroom. I can't look at her like that again. I stay downstairs instead.

The lodge seems to feed on my doubt. The walls creak and groan, the sound echoing through the house like the slow, deliberate exhale of some great beast. The mood has descended deeper now, as though it's pressing down on me, forcing me to stay in place. I feel like I'm suffocating, but no matter how deeply I breathe, I can't seem to get enough air.

By midday, the lodge's malevolence had reached a fever pitch. The walls were breathing again, their wooden surfaces expanding and contracting with an unnatural rhythm. The sound was faint but constant, like the inhalation and exhalation of something alive. The air felt heavy, thick with an almost electric charge, and I found myself flinching at every creak, every groan, every whisper.

I was in the study when I found the glass.

It was sitting on the edge of my desk, its rim cracked and uneven, the faint scent of whiskey still clinging to it. I didn't remember leaving it there, and as I picked it up, my thumb grazed the sharp edge of the break. Blood welled up immediately, a bright red bead that dripped onto the papers scattered across the desk. I cursed, grabbing a tissue to press against the cut, but my eyes kept drifting back to the glass.

The break wasn't natural. It was deliberate. The smashed edges were too precise, too clean, as though someone had taken the time to shape it into a weapon.

Harper's face flashed in my mind, her eyes dark and accusing, her smile sharp and cold. I shook my head, trying to banish the image, but the unease remained. She couldn't be here. She wasn't here.

But the glass said otherwise.

The tricks continued. That evening, I found shards of broken ceramic scattered across the floor just outside the study door. They were positioned perfectly to catch me if I'd stepped out without looking, sharp enough to slice through my slippers. I cleaned them up quickly, my hands shaking as I gathered the pieces into a dustpan.

"She's not gone."

The whispers grew louder, their words hissing and sharp, burrowing into my mind like parasites. The shadows in the corners seemed to stretch toward me, reaching for my throat. I stumbled back, my chest heaving, my vision swimming with dark spots.

"Harper!" I shouted, my voice breaking. "What do you want from me?"

My words echoed through the empty lodge, bouncing off the walls and fading into nothing. No answer came. Only the sound of the lodge breathing, its slow, deliberate rhythm mocking my desperation.

By the time night fell, I was on edge, every muscle in my body wound tight. The lodge's energy was unbearable, a living, pulsating force that seemed to seep into my very bones. I barricaded myself in the study, locking the door and pushing a chair against it for good measure. The fire in the hearth burned low, casting flickering shadows across the room, and I sat hunched over the desk, my head in my hands.

"She's not gone," the whispers said, soft and mocking.

"Leave me alone," I muttered, my voice hoarse.

The shadows on the walls shifted, dark figures forming and dissolving, their movements too fluid, too deliberate to be a trick of the light. My breath hitched as one of them broke away, slithering across the floor toward me. It stopped just short of my chair, its form pulsating, and for a moment, I thought I saw Harper's face staring back at me from within the darkness.

I blinked, and it was gone.

Somewhere in the lodge, I heard a door slam, the sound

reverberating through the walls like a gunshot. I flinched, my heart pounding, my hands gripping the edge of the desk. I couldn't tell if it was real or another of the lodge's tricks, but either way, I knew one thing for certain.

Harper's angry spirit was still here.

And she wasn't done with me yet.

25

THE ESCAPE

The lodge is alive, and it knows us—knows *me*. It knows Michael. It knows the secrets we bury and the lies we tell ourselves to keep breathing. It sees every crack in our façade, every wound we try to hide, and it digs its claws into those places, prying them open just to watch us bleed. It feeds on us, on our fear, our anger, our desperation. The more we fight it, the tighter its grip becomes.

But I've learned something it didn't expect. I can feed off it too. The lodge isn't invincible, and neither is Michael. They both think they control me, that I'm just a pawn in their game. But they're wrong. They're so wrong.

I stood in the shadows, my breath slow and measured, watching as Michael clawed at the front door. His desperation was palpable, raw and unhinged, and it filled me with a strange, twisted satisfaction. He thought he could leave, that there was a way out. I almost laughed. There was no escape from this place. There never had been. The lodge wouldn't let him go. And neither would I.

Michael was unraveling.

His shoulders slumped as he slammed his fists against the

door, his knuckles bruising, his breath coming in ragged gasps. His hair was plastered to his forehead with sweat, his shirt wrinkled and stained. He looked like a man who had been running from something for days but couldn't find the strength to take another step.

"Why?" he muttered, his voice barely audible. "Why won't it let me go?"

I leaned against the wall, the shadows wrapping around me like a cloak. My fingers brushed the cold wood of the paneling, and for a moment, I thought I felt it pulse beneath my touch, like a heartbeat. The lodge was watching him, toying with him, and I could feel its amusement, its dark, insidious joy.

But it wasn't just the lodge. I was part of this now. I'd set the traps, placed the broken glass, spilled the salt. Each little act was a thread in the web I was spinning, a game to see how far he would unravel before he realized it was me. I should have felt guilty, but I didn't. Not anymore.

Michael was the one who started this. He brought me here, into this living nightmare, and then he betrayed me. He used me. And now, I was using him.

He turned away from the door, his body sagging, as if the lodge was finally crushing him. His eyes darted around the room, flickering over the shadows that stretched and twisted along the walls. I saw the fear in his face, the growing realization that he was trapped, that he couldn't outsmart this place.

"Harper," he said, his voice cracking. "Harper, if you can hear me... I'm sorry. I'm so sorry."

The words should have meant something, but they didn't. Not anymore. They were hollow, desperate, spoken more for his benefit than mine. He wasn't apologizing to me; he was pleading with the lodge, trying to bargain with a force he couldn't comprehend.

I wanted to step out of the shadows, to confront him, to see his face when he realized I wasn't gone. But I didn't. The lodge wouldn't let me. It wanted him to squirm, to suffer, to break. And I... I wanted to see what he would do when there was nothing left to hold on to.

The lodge pulsed again, a low, rhythmic thrum that vibrated through the floorboards and up into my chest. It was speaking to me, though not in words. Its intentions were clear, carved into the very fabric of the house. It wanted more than our fear, more than our pain. It wanted to consume us completely, to strip away everything that made us human until we were nothing but hollow shells, echoes of who we used to be.

The lodge wanted our souls.

It was already happening to Michael. I could see it in the way he moved, the way he spoke. He wasn't the man I married anymore. He was something else, something the lodge had twisted and warped into its image. And I... I wasn't far behind him.

But I wasn't going to let it win. Not yet.

I still had a role to play.

Michael stumbled toward the staircase, his hand gripping the banister as though it were the only thing keeping him upright. He paused, his head tilting slightly as though he'd heard something. I held my breath, pressing myself deeper into the shadows. He turned slowly, his eyes scanning the hallway, and for a moment, his gaze lingered on the spot where I stood.

"Harper?" he whispered, his voice trembling. "Are you there?"

I didn't move. The lodge shifted around us, the walls groaning as the shadows deepened. Michael's hand tightened on the banister, his knuckles white, and I saw a flicker of something in his eyes—hope, fear, maybe both.

"I know you're here," he said, louder this time. "I can feel you."

He took a step toward me, and I felt the pulse of the lodge quicken, its energy crackling in the air like static. It was watching, waiting, urging me to act. But I stayed still, my fingers brushing the wall as I let the moment stretch out, the tension building like a taut wire ready to snap.

"Please," Michael said, his voice breaking. "I don't know what to do. I don't know how to fix this."

I almost pitied him. Almost. But then I thought about the notes, the journal, the way he'd treated me like an experiment, like I was something to be studied and controlled. He'd brought me here, to this place, to this *thing*, and now he was begging for my help.

The lodge hummed again, its presence pressing against me like a heavy fog. It wanted me to step forward, to show myself, to give Michael the confrontation he was so desperate for. But I wasn't ready. Not yet.

Instead, I slipped away, my footsteps silent on the cold wood as I moved deeper into the house. Michael's voice followed me, echoing through the empty hallways, but I didn't look back.

The lodge had its plans, and so did I. It thought it could manipulate me, bend me to its will, but it didn't understand what I was capable of. I wasn't just another victim. I wasn't just another pawn in its game.

I was something else entirely.

But I should have known the lodge would play a new hand eventually and it caught me off guard with the dream and I have to say it dug deep and unearthed a secret that I thought I'd wiped from my psyche. I was wrong which was why I had to endure a foray into my past. The lodge took me back in time, via a dream.

. . .

I'd taken to sleeping in one of the unused bedrooms on the floor above Michael's. Not that he slept there much, and I knew he was too traumatized to go searching for me. In the dream I was standing in the hallway observing my husband, and then gradually the walls melted away completely, the lodge's cold embrace replaced by the smothering heat and crackle of fire. I was no longer in the shadowed corridors of the lodge. I was home—or what was left of it. My childhood home stood before me, just as I remembered it, every detail sharpened by the flames licking hungrily at its edges.

The floorboards beneath my feet groaned as I moved, warped and blackened by the heat. The wallpaper ripped, rolling downwards in sheets, the furniture now a distorted, melting mess. Smoke billowed from the corners of the room, heavy and thick, wrapping around me like a shroud. I gagged on the acrid scent of burning wood and something darker—something that smelled of flesh.

The living room was as familiar as it was horrifying. The old couch, its cushions flattened from years of use, was consumed by fire, its fabric disintegrating into ash. The bookshelf my father had built with his own hands was collapsing under the weight of the flames, the books bursting into brief flashes of light before crumbling into nothingness. The clock on the mantel—the one that had chimed every hour since I could remember—was frozen at 11:17, the glass face cracked and distorted by the heat. Its pendulum hung still, as if the fire had devoured even the concept of time.

I couldn't breathe. My lungs screamed for air, but all they got was smoke. The heat was unbearable, scorching my skin, and I could feel my clothes sticking to me, damp with sweat and fear. My legs felt like lead, rooted to the floor as the room around me dissolved into chaos.

The voices started again, faint at first, hidden beneath the roar of the flames. They were distant, distorted, but unmistakable.

"You let us burn."

I spun toward the staircase, my heart lurching as I saw the fire crawling upward, devouring each step with a sinister, deliberate hunger. My gaze traveled upward, to the landing where the flames hadn't yet reached. And there they were.

My mother stood at the top of the stairs, her nightgown tattered and singed, her hair hanging in soot-streaked tangles. Her face was gaunt, her skin pale and waxy, her eyes wide and unblinking. Beside her stood my father, his shoulders hunched, his once-strong frame now gaunt and skeletal. And then there was Emma.

Emma, my little sister, was clutching her stuffed rabbit—the one I'd given her for her fifth birthday. The edges of its fur were singed, its button eyes hanging by threads. She stared down at me, her small frame trembling, her lips moving soundlessly.

I opened my mouth to call out to them, but no sound came. My throat burned; the words strangled by the smoke that filled the room. Tears streamed down my face, mixing with the sweat and ash, as I raised my hands in a feeble gesture of apology, of helplessness.

"I'm sorry," I choked out, my voice barely audible. "I'm so sorry."

My mother's head tilted to the side, her expression cold and unfeeling. "You let us burn," she said, her voice hollow and echoing, like it wasn't her own.

"No," I whispered, shaking my head. "No, I didn't—"

"You could have saved us," my father interrupted, his voice a low growl that sent chills down my spine. "But you ran. You left us."

"That's not true!" I screamed, my voice breaking. "I tried—I did everything I could!"

The flames surged, the heat blistering my skin as the walls groaned and splintered around me. Emma took a step forward, her bare feet leaving blackened, charred imprints on the floor. Her wide, innocent eyes glistened with tears, but her expression was unreadable—somewhere between sorrow and anger.

"You left me," she said softly, her voice trembling. "You left me, Harper."

I collapsed to my knees, my legs giving out beneath me. My chest heaved as I sobbed, the poison of her words seeping into me. "I didn't mean to," I cried. "I didn't want to—I was scared, Emma. I was so scared."

Her lips curved into a small, sad smile, but it didn't reach her eyes. "You let me die," she said, her voice laced with quiet accusation. "You let all of us die."

"No," I whispered, shaking my head frantically. "No, no, no..."

The room shifted; the fire roaring louder as the ceiling above me began to collapse. Burning beams crashed to the floor, splintering into sparks and ash. The air grew hotter, denser, and I felt my vision blur, the edges of the room fading into a hazy swirl of orange and black.

And then I was in my bedroom.

It was untouched by the flames—exactly as I'd left it on that night so many years ago. The pink comforter on the bed, the posters of boy bands on the walls, the stack of books on the nightstand—it was all there, pristine and perfect. But the door was open, and beyond it, I could see the fire raging, its orange glow spilling into the room like an unwelcome intruder.

I turned toward the window, my breath catching in my throat as I saw myself reflected in the glass. It wasn't me—not really. It was a younger version of me, wide-eyed and trembling, her hands pressed against the windowpane as though she were trying to escape.

"You ran," she said, her voice low and accusing. "You ran, and you left them to die."

I stumbled backward, shaking my head. "I didn't—I couldn't—"

"You're a coward," she spat, her voice rising. "You always have been."

The flames surged into the room, consuming everything in their path, and I screamed as they closed in around me. The heat was unbearable, the air thick and choking, and I could feel my skin blistering, peeling away.

And then it was gone.

I was back in the lodge, collapsed on the floor, my chest heaving as I gasped for air. The smell of smoke lingered, clinging to my clothes and hair, and I could still feel the heat on my skin, as though the fire had followed me back.

I pressed my hands to my face, my body trembling. The lodge had shown me my greatest failure, dredged it up from the deepest, darkest corners of my mind. It had made me relive it, feel it, like it was happening all over again. The night I let my parents die, just to block out the sounds of them fighting. I thought it would shut them up, punish them for making me sad and scared. I didn't know they'd die. But they did, because I waited and waited downstairs until the fire took hold and there was no way to escape and by the time I went for help, Emma and her bunny had burnt to death. I'd forgotten about my sister. The innocent victim in all of it.

I had told myself for years that it wasn't my fault, that there was nothing I could have done. But that was a lie. One I'd stuck to throughout the years in care, adolescence, until it became my truth. The lodge had a way of twisting things, of making me question everything I thought I knew.

And then there was Michael.

The lodge was breaking him, turning him into something

unrecognizable. But was I any better? I had set traps, played games, fed into the chaos. Was it revenge? Self-preservation? Or was I becoming just as cruel, just as twisted as the lodge itself?

I didn't know anymore. All I knew was that we were both falling, and the lodge was waiting at the bottom, ready to catch us.

26

THE EXORCISM

The lodge was Harper now. I could feel her everywhere. Watching, whispering, pressing her presence into every corner of my mind. She had slipped through the cracks in the walls, seeped into the floorboards, taken root in the air I breathed. It wasn't just a suspicion anymore; it was a fact. Harper *was* the lodge, and she wanted to destroy me.

The realization should have terrified me, but all I felt was fury. A blinding, consuming fury. My heartbeat thundered in my ears, and every rational thought evaporated under the force of my anger. She thought she could trap me here. She thought she could win.

I would burn this place to the ground before I let that happen.

The shattered mirrors weren't enough. Their broken fragments stared back at me from the floor like glittering eyes, refracting a thousand distorted versions of my face. Each one mocked me, their spiked edges twisting my reflection into something monstrous. Or maybe they were finally showing me the truth.

The poker was still in my hand, its metal cool and steady despite the chaos raging inside me. I gripped it tighter, my knuckles white, as I turned to face the walls. They moving again, the wood groaning and shifting, the grain rippling like muscle under skin. I swung the poker blindly, the impact reverberating through my arms as it splintered the paneling.

"Get out!" I roared, my voice cracking. "You don't belong here! You don't belong *in me*!"

The lodge seemed to respond, a vibration in the air deepening into a resonant thrum that invaded my bones. The shadows in the corners stretched and writhed, their movements deliberate, predatory. I could feel their eyes on me, cold and calculating, waiting for me to break.

"Harper!" I screamed, slamming the poker into the wall again. The wood splintered further. "Is this what you wanted? Is this what you've become?"

The only answer was her laughter, soft and hollow, echoing through the room. It wasn't coming from the walls this time. It was coming from *inside me.*

I staggered back, my breath coming in ragged gasps, my chest heaving as I clutched my head. The laughter wouldn't stop, reverberating through my skull like a hammer. It was hers, but it was mine too, a twisted amalgamation of our voices that sent a chill down my spine.

"You brought us here," the voice hissed, low and venomous. "You made this happen."

"No," I muttered, shaking my head. "No, that's not true."

"You wanted control," it continued, its tone mocking. "You wanted to fix her, to mold her, to make her yours. But you couldn't, could you? And now she's stronger than you'll ever be."

"Shut up!" I shouted, swinging the poker wildly at the air. "You don't know anything!"

But it did. It knew everything. The lodge had wormed its way into my mind, pulling apart every memory, every failure, every regret. It twisted them, reshaped them, turned them into weapons to use against me.

I saw Harper in my mind's eye, the way she used to be—vibrant, determined, unshakable. I'd hated that about her. No, not hated. Resented. She'd never needed me the way I needed her, and that imbalance had eaten away at me, little by little, until I couldn't see her as my partner anymore. She'd become my project, my responsibility, my burden.

And now, she was my tormentor.

The lodge groaned, its walls shifting as though in response to my thoughts. The shadows tightening like a noose, and I lashed out again, the poker striking a chair and sending it crashing to the floor. The sound was deafening in the mute space, a sharp, violent crack that seemed to shake the room.

I turned to the fireplace, the flames burning low and sullen, casting long, flickering shadows on the walls. The mantle was bare now, the shattered mirror lying in pieces on the hearth. I could see my reflection in the fragments, each shard showing a different part of my face—my eyes wild, my mouth twisted in a snarl, my skin pale and slick with sweat.

I looked like a man possessed. Maybe I was.

"You can't have me," I whispered, my voice trembling. "You can't win."

The fire surged suddenly, the flames leaping higher, brighter, as though in response to my defiance. Her face appeared in the fire again, her smile cruel and knowing, her eyes glinting with malice.

"You're mine," she said, her voice a low, melodic hiss. "You've always been mine."

The laughter returned, louder this time, drowning out the

crackle of the fire and the creak of the walls. I dropped the poker, the metal clattering against the stone hearth as I stumbled back, clutching my head. My thoughts were a cacophony, Harper's voice weaving through them like a thread, pulling them tighter and tighter until I thought my skull might split open.

"You're not real," I whispered, my voice hoarse. "You're not real."

But she was. She was everywhere. In the walls, in the fire, in the shadows that stretched toward me like claws. She was the lodge, and the lodge was her, and they were both pulling me apart, piece by piece.

I fell to my knees, my breath coming in shallow, uneven gasps. The room spun around me, the shadows shifting and twisting. The lodge's pulse thrummed beneath me, a steady, unrelenting beat that matched the pounding in my head.

I was losing. I could feel it. The lodge was inside me now, burrowing deeper with every passing moment, turning my own thoughts against me. Harper wasn't just a part of the lodge anymore. She was a part of me.

And I didn't know how to make her stop.

The fire burned low again, its flames flickering weakly as though it, too, was mocking me. I stared into the embers, my vision blurring, and for a moment, I thought I saw something moving within them—a figure, small and indistinct, but undeniably familiar.

Harper.

She wasn't smiling anymore. Her face was cold and expressionless, her eyes fixed on mine as though daring me to look away. I couldn't. I was trapped, frozen, as her lips moved, forming a single, silent word.

Coward.

Something snapped inside me then, a sharp, visceral crack that left me hollow. The anger drained away, replaced by a cold, sinking dread that settled deep in my chest. I wasn't just losing to the lodge. I was losing to her.

And maybe that was what I deserved.

27

THE HIDDEN ROOM

It was during one of her endless, restless wanderings that she found the door. She wasn't sure what had drawn her to the farthest corner of the lodge's labyrinthine corridors—perhaps the faint draft of cold air seeping from beneath the doorframe or the almost imperceptible sound of something shifting on the other side. Whatever it was, it stopped her in her tracks.

The door was unlike the others in the lodge. While the others were heavy and ornate, their surfaces carved with intricate patterns, this one was plain and unassuming, its wood warped and darkened with age. It was almost hidden in the shadows of the corridor, as though the lodge had deliberately tried to obscure it.

Harper's hand trembled as she reached for the handle, her breath hitching in her throat. The brass was ice-cold beneath her fingers, and for a moment, she hesitated. The lodge had been leading her somewhere for days now, luring her into its depths, and she wasn't sure she wanted to see what lay on the other side.

But she couldn't stop herself. She turned the handle and pushed the door open.

The room beyond was dark and claustrophobic, lit only by the faint, flickering glow of a single bulb hanging from the ceiling. The air was thick with the smell of mildew and decay, and Harper gagged as she stepped inside, her eyes adjusting to the dim light. The walls were lined with shelves, their surfaces cluttered with an array of objects that seemed utterly out of place in the cold, empty lodge.

There were photographs—faded, yellowed images of couples smiling stiffly at the camera, their faces frozen in expressions of strained happiness. Some of the photos were framed, others tucked into dusty albums, their pages tattered with age. Beneath the photographs were trinkets and keepsakes: lockets, wedding rings, dried bouquets tied with fraying ribbons. There were letters, too, their edges brittle and torn, the ink smeared and faded but still legible enough to convey their desperate, pleading tones.

Harper's eyes traveled across the shelves, her heart pounding as she tried to make sense of what she was seeing. It wasn't just the objects themselves that unnerved her—it was the way they were arranged, each item carefully placed as though curated by an invisible hand. They weren't random artifacts. They were pieces of lives, fragments of relationships that had been torn apart.

The lodge had collected them.

Her gaze fell on a framed photograph propped up against the wall, and she knelt to pick it up, her fingers brushing the layer of dust that covered the glass. The couple in the photo looked young, their smiles wide and genuine, but there was something in their eyes—something that spoke of cracks beneath the surface. The background was familiar, though it took Harper a moment to place it: the front porch of the lodge.

She turned the frame over, her hands trembling as she read

the names scrawled on the back in faded ink: *Margaret and William—1956.*

Harper committed the date to memory. She turned to the shelves again, her eyes darting from photo to photo, and realization struck her like a physical blow. Every couple in the photographs had stayed here. They had all been drawn to the lodge, just as she and Michael had been. And judging by the worn, broken artifacts left behind, none of them had left whole.

A chill ran down her spine as she moved to another shelf, her fingers brushing against a worn leather-bound journal. She opened it, her eyes scanning the pages, and her heart sank as she read the entries. They were full of paranoia, accusations, pleas for forgiveness.

She's lying to me. I can see it in her eyes.

He's trying to break me down. I don't know what's real anymore.

The words echoed her own thoughts, her own fears. She dropped the journal, her breathing shallow as she backed away from the shelves.

The lodge hadn't just been feeding on her and Michael. It had been doing this for decades.

In the far corner of the room, Harper's eyes fell on a stack of old newspaper clippings pinned to a corkboard. The edges were yellowed, the headlines faded but still legible. She stepped closer, her hands shaking as she reached for the topmost article.

LOCAL COUPLE MISSING AFTER WINTER RETREAT.

The article was dated January 1978 and detailed the disappearance of a young married couple, James and Betty Parker, who had been staying at the lodge. Their car had been found buried in snow outside, but there was no sign of the couple. Friends described their relationship as "strained" in the months leading up to their disappearance, with several pointing to James's controlling behavior and Evelyn's increasing paranoia.

Beneath it was another clipping, dated March 1965:

MAN FOUND DEAD IN REMOTE MOUNTAIN LODGE—WIFE STILL MISSING.

The accompanying photo showed the lodge's front porch. The article described a man, Thomas Groves, who had been found in one of the bedrooms, his body covered in deep gashes. His wife, Lillian, was never found. Authorities speculated she might have fled into the snowy wilderness, though no tracks were ever discovered.

Harper's stomach churned as she flipped through the articles, each one more horrifying than the last. The lodge had been a magnet for tragedy for decades, perhaps longer. It wasn't just a place. It was a predator, and it had been feeding on people like her and Michael for generations.

The sound of footsteps snapped her out of her trance. They were heavy and uneven, growing louder as they approached the room. Harper froze, her pulse quickening as the door creaked open and Michael stepped inside.

His face was pale, his eyes sunken and wild. He looked like he hadn't slept in days, his hair disheveled, his clothes rumpled and stained. His gaze locked on her immediately, his expression unreadable as he took in the scene. She expected him to remark on her appearance, that she wasn't dead or slashed to pieces. Instead, he seemed to accept that what he was seeing might not be real so asked a question instead.

"What... what is this?" he asked, his voice low and hoarse.

Harper swallowed hard, her hands trembling as she gestured to the shelves. "It's... it's them," she said. "The others. The people who came before us."

Michael stepped closer, his eyes scanning the photographs and trinkets. His jaw tightened, and for a moment, Harper thought she saw something flicker in his expression—fear, maybe, or anger. He picked up one of the photographs, his fingers brushing against the glass, and stared at it for a long moment before setting it back down.

"Did you know about this?" he asked, his voice sharp.

"No," Harper said quickly, shaking her head. "I just found it."

Michael's gaze snapped to hers, his eyes narrowing. "You expect me to believe that?"

"Yes!" Harper's voice rose, her frustration bubbling to the surface. "Michael, look around you! This is what the lodge does. It manipulates people. It feeds on them. Once they're dead their souls haunt this place and become part of the game. Don't you see that?"

But Michael didn't answer. His eyes flicked back to the shelves, his brow furrowing as he studied the artifacts. "So, what?" he muttered, more to himself than to her. "This place just... eats people alive? Is that what you're saying?"

"Yes," Harper said, her voice trembling. "And it's doing the same to us."

Michael's lips pressed into a thin line, and for a moment, Harper thought he might believe her. But then his expression hardened, and he turned to face her fully, his shoulders tense.

"Convenient," he said, his tone icy.

Harper stared at him, her chest tightening. "Michael—"

"You think this is some... some ghost story?"

"It's not a ghost story!" Harper shouted, her voice cracking. "It's real, Michael! Can't you feel it? Can't you see what it's doing to us?"

Michael's laughter was bitter and hollow, and it sent a chill down Harper's spine. "The only thing I see," he said, stepping closer, "is a woman who's been looking for someone to blame for killing her family, her entire life."

Harper's palms were damp. "And the only thing I see," she said, her voice low and steady, "is a man who can't admit he's lost control."

The tension crackled like electricity, and the lodge seemed to tap its feet, its walls vibrating with malicious glee. The artifacts loomed around them, silent witnesses to the horrors that had unfolded within these walls. The lodge wasn't just watching—it was feeding, drawing strength from their fury.

28

THE STRUGGLE

Michael stood before me, his chest heaving, his eyes wild and unblinking. He looked like a man on the verge of collapse, his hair disheveled, his clothes hanging loose on his frame. There was a sheen of sweat on his brow, despite the cold, and his hands were clenched into trembling fists at his sides.

"You think you're so clever," he said, his voice low and venomous. "Don't you, Harper? You think I don't see what you've been doing? They told me, they told me the truth about you."

I took a step back, his words making me recoil. "Michael," I said, my voice trembling but firm. "You're not making any sense."

"Don't patronize me!" he snapped, his voice rising to a shout that echoed through the room. The lodge responded, its walls groaning faintly as though in agreement. "You've been plotting against me since the day we got here. Setting traps, sabotaging me, trying to make me think I'm losing my mind."

I shook my head, the anger bubbling up inside me now. "You don't need my help to lose your mind, Michael. You're doing just fine on your own."

The words hit him like a slap, and for a moment, I thought

he might lunge at me. His jaw tightened, and his eyes burned with a mix of fury and desperation. But then he laughed—a bitter, hollow sound that sent a chill down my spine.

"You've always been like this," he said, his voice dripping with disdain. "Twisting the truth, turning everything back on me. You've never taken responsibility for anything, Harper. Not for your career, not for us, not your family, not for this."

He gestured wildly to the room around us, his movements jerky and unhinged. The flickering light cast strange, distorted shadows across his face, making him look almost inhuman. For a moment, I saw something else in his eyes—something darker, something that didn't belong to him.

The lodge.

"I'm not the one who brought us here," I shot back, my voice steady despite the fear clawing at my chest. "That was all you. You wanted to fix me, remember? You wanted to play the hero, the savior. But look at us now, Michael. Look at what you've done."

The shadows surged around us, working their way up the walls and stretching toward the ceiling like smoke. The room felt smaller somehow. The lodge tightened its grip, feeding on our anger, our fear. I could feel its malevolence, its hunger, pressing against my skin, filling the space between us.

Michael's face twisted into a snarl, his fists clenching tighter. "You've been sabotaging me since the day we met," he said, his voice trembling with rage. "Always undermining me, always trying to make me look like the bad guy. But I see you now, Harper. I see what you really are."

"And what's that?" I demanded, my voice sharp and defiant. "Go on, Michael. Say it."

"You're a parasite," he spat, his voice venomous. "You've been feeding off me for years, dragging me down, tearing me apart. And now you want to finish the job."

I laughed then, a harsh, bitter sound that seemed to echo off the walls. "That's rich," I said, taking a step closer. "Coming from the man who's spent our entire marriage trying to control me, to break me, to turn me into someone I'm not. You want to talk about parasites? Take a good look in the mirror, Michael."

The lodge groaned loudly, the sound reverberating through the room like a warning. The shadows danced wildly now, their movements erratic and violent, as though mirroring the storm inside us. I could feel its presence growing stronger, wrapping around us like a shroud, pushing us closer to the edge.

Michael took a step forward, his eyes blazing. "You've been lying to me since the day we walked through that door," he said, his voice low and dangerous. "But I won't let you win, Harper. I won't let you destroy me."

"Destroy you?" I repeated, my voice rising. "You've been destroying yourself since the moment we got here. I'm just watching the pieces fall."

His hand shot out suddenly, grabbing my wrist with a force that made me wince. His grip was bruising, his fingers digging into my skin as he pulled me closer. "You don't get to twist this," he hissed, his breath hot against my face. "Not this time."

The shadows surged around us, their edges blurred, and I could feel the lodge urging us on. It wanted this. It wanted us to break, to shatter, to tear each other apart.

But I wasn't going to let it win.

I twisted my wrist sharply, breaking free from his grip, and shoved him back with all the strength I could muster. He stumbled, his back hitting the edge of the bed, and for a moment, he looked stunned, his eyes wide and disbelieving.

"You think you're so strong," I said, my voice trembling with anger. "But you're just as weak as I am, Michael. Maybe even weaker. And now look at you. You're falling apart."

His face twisted in fury, but I didn't give him a chance to

respond. I took a step closer, my voice steady and cold. "You've spent so much time trying to break me, trying to make me doubt myself; to make me think I'm the problem. But guess what? I see you now. I see you for what you really are."

The lodge hummed louder, its pulse matching the frantic rhythm of my heartbeat. The shadows writhed wildly, their movements frantic and chaotic, as though they were feeding off our fury.

Michael's shoulders sagged suddenly, his anger draining away as he sank onto the edge of the bed. He looked up at me, his eyes hollow and defeated, and for a moment, I almost felt sorry for him.

"Harper," he said softly, his voice trembling. "I didn't mean for it to be like this. I... I didn't know."

But it was too late. The damage was done, and the lodge wasn't finished with us yet.

29

ALIVE

The lodge was waking up.

The walls seemed to shift ever so slightly, pressing inward, their edges bending like ribs around a living heart. The air thickened, clinging to Harper's skin as if it were trying to seep inside her. She could feel it—its hunger, its malevolence.

Harper stood in the middle of the great room, her arms wrapped tightly around herself, as if she could shield her body from the lodge's creeping tendrils of cold. The once-grand fireplace loomed over her, its charred stone mouth agape and blackened as though it had swallowed its last warmth centuries ago. The shadows around her were restless, darting across the walls like silent predators.

Michael was upstairs—she could hear him pacing, his footsteps erratic, sharp bursts of sound breaking the quiet. It sounded like he was searching for something, but Harper knew the truth. He wasn't searching. He was *running*. From what, she didn't know. The lodge? Himself? Or maybe even her.

She stayed frozen in place, her breath shallow and quick, her eyes fixed on the distorted reflection of herself in the shattered glass of the mantel mirror. Her face looked stretched and warped, her wide, frightened eyes staring back at her from a face she barely recognized. The room trembled, and somewhere deep within the walls, the lodge groaned like an ancient creature stirring from a long slumber.

And then the first crack came.

The sound was sharp and splintering, like brittle wood snapping under immense pressure. Harper flinched as a fine shower of dust rained down from the ceiling, the delicate particles catching in the dim, flickering light. She staggered backward, her hands instinctively coming up to shield her head. The walls shuddered, the sound of groaning timber reverberating through the room, and the air grew colder, icy, cutting through her like knives.

The shadows, which had been lurking passively in the corners, began to move. They crawled along the walls, seeping onto the floor like ink bleeding through paper. Harper's breath caught as she watched them gather, pooling together and then breaking apart like living things. Their movements were deliberate, and she could feel their attention—an unnatural awareness that sent shivers down her spine.

The whispers started then.

"*Harper... Harper...*"

A sing song, directly into her ear. Her legs trembled, threatening to give out beneath her, but she forced herself to stay upright. "No," she whispered, shaking her head. "No. You're not real."

The whispers didn't relent. They grew sharper, more insistent, wrapping around her like tendrils of smoke. She stumbled backward, her chest tightening as the voices shifted tone, becoming cold, accusatory.

"*Why are you still here?*" they demanded, their words laced with venom. "*Why didn't you leave?*"

"I don't know," Harper choked out, her voice trembling. "I don't know."

A low, mocking laugh rippled through the air, the sound vibrating in her bones. "*Liar.*"

The room around her shifted. The walls seemed to breathe, expanding and contracting in slow, rhythmic pulses. Harper felt the floor beneath her feet ripple as though she were standing on water, and she staggered, clutching at the edge of the mantel for support. The cold stone was rough beneath her palms, grounding her for a fleeting moment—until her gaze was drawn upward.

The mirror above the fireplace was intact again.

Harper froze. She knew it had been shattered—she'd seen the shards scattered across the floor just hours ago. But now it was whole, its surface smooth and gleaming, reflecting the dim light of the room. And her.

But it wasn't her.

The reflection tilted its head, a motion Harper hadn't made, and a small, knowing smile played on its lips. "You didn't stay because you loved him," it said, its voice soft and laced with quiet malice. "You stayed because you didn't know who you were without him."

Harper's stomach twisted, and she shook her head violently. "That's not true," she whispered, her voice barely audible. "That's not true."

The reflection's smile widened, its teeth sharp and glinting in the flickering light. "Isn't it?" it asked, leaning closer to the glass. "You let him take everything from you. Your career. Your independence. Your *self.* And you stayed. Because without him, you're nothing."

"Stop it!" Harper screamed, her voice breaking. She swung her fist at the mirror, the glass shattering under the force of the blow. Cracks spiderwebbed across its surface, but the reflection didn't disappear. It stared back at her, fractured and broken. Its rictus grin unchanged.

Upstairs, Michael's footsteps thundered across the floorboards. He was running now, his movements frantic, erratic. His breath came in sharp, ragged bursts as he slammed into the study and locked the door behind him. The room was dim, the single lamp to weak for the task of lighting a room.

He pressed his back against the door, his chest heaving, and closed his eyes. But the whispers followed him, seeping through the cracks in the wood like a toxic fog. They weren't just in the room—they were in his mind.

"*Failure... Manipulator... Coward...*"

Michael's hands shot up to cover his ears, his nails pressed into his scalp. "No," he muttered, his voice trembling. "No, that's not true. I'm not... I'm not a coward."

"*You brought her here,*" the voices hissed. "*You destroyed her.*"

"I was trying to help her," Michael said, his voice rising in desperation. "I was trying to save her."

The shadows in the study twisted, coiling around him like snakes. The voices grew louder, overlapping and distorting until they became a single, unified tone—Harper's voice.

"*You can't save someone who doesn't want to be saved,*" it said, soft and mocking. "*You loved the idea of her, Michael. You loved the control*

Downstairs, Harper collapsed to the floor, her back pressed against the cold stone of the hearth. The lodge's voice surrounded her now, a constant, inescapable presence that filled the room. It wasn't mocking her anymore. It was asking her a question.

"*Why did you stay?*"

Harper buried her face in her hands, her shoulders shaking as sobs wracked her body. "I don't know," she whispered. "I don't know."

"*Liar,*" the lodge said again, its voice sharper now, cutting through her like a blade. "*You stayed because you were afraid. Afraid of losing him. Afraid of losing yourself.*"

"I didn't want to be alone," Harper cried, her voice breaking. "I didn't want to lose everything I'd built. Everything I thought we had."

The lodge's tune deepened, vibrating through the floorboards. For a moment, the whispers stilled, leaving only the sound of Harper's sobs echoing through the room. And then it spoke again, its voice colder, harsher.

"*You've already lost yourself.*"

The house groaned, the walls trembling as though the lodge was laughing. The whispers rose again, louder now, deafening, as though every voice trapped within the lodge had joined the chorus. Harper pressed her hands to her ears, screaming for them to stop, her voice raw and broken.

Upstairs, Michael did the same, his knees buckling as he collapsed to the floor. He clutched his head, his breath coming in short, panicked gasps, as the shadows closed in around him.

The lodge had them. And it wasn't going to let them go.

30

MALICE

I stood at the top of the staircase, staring down into the black void of the ground floor, where I could hear Michael's uneven footsteps pounding across the floorboards below me. His pacing had taken on a frantic rhythm, erratic and uneven, like a man trying to outrun something that wasn't there.

I clutched the banister, the cold wood biting into my palm, and forced myself to call out. "Michael?" My voice cracked, barely carrying. "Michael, where are you?"

For a moment, nothing. Just the sound of his footsteps, the creak and groan of the wood bending under the load. And then his voice came, drifting up the staircase like a ghostly echo.

"Harper," he said, his tone soft, but wrong. Like a thread stretched too tight, ready to snap. "Come downstairs."

The ground floor was colder, sharper. Each step I took down the staircase felt like I was descending into some frozen pit. My breath came in shallow bursts, visible clouds of white that evaporated into the dim light.

I saw a faint, flickering glow spilling from the study, its light casting long, indistinguishable shapes that clawed at the walls.

I moved toward it, my steps slow and hesitant, each one an

act of will against the fear clawing at my chest. The lodge groaned beneath my feet, the sound vibrating up through my legs. The whispers began again, faint and indistinct at first, but growing louder, sharper, with every step I took.

"*Failure. Manipulator. Parasite.*"

The words sliced through the air like blades, their venomous tone leaving no room for doubt. They weren't just speaking—they were accusing. And they weren't speaking to me.

They were speaking to Michael.

I reached the doorway of the study, my heart pounding so loudly in my chest that it drowned out the whispers for a moment. The air inside the room was colder than the hallway, sharp and biting.

Michael was on the floor in the center of the room, his back to me. His shoulders were hunched, his head bowed, and his hands hung limply at his sides. The shadows clung to him, swirling and twisting around his body.

"Michael?" My voice trembled as I stepped into the room, my feet hesitant on the creaking floorboards. "What's going on? What are you doing?"

He didn't respond immediately. His shoulders twitched, and then I heard it—a low, bitter laugh that sent a chill down my spine. It was hollow, broken, and entirely unlike the Michael I thought I knew.

"You were right," he said finally, his voice low and uneven. "You were always right."

I took another cautious step forward, my hands trembling at my sides. "About what?" I asked, though I wasn't sure I wanted to know the answer.

He turned his head slightly, just enough for me to see the side of his face. His eyes were red-rimmed and glassy, his jaw clenched tight, his lips twisted into a bitter smile.

"About us," he said, his voice cold and flat. "About everything. This... this was a mistake."

The floor seemed to tilt beneath me, and I reached out, gripping the edge of the doorway to steady myself. "What are you talking about?" I asked, my voice small and shaky.

"I never loved you," he said, his voice sharp and final, like a blade slicing through the air. "Not really."

The words hit me like a physical blow, and for a moment, I couldn't breathe. My mouth opened and closed, but no sound came out. "What?" I finally managed to whisper. The word barely audible.

Michael's smile twisted; his teeth bared in something that wasn't quite a grin. "I thought I did, at first," he said, his voice dripping with disdain. "You were... strong. Driven. Ambitious. You were everything I thought I wanted. But then I saw the cracks. The flaws. And I thought... I can fix this. I can fix *you*."

My stomach churned, bile rising in my throat as his words sank in. "You... you saw me as a project," I said, my voice breaking. "Not a partner. Not your wife."

He let out a sharp, bitter laugh, shaking his head. "You were never my equal, Harper," he said, his tone mocking. "You were my responsibility. My burden."

The shadows around him surged forward then, their movements frenzied and violent, and Michael's smile faltered. His hands shot out, clawing at the air as the darkness wrapped around his arms and legs, pulling him down toward the floor.

"Michael!" I screamed, rushing toward him, but the air in the room turned thick and heavy, freezing me in place. My legs refused to move, and I could only watch in horror as the shadows consumed him.

Michael's screams filled the room, raw and guttural, as the shadows enveloped his torso, his neck, his face, then began slicing his skin with fingerlike knives. Blood seeped from the wounds, dark and glistening, pooling on the floor beneath him as the lodge seemed to drink it in, its cheers growing louder, more triumphant.

His eyes met mine, wide and terrified, and for a moment, I thought I saw the man I had once loved—the man who had stood beside me on our wedding day, who had held my hand and promised to build a life together. But that man was gone, buried beneath the lodge's malevolence.

"Help me," he choked out, his voice barely audible over the sound of the shadows tearing into him. "Harper... please..."

Tears streamed down my face as I struggled against the invisible force holding me back. "I can't!" I cried, my voice breaking. "I can't, Michael!"

The shadows surged one final time, engulfing him completely. His screams cut off abruptly, leaving only the sound of the lodge's low, pulsing melody. The darkness retreated slowly, slithering back into the corners of the room, leaving nothing behind but a faint stain on the floor where Michael had been.

I sank to my knees, my body trembling, as a hush fell over the room. The air was still and heavy, the shadows motionless in their corners. Michael was gone. The lodge had taken him.

And now it would be coming for me.

31

THE WOODSHED

I tried to tell myself to move, to run, to get out of this cursed place, but my legs refused to cooperate. I was frozen, my knees rubbing on the floor, my hands trembling as they clutched the edges of Michael's desk for balance. The song of the lodge vibrated through the room, deep and rhythmic, like the heartbeat of some ancient, unearthly thing. It wanted me now. I could feel its hunger, its malevolent intent.

And then the whispers began.

"*Harper... Harper...*"

I pressed my hands to my ears, trying to drown them out, but it was no use. The voices weren't just in the room—they were in my head, burrowing into my thoughts, filling every corner of my mind with their relentless accusations.

"*You stayed too long.*"

"*You should have left.*"

"*This is your fault.*"

"No!" I screamed, my voice cracking. "Leave me alone!"

The whispers twisted into mocking laughter, and the air around me grew colder, sharper, biting into my skin like tiny needles. The shadows began, converging toward me with a deliberate, predatory intent.

The desk behind me slid across the room and slammed into the wall with a deafening crack. The lamp on the desk flickered violently before going out completely, plunging the room into darkness.

And then I felt it—a pull, faint at first but growing stronger by the second. It was like an invisible hand had wrapped itself around my chest, dragging me toward the center of the room, toward the very spot where Michael had disappeared. The floorboards beneath me shifted, the cracks between them widening into gaping voids. I could see something beneath them —something dark and moving, writhing like a nest of snakes.

"*No... no...*" I whispered, my voice trembling. My hands clawed at the floor, desperate for something solid to hold onto, but the pull grew stronger, dragging me closer to the center of the room. The shadows moved around my legs, cold and slimy, tightening their grip with every passing second.

"*Harper...*" the whispers taunted, their voices low and mocking. "*It's your turn now.*"

I didn't know where the strength came from, but some part of me—the part that still wanted to survive, to fight—surged to the surface. My hand shot out, grabbing the edge of the desk, and I pulled myself forward with all the strength I could muster. My fingers found the journal—Michael's journal—where it had fallen on the floor during the chaos, and I clutched it tightly against my chest as though it were a lifeline.

The pull didn't stop, but I forced myself to my feet, stumbling toward the door. The floorboards buckled beneath me, the walls leaning inward as though they were trying to trap me, but I kept moving. My hand grasped the doorknob, the cold metal biting into my palm, and I wrenched it open.

The lodge wasn't letting me go without a fight. The walls

seemed to groan in protest, the floor trembling beneath my feet, but I forced myself forward, clutching the journal like it was the only thing keeping me tethered to reality.

The front door was sealed. I had tried it countless times before and knew better than to waste precious seconds trying again. Instead, I made my way toward the back of the house, where I knew the door to the woodshed stood. The whispers followed me, growing louder, more frantic, their voices rising into a shrill, piercing wail that made my head throb with pain.

The kitchen was ice-cold, the windows frosted over from the inside. My breath came in shallow, visible puffs as I stumbled toward the back door, my hands trembling so badly that it took me three tries to get the latch open. The air outside hit me like a slap, sharp and freezing, but it was cleaner, lighter. For the first time in hours—or maybe days—I could breathe.

I didn't stop. The snow crunched beneath my boots as I ran toward the woodshed, the journal clutched tightly against my chest. The shadows didn't follow me outside, but I could feel the lodge's presence still, pressing against the walls, watching me from every window. It didn't need to chase me—it knew I had nowhere else to go.

The woodshed was small and dark, its single window fogged over with frost. I stumbled inside, slamming the door shut behind me and bracing it with my body. My breath came in ragged gasps, my chest heaving as I slid down to the floor, my back pressed against the rough wood of the door.

The journal in my hands was heavy, its leather cover cold and worn. I opened it with trembling fingers, flipping through the pages filled with Michael's handwriting. The words blurred before my eyes, but I forced myself to focus, to read.

The last few entries were different—disjointed, frantic, filled with scribbles and crossed-out words. He had been unraveling, just like I was.

The final entry stopped me cold.

"The lodge doesn't just take. It consumes. It feeds. It won't stop until there's nothing left of us. Not her. Not me. Not anyone."

Tears blurred my vision, dripping onto the page and smearing the ink. I clutched the journal tightly against my chest, my body shaking with silent sobs. Outside, the lodge loomed, its dark silhouette barely visible through the frost-covered window. It was still watching, still waiting.

A gust of wind rattled the walls of the woodshed, and I looked up, my eyes darting toward the frost-covered window. I looked down at the journal again, my fingers gripping the edges of the pages so tightly they threatened to tear. Michael had lost his mind. That much was clear. But had it been the lodge that broke him? Or had it only brought out what had been there all along?

I knew I couldn't stay in the woodshed forever. The cold was seeping into my bones, and the journal wouldn't giving me the answers I needed. If I wanted to survive—if I wanted to escape—I had to face the lodge again. But the thought of stepping back inside sent a wave of nausea rolling through me. The shadows. The whispers. The way it *felt* alive, like it was breathing, waiting, hungering.

I pushed myself to my feet, my legs trembling beneath me, and pulled my coat tighter around my body. The journal was clutched against my chest, its presence both comforting and debilitating. I couldn't risk taking it back inside, so I stuck it under a pile of kindling and scraped an extra layer over the top. I opened the door cautiously, the icy wind slicing across my face as I stepped out into the snow. The path to the lodge stretched before me, and I swallowed hard then forced my feet to move. It felt like walking into the jaws of a predator, each step echoing with the silent promise of danger.

Once inside, I ran through the kitchen into the great room,

my eyes darting toward the study. The door was ajar, its dark interior beckoning me like an open grave. I hesitated in the doorway, my fingers brushing against the cold wood of the frame. The stain on the floor where Michael had disappeared was still there, dark and glistening, as though it had never dried. As I stared at the space where he was no longer, I sucked in fetid air and steeled myself for whatever came next, then told myself I needed a plan.

32

THE OWNER

The knock on the door echoed through the lodge like a gunshot, sharp and startling in the void of quietude. Harper froze. Her eyes darted toward the door, wide and unfocused, as if she wasn't entirely sure she'd heard correctly. It had been weeks—months, maybe—since anyone had come near the lodge. The snow-covered grounds outside seemed to stretch endlessly, a desolate barrier between her and the rest of the world. No one was supposed to be here. No one could be here.

Another knock, louder this time, reverberated through the walls.

The shadows in the corners of the room stirred, restless and agitated. Harper felt their unease as a prickling at the back of her neck, an instinctual warning that tightened her chest and quickened her breath.

The third knock was accompanied by a voice. "Hello? Is anyone home?"

The voice was firm, authoritative, but not unkind. It carried a note of curiosity, as though the speaker wasn't entirely sure they'd find anyone inside. Harper hesitated; her feet rooted to the floor. The lodge didn't want her to answer. She could feel it in the way the air thickened around her, the way the shadows stretched longer, darker, as if to block her path. But the voice called again, and something inside her stirred—a faint, flickering memory of the world beyond the lodge, of people, of normalcy.

She moved toward the door, her steps slow and hesitant. The shadows seemed to recoil, retreating into the corners, but their presence lingered, a watchful, malevolent force pressing against her back. Harper reached the door and paused, her hand hovering over the doorknob. The wood beneath her palm felt colder than it should have, almost icy, as if the lodge itself were trying to dissuade her.

But she turned the knob anyway.

The man standing on the porch was tall and thin, his face lined with age and framed by a well-groomed beard that was flecked with gray. His eyes were sharp, calculating, but there was a kindness in their depths that softened the edges of his stern expression. He wore a long, dark coat, buttoned to his chin, and a thick scarf wrapped around his neck, though it did little to shield him from the biting wind that swirled around him. Snow clung to his boots and the hem of his coat, a testament to the long trek he'd made to reach the lodge.

"Ms. Harper, I presume?" he said, his voice warm but measured.

Harper nodded, her grip tightening on the edge of the door as she studied him. There was something familiar about him, though she couldn't quite place it. He looked past her, his gaze sweeping over the dimly lit interior of the lodge, and his lips pressed into a thin line.

"I'm Peter Grayson," he said, extending a gloved hand. "I'm the owner of the lodge."

Harper stared at his hand for a long moment before finally

reaching out to shake it. His grip was firm, steady, a stark contrast to her trembling fingers.

"I wasn't expecting anyone," Harper said, her voice soft and uncertain.

"I imagine not," Grayson replied, stepping past her into the foyer without waiting for an invitation. He shrugged off his coat, draping it over the back of a nearby chair, and glanced around the room with an air of quiet authority. "It's been a long time since I've been up here myself. I wanted to check on the place, make sure it's being well cared for especially after the snowstorm. It really was quite something, wasn't it."

Harper closed the door, her movements slow and deliberate, as though she were trying to delay the inevitable. "It's fine," she said. "I've been looking after it."

"So I see," Grayson said, his gaze lingering on the room, where the shadows seemed to gather and shift, just out of sight. He turned back to Harper, his expression thoughtful. "How long have you been here, Ms. Harper?"

"I don't know," Harper admitted, her voice barely above a whisper. "A few months, maybe. I lost track."

Grayson nodded slowly, his sharp eyes studying her face and her appearance which wouldn't inspire confidence in her housekeeping skills. "Where's your husband? I was told a couple were renting the house."

The question hit her like a blow, sharp and sudden, and for a moment, she couldn't breathe. The lodge seemed to tighten around her, its presence pressing against her chest, wrapping around her throat.

"He's gone," she said finally, her voice flat and emotionless. "The lodge... it took him."

Grayson's brow furrowed, and he took a step closer, his hands clasped in front of him. "What do you mean, 'it took him'?" he asked, his tone gentle but insistent.

Harper's gaze drifted to the floor, her hands clutching the journal so tightly that her knuckles turned white. "It consumed him," she said, her voice trembling. "The shadows... they came for him, and now he's gone. He's part of the lodge now."

Grayson's expression darkened, his jaw tightening as he studied her. "Ms. Harper," he said carefully, "I know this place can be... unsettling. It has a way of getting under your skin. I bought it many years as an investment and could never settle, hence why I rent it out. But—the lodge is just a house. It's old, yes, and it has its quirks, but it's not alive. Whatever you think happened here... it didn't."

"You don't understand," Harper said, her voice rising. She took a step back, her eyes wild and unfocused. "The lodge *is* alive. It's watching us, listening to us. It took Michael, and it's not going to let me leave."

Grayson raised his hands in a calming gesture, his expression softening. "You've been through a lot, stuck here on your own in the storm," he said gently. "I can see that. But you don't have to stay now. You can leave, Ms. Harper. You can come back to town with me and we can ask someone to help look for you husband."

Harper shook her head violently, her hair falling into her face. He clearly thought she was mad. "You don't get it," she said, her voice breaking. "I can't leave. The lodge won't let me. It's part of me now. I belong here."

Grayson took another step forward, his voice firm but compassionate. "No, Harper. You don't belong here. This place isn't your home."

The shadows in the corners of the room shifted and Harper felt the lodge's anger like a physical force. It didn't want her to leave. It wouldn't let her. She twisted her hands, her breath coming in shallow gasps, and took another step back.

"I'm not leaving," she said, her voice trembling but resolute. "This is my home now. This is where I'm supposed to be."

Grayson opened his mouth to respond, but the words seemed to catch in his throat. His sharp eyes flickered to the shadows, his expression hardening as he took in the room once more. For the first time, he looked uncertain, his confidence faltering in the face of something he couldn't quite explain.

"Harper," he said softly, "Is there someone I can call, a relative perhaps?"

"You can't, there's no signal. We haven't had one since we arrived." Harper could feel anger building inside her. This man thought she was stupid, she could tell.

Grayson smiled, kindly, no hint of derision. "There is always a signal here, Harper, thanks to the mast on the other side of the forest which serves the surrounding area," he pulled his phone from his pocket and held up the screen so she could see and sure enough, he had full service.

"No," Harper said, her voice firm and unyielding. "That can't be right and anyway how did you get here? The road is totally blocked... unpassable."

"Yes, that's correct, but there's a single track that runs through the forest on the far side and with the right tires and vehicle you can get through. It says so in the information booklet that should have been on the counter in the kitchen when you arrived. Did you read it?" Grayson cast a look towards the kitchen and then back to Harper, a flicker of something crossing his face that she couldn't quite fathom.

That's when the room seemed to darken around them, the air growing colder, heavier. Grayson's jaw tightened, and he straightened, his expression grim. "Look, I need to make a call because I'm worried about your husband and I think we need to look for him, get some help up here. Do you agree?"

"No, no it's fine... he's probably just out walking... you should go. Please, leave now. It's for your own good. You shouldn't stay here because it's not safe and they'll come after you, too." With that, feeling panic rise and her throat constrict, Harper grabbed the man's coat and thrust it into his arms, yanking the door open and indicating that he should go.

She wasn't sure if it was the creak of a floorboard just behind him or the banging screech of a crow in the garden beyond that unnerved him but as though being shaken into action, Grayson gave a curt nod and silently did as she asked.

Harper watched him go, her heart pounding as the door closed behind him.

The room felt impossibly still after Grayson left, the echo of the door closing reverberating through the lodge like the final toll of a bell.

Grayson's words lingered in her mind, unwelcome and invasive, cutting through the haze that had enveloped her for so long. *There's always a signal. There's a single track that runs through the forest.* So why... how had they become trapped for so long?

It was the house, she knew it. It had needed time to show her the truth about herself, about Michael, about everything. And why hadn't she taken the man up on his offer? It was as though she'd become institutionalized. She couldn't leave. She didn't *want* to leave.

But something deeper stirred within her, a faint, flickering memory of who she had been before. The Harper who had laughed freely, who had fought for her career, who had loved Michael with all the fire and passion of someone who believed love could fix anything. That Harper was buried now, smothered by the lodge's presence, but some of Grayson's words had reached her, pulling at threads she thought had long since unraveled.

She turned slowly, her gaze drifting toward the mirror above the fireplace.

It was cracked, lines spiderwebbing across its surface, but it still reflected her image. Or at least, something that *looked* like her.

She stepped closer, her breath catching in her throat as she studied the woman staring back at her. Her face was pale, almost gray, her cheeks hollow, her eyes sunken and rimmed with dark shadows. Her hair hung limply around her shoulders, dull and lifeless, and her lips were dry and cracked. She reached up to touch her face, her fingers trembling, and the reflection mimicked her, its movements hesitant and strange, as though it were imitating her rather than reflecting her.

"This isn't me," she whispered, her voice barely audible. The reflection tilted its head, its sunken eyes narrowing, and for a moment, she thought she saw something else beneath the surface—a flicker of movement, a shadow curling just behind her.

The lodge's whispers rose, low and insistent, wrapping around her thoughts like smoke. *You belong here,* they said. *You are one of us now. Don't leave.*

But Grayson's voice cut through them, sharp and unwavering. *This isn't your home.*

Harper closed her eyes, her breath coming in shallow, uneven gasps. The lodge's pull was stronger than ever, but Grayson's words had planted a seed of doubt. She opened her eyes again, staring at her reflection, and for the first time, she saw the truth. The lodge had consumed her, just as it had consumed Michael. It had taken everything she was and twisted it into something unrecognizable.

She turned away from the mirror, her chest tight, and moved toward the door. The shadows stirred, their edges sharper than before. It didn't want her to leave. She could feel its anger, its desperation, as though it were trying to wrap itself around her and pull her back.

"I have to go," she said aloud, her voice trembling. The shadows recoiled slightly, their movements hesitant, but they didn't disappear. "I can't stay here anymore."

She thought of Michael, of his final moments, of the way the lodge had taken him piece by piece until there was nothing left. She thought of his journal, of the words he had written in those final days, his descent into madness mirrored in her own. And then she thought of the lodge itself—the way it had held her, nurtured her, shown her who she truly was.

"I'm sorry," she whispered, her voice cracking. "I'm sorry, Michael. I'm sorry... my love."

She wasn't sure who her final, unbidden words were for. Michael or the lodge that had possessed her like an invisible lover.

In a manic bid for freedom, she flung open the door just as Grayson was swinging his car around, preparing to head back into town and as she took the steps three at a time, waving her arms in a bid to stop him, she heard the unearthly wails of souls still trapped inside the lodge. The sound, like banshees from hell nipping at her heels caused her to run and fling open the passenger door of Grayson's car.

"Take me away, please, hurry, take me away now before they catch me and make me stay. Harper pleaded and could hear the hysteria in her own voice as she slammed the door shut and felt the car speed away from the lodge.

The drive down the long, snow-covered track was surreal, the world outside the windshield a blur of white and gray. She had packed nothing, leaving everything behind—the journal, her clothes, even her memories. She hadn't even looked back at the lodge as they'd driven away, afraid that if she did, the sight of whatever she'd left behind would haunt her for the rest of her days.

33

THERAPY

It's been a month since I left the lodge, but I might as well still be there. The streets of Princeton, so familiar once, feel like a distant memory that I've stumbled into by accident. The city hasn't changed—the same gray buildings lining the same orderly streets, the same coffee shops with their bustling crowds of students and professors, the same dull rota of life that I used to find comfort in. But I don't belong here anymore. I'm not the same.

When I walk these streets now, I keep my head down, blending into the crowd like a ghost haunting its former life. A spy gone dark. The people rushing past me have no idea I'm here, or maybe they do, and they just don't care. No one asks where I've been. No one asks why I was gone. It's easier that way, really. If someone did stop to ask, I wouldn't know what to tell them. How could I possibly explain what happened at the lodge? How could I tell them about Michael, about the shadows, about the way the walls breathed and whispered my name? No, I told myself. It's better this way.

I haven't told anyone that I hear them calling still. My suitcase sits by the door, packed, ready to go, like it's waiting for me to leave again. I don't need much—just a few clothes, a toothbrush, the bare essentials. The truth is, while I am glad to be free of the lodge I am having trouble accepting that I'm here to stay, that all that is behind me, that I've closed that chapter of my life. And I can't. Not yet.

The apartment feels smaller than it used to. I sit by the window most nights, staring out at the city below, but my mind always drifts back to the lodge. It's still with me, its presence lingering in the corners of my thoughts, muttering to me in the quiet moments.

I started seeing Dr. Vargas a week after I returned. My therapist before the lodge had referred me to her, someone with "expertise in trauma-related psychosis," though no one said those words outright. I could feel their judgment in every polite email, every carefully worded message. They didn't understand. How could they?

Dr. Vargas's office is small but inviting, with warm yellow walls and a bookshelf lined with titles on psychology and self-help. A pot of tea sits on a tray between us, its steam misting the air, but I don't touch it. The smell of chamomile makes me nauseous for reasons I can't quite explain. Dr. Vargas watches me from across the room, her expression calm and attentive, her pen poised over her notepad.

I lean forward, my hands twisting together in my lap, my fingers pale from the pressure. "I know what you're thinking," I say, my voice trembling but steady enough to be heard. "You think I've lost my mind."

"I think you've been through a lot," Dr. Vargas replies gently, her eyes soft but sharp, dissecting every word I say. "And that it's going to take time to process everything you've experienced. Has there been any news of him? An update from the police."

I laugh, a brittle sound that breaks the stillness of the room. "No, nothing but they won't find him will they. No matter how many search teams comb the forest, how many sniffer dogs roam the pathways. He's gone somewhere nobody can reach him. Into the lodge."

Dr Vargas simply waits, saying nothing.

"You don't believe me, do you?" I ask. "About the lodge. About what happened there. Michael's disappearance."

Dr. Vargas sets her pen down, folding her hands in her lap. "Why don't you tell me more about it?" she says. "Help me understand."

I take a deep breath, my chest tight, and begin. "The lodge wasn't just a house," I say, my words tumbling out in a rush. "It was alive. I could feel it—its heartbeat, its breath, its eyes watching me. It wasn't just a place. It was... something else. Something alive. And it wanted us."

Dr. Vargas doesn't flinch, doesn't look away. Her face remains neutral, her head tilted slightly as though she's trying to see me from a better angle. "When you say it wanted you," she says carefully, "what do you mean?"

"It fed on us," I say, my voice rising. "On our fears, our emotions, our... our relationship. It took Michael. It consumed him. And it almost took me too."

Dr. Vargas nods slowly, her pen moving across her notepad in quick, deliberate strokes. "You feel like the lodge was a presence," she says. "Like it had a consciousness. Is that right?"

"Yes," I say, my voice breaking. "It wasn't just a house. It was alive. And it hated us."

She leans forward slightly, her hands still folded. "Do you think it's possible," she says, her tone calm and measured, "that the lodge was a reflection of what you and Michael were going through? A manifestation of the tension, the struggles, the pain you were carrying?"

I stare at her, my chest tightening. "You think I imagined it," I say flatly.

"I think trauma can affect the way we perceive the world around us," she says gently. "It can amplify our fears, distort our memories, make things feel more real than they are."

"It was real," I snap, my voice sharp enough to make her blink. "The shadows. The whispers. The way the walls moved. The curtains had faces. I didn't imagine that. I couldn't have."

Dr. Vargas doesn't argue. She doesn't even flinch. "I'm not saying you're lying," she says. "What you experienced was real to you. And that's what matters. But what if the lodge wasn't alive? What if it was your mind's way of processing everything you were going through with Michael?"

Her words hang in the air between us, heavy and loaded. I shake my head, my hands clenching into fists. "You don't understand," I say, my voice trembling. "It wasn't just in my head. It was real. It *is* real."

Dr. Vargas doesn't respond right away. She watches me for a long moment, her gaze steady and unyielding. "It sounds like the lodge left a deep impression on you," she says finally. "And that's something we can work through together."

I leave the session feeling hollow, her words echoing in my mind. *A reflection of your trauma. A projection of your fears.* I want to believe she's wrong. I want to believe the lodge was real, that it wasn't just a manifestation of everything broken between Michael and me. But the more I think about it, the more the edges blur, the more the memories twist and fray at the corners.

The nightmares don't stop. Every night, I'm back at the lodge, standing in the great room, the shadows crawling towards me. Michael's voice is always there, soft and pleading, calling to me from somewhere I can't reach.

"*You left me,*" he says. "*You left us.*"

"I didn't," I whisper back, tears streaming down my face. "I didn't have a choice."

"*It's waiting for you,*" he says. "*It's calling you back.*"

I wake up gasping, the sound of his voice lingering in the stillness of the room. And in those quiet moments before dawn, I wonder if he's right. If the lodge is waiting. If it will always be waiting.

34

THE MEMOIR

The words don't stop, not even when I try to sleep. They fill my head, tumbling over one another like a frantic crowd trying to escape a burning building. My fingers ache from gripping the pen too tightly, but I can't stop. I have to get it all out—everything that happened at the lodge, everything Michael did, everything I saw. If I don't write it down, it might slip away, swallowed up by the shadows that still linger at the edges of my vision.

The apartment is silent except for the scratch of my pen on the paper. Outside, the world moves on without me—cars honk, people shout, a dog barks somewhere in the distance—but it all feels so far away. Princeton might as well be another universe. The lodge is still with me, its presence like a second skin, and the further I try to run from it, the tighter it clings.

My notebook is nearly full now, the pages covered in my cramped, hurried handwriting. The story flows in fits and starts, fragments pieced together from memory and nightmare. Michael's voice weaves through it all, his words twisted and distorted, echoing in the back of my mind. I tell myself it's just the residue of grief, the ghost of him lingering in my thoughts. But I know better. The lodge doesn't let go. Not really.

It was late last night when I first noticed the suitcase.

I had shoved it into the corner of the living room, leaving it there to gather dust along with the rest of my life. But as I sat at the desk, scribbling furiously, I felt it—a faint pull, an itch at the edge of my awareness that I couldn't ignore. My eyes drifted to the case, a dark shape slouched against the wall, and I felt the lodge's presence stir.

At first, I thought it was just my imagination. Another trick of the shadows, another whisper from a voice I couldn't place. But the feeling didn't go away. It grew stronger, more insistent, until I couldn't stand it anymore. I left my pen and notebook on the desk and crossed the room, my footsteps silent on the carpet.

The small suitcase felt different, unfamiliar. My fingers trembled as I unzipped it, the sound sharp in the quiet room, and my breath caught when I saw what was inside.

Michael's journal.

I left with nothing. Grayson had what personal belongings the housekeeper found packed and send back to me. The box with Michael's clothes is in the spare room, in the closet hidden under blankest because I can't bear to look inside.

I'd left his journal hidden in the woodshed but there it was, nestled among my clothes like it had been waiting for me. My hands shook as I pulled it out, the leather cover cool and smooth beneath my fingers. It felt alive in my hands, like it had absorbed some part of him, like it was still connected to the lodge in ways I couldn't understand.

I opened it slowly, the pages crackling with age and dampness. Most of the entries were familiar—I had read them before, back in the lodge, when I was trying to piece together the fragments of Michael's unraveling mind. But as I flipped through the pages, I found something new. Something I hadn't seen before.

A final entry, scrawled across the last page in uneven handwriting.

"You can leave the lodge, but the lodge never leaves you."

The words stared back at me, sharp and menacing, as though they were alive. My breath caught, my chest tightening, and I dropped the journal, the sound of it hitting the floor echoing in the silent room. My hands flew to my mouth, stifling a sob, and I sank to my knees, my heart pounding in my chest.

Michael was gone. The lodge had taken him. But his words... his words were still here. And they were true. I could feel it, deep in my bones, in the marrow of my very being. The lodge hadn't let go. It never would.

A mirror hangs above the faux fireplace, its frame ornate and tarnished, a relic from another time. I avoid looking at it whenever I can, but tonight, I can't help myself. The journal lies open on the floor, the final entry glaring up at me like a challenge, and I feel its pull, dragging my gaze upward.

At first, my reflection looks normal. Pale, gaunt, hollow-eyed, but normal. It's me, or at least the version of me that the lodge left behind. I lean closer, studying the shadows under my eyes, the sharp lines of my cheekbones, the tight set of my jaw. I look like someone I don't recognize, someone who has been hollowed out and filled with something else.

And then it happens.

My reflection smiles.

It's slow, deliberate, the corners of its lips curling upward in a way that feels wrong, unnatural. My own face remains frozen, my lips pressed into a thin line, but the reflection grins at me, its eyes glinting with something dark and dangerous. My stomach twists, nausea rising in my throat, and I stumble back, my heart hammering in my chest.

"No," I whisper, shaking my head. "No, that's not real. That's not me."

The reflection doesn't move, its grin widening as it watches me. The lodge's whispers rise in the back of my mind, soft and insistent, wrapping around my thoughts like smoke.

"You can leave the lodge, but the lodge never leaves you."

I sink to the floor, my knees hitting the carpet, and bury my face in my hands. The journal lies beside me, its pages fluttering in an invisible breeze, and the words blur together in my mind, their meaning slipping away like water through my fingers.

The lodge is still with me. It always will be. And no matter how far I run, no matter how hard I try to escape, I know the truth.

It's calling me back.

35

THE RETURN

Harper had tried to resist the voices at first, chalking them up to remnants of her fractured mind, echoes of a trauma she was still clawing her way out of. But over the past week, they had grown louder, more distinct. They didn't hiss or whisper like the lodge's old whispers had. These voices were clear and soothing, a steady, melodic cadence that brushed against her ears like a mother's lullaby.

"Harper," they called softly. "Come home."

It didn't feel like an order or even a plea. It felt like a gentle invitation; spoken with a kind of warmth she hadn't felt in years. A lost lover trying to reconnect. The voices wrapped themselves around her like a quilt, reassuring her, coaxing her. They didn't frighten her the way the nightmares did. Instead, they filled her with an overwhelming sense of calm, a certainty that if she just listened, if she followed their guidance, everything would make sense again.

She had stopped seeing Dr. Vargas. Therapy felt pointless now, an attempt to untangle a web that wasn't hers to undo. The lodge was calling her back, and she had started to believe it wasn't madness—it was destiny. She had been wrong to leave. It was never about running or escaping. It was about understanding. About finishing what had been started.

The drive to the lodge felt shorter this time, the roads now clear of snow winding beneath her wheels like an old, familiar path. The trees on either side of the road seemed taller, darker, their branches arching overhead to form a canopy that blocked out the sky. The world outside the car felt distant, muted by the layers of snow that remained, as though she had already begun crossing a threshold into another reality.

The voices grew louder the closer she got. They no longer just called her name—they spoke to her, soothing her frayed nerves, guiding her thoughts.

"It's where you belong," they murmured. "You'll find the answers there."

By the time the lodge came into view, Harper's hands were trembling on the steering wheel. She parked the car at the edge of the property, her headlights cutting through the swirling snow to illuminate the hulking silhouette of the house. It stood silent and still, its windows dark, its door shut tight. For a moment, she hesitated, gripping the keys so hard that the metal dug into her palm.

The lodge didn't feel threatening anymore. It felt... empty. Hollow. Like a spurned lover, bereft.

The front door was locked, but Harper found a loose window on the side of the house. The latch gave easily under her hands, and she hoisted herself inside, landing softly on the creaking wooden floor. The air inside was cold but not stale like before, the faint scent of mildew and decay relaced my disinfectant and furniture polish. The housekeeper had done a good job for Grayson.

She waited for a moment, letting her eyes adjust to the dim light, and then the voices came again.

"Upstairs," they said. "It's in the attic."

Harper moved without hesitation, her footsteps echoing in the vast, empty space. The lodge felt different now. The essence that had once suffocated her was gone, replaced by a strange sense of purpose. The shadows still lingered in the corners, but they didn't seem alive anymore. They were just shadows.

The attic door was hidden behind a narrow hallway on the top floor, its edges warped and splintered with age. Harper pulled it open, her breath puffing in the cold air, and stared up at the wooden ladder that led into the darkness above. The voices were louder now, their tone almost excited, urging her forward.

"Go on," they said. "It's waiting for you."

She climbed slowly, her hands gripping the sides of the ladder, the wood rough and splintered beneath her fingers. The attic smelled of dust and old wood, and as her head emerged into the space, she saw it was filled with the detritus of past lives: broken furniture, crates overflowing with yellowed papers, cobwebs stretched across forgotten belongings.

And there, in the center of the room, was a single wooden box.

Harper knelt in front of the box, her heart pounding in her chest. It was small, unassuming, its surface scuffed and faded with age. A brass latch held it closed, and when she flipped it open, the lid creaked loudly.

Inside, she found an assortment of personal items: a comb with a few strands of jet-black hair caught in its teeth, a delicate silver bracelet, a stack of letters tied together with a frayed ribbon. She picked up one of the letters, her fingers trembling, and unfolded it carefully.

The paper was brittle, the ink faded but still legible. The handwriting was neat and precise, the words flowing across the page in tight, even lines.

It began.

I hope this letter finds you well, though I fear the lodge has already begun its work. It will make you feel safe at first, as though it understands you, as though it can give you everything you've ever wanted. But don't trust it. The lodge demands more than it gives. And once it takes what it wants, it will never let you go.

Harper's breathing came in short gasps, her hands shaking as she read. The letter went on to describe the writer's suspicions about the lodge, how it seemed to thrive on conflict, how every couple who stayed there came to ruin.

I've seen what it does to people. It twists them, breaks them, until there's nothing left but the lodge itself. If you can, leave, leave before it's too late. Never go there, never stay under its roof.

The letter was unsigned, but as Harper read it, a cold dread seeped into her bones. She glanced back at the box and found more letters, all written in the same careful hand, all addressed to Rebecca. But in another hand, written in red, the lines scored deep into the page as though drawn in anger, were strange symbols. Harper had no idea what they meant but they reminded her of the occult, something evil.

Beneath the letters were other items: books, and when she turned the pages they too were defaced with red symbols causing Harper to shudder and slam them shut. A photograph of a smiling couple standing in front of the lodge, their faces bright with the joy of newlyweds; a man's wedding ring, tarnished and scratched; a woman's scarf, its edges frayed.

The voices in Harper's head grew quiet, as though they were waiting for her to process what she had found. She stared at the photograph, her thumb brushing over the smiling faces of the couple. The date scrawled on the back read *November 1950*. The woman in the photo must have been Rebecca, Harper realized, and the man her husband. They looked so happy, so oblivious to the darkness that had awaited them.

She thought of Michael, of their own arrival at the lodge,

and felt a sickening twist in her stomach. Had the lodge been waiting for them, too? Had it seen the fractures in their marriage and decided they were ripe for the taking? Harper sifted through the letters again, her mind racing as she pieced together the pattern. Every couple who stayed at the lodge seemed to have met the same fate: violence, madness, destruction.

And now it was her turn.

36

CARVINGS

I feel her before she even reaches the property. Harper. My Harper. The one who left but never really left. She thought she could run, that the road stretched long enough to sever my hold on her. But she was wrong. She is mine, as she has always been. Every tear she shed, every seared edge of her broken mind, every fractured part of her spirit—they stitched themselves into me the moment she crossed my threshold. She might have walked away, but I never let go. I don't let go.

But she isn't alone this time. He's here too, though not as she remembers him. Michael, or what's left of him. His body still moves, his hands still work, but his will is mine now. The lodge speaks through him, guiding his movements, driving his purpose. He moves through my halls like a puppet, the strings of his humanity frayed but not yet severed.

He carves into my walls with single-minded precision, his blade scraping symbols into the wood, each cut a whisper of ancient power that resonates through my foundations. The air pings with the energy of his work, reverberating with an almost inaudible frequency that would drive a lesser mind to madness.

But Michael doesn't hear it. He is too far gone, too hollowed out, too consumed by what I've made him.

I guide him as I guided the others before him, each cut feeding me, deepening my hold. These marks are not random; they are the language of hunger, the words that tether me to this world. And though Michael doesn't understand their meaning, his hands move as if they've always known.

Harper enters the lodge with the caution of someone stepping into a predator's den. She doesn't speak. Her breathing is shallow, her footsteps deliberate, as if she believes she can move silently enough to escape my notice. But I know every creak of the floorboards, every ripple of air her presence stirs. I watch her as she moves, her gaze darting to the shadows that stretch along the walls. She feels me here, though she won't admit it yet. The lodge is already seeping back into her, threading its way through the cracks in her resolve.

I observe as she returns from the attic, where I left her a gift, a tease really, to see if she would flee or stay once she read the letters to dear Rebecca.

It doesn't take her long to find him.

She stops in the doorway to the dining room, her body going rigid as her eyes lock onto Michael's hunched figure. He is standing by the far wall, his back to her, his hand moving in slow, deliberate strokes as the blade of the knife cuts into the wood. The sound is rhythmic, almost hypnotic, a scraping that echoes through the room like the ticking of a clock. For a beautiful moment in which I absorb her shock, Harper doesn't move. She barely breathes. It is a beautiful moment.

The light in the room is dim, casting long shadows that dance across Michael's frame. He looks thinner than Harper remembers, his clothes hanging loose on his body, his shoulders sharp and angular beneath his shirt. His hair is falling out now, bald patches dot his scalp, his skin pale, and his movements are mechanical, almost inhuman, as though his body is being piloted by something outside himself.

"Michael?" Harper's voice is barely above a whisper, trembling and uncertain.

He doesn't respond. The knife in his hand continues its path, carving a primitive symbol into the wall. The symbol glows faintly, its lines pulsing with a sickly light that seems to come from within the wood itself. Harper takes a hesitant step forward, her breath catching in her throat.

"Michael, where have you been?" she asks, louder this time.

His hand stills, the blade poised mid-cut, and for a moment, the room is silent except for the sound of Harper's breathing. Then he speaks, his voice low and distorted, as though it's coming from somewhere deep within me.

"It's not enough," he says. "It's never enough."

Harper feels the thump of his words like a blow, her knees threatening to buckle beneath her. She looks past him to the wall, her eyes tracing the lines of the symbols he's carved. They are ancient and unfamiliar, their edges radiating a malevolence that makes her stomach churn. She's seen them before—in Rebecca's letters, in the books she found in the attic. They are symbols of power, of hunger, of sacrifice.

"Michael, stop," she says, her voice trembling. "You don't know what you're doing."

He turns to her slowly, his movements unnaturally smooth, and when she sees his face, a gasp escapes her lips. It's him, but it isn't. His skin is waxy and pale, his eyes sunken and rimmed with darkness, and his lips are twisted into a faint, knowing smile. There's a hollowness in his gaze, an emptiness that wasn't there before. It's as if the man she knew has been gutted, his body left behind as a shell.

"I know exactly what I'm doing," he says, his voice calm and flat, devoid of emotion. "I'm giving it what it needs."

Harper takes another step back, her pulse pounding in her ears. "What are you talking about? What does it need?"

Michael tilts his head, studying her with a detached curiosity, as though she's the subject of one of his experiments. "You already know," he says. "You've felt it, haven't you? The hunger. The lodge saw us, Harper. It saw what we had to give. And now it's time to pay."

"No," she whispers, shaking her head. "No, you wouldn't do this. You wouldn't—"

"Wouldn't I?" he interrupts, his smile widening. "Are you sure about that? Are you sure this isn't who I've always been?"

The question cuts through her like a blade, dredging up memories she's tried to bury. She thinks of his journal, the way he documented her every move, dissecting her like a specimen under a microscope. She thinks of the lies, the manipulations, the subtle ways he exerted control over her life. And she wonders: Was this always in him? Did the lodge simply bring it to the surface? Or has it reshaped him entirely, molding him into something unrecognizable?

"You did this," she says suddenly, her voice rising, her anger spilling over. "The lodge did this to you. It twisted you, turned you into... into this."

Michael takes a step toward her, the knife still in his hand, the blade glinting faintly in the dim light. "The lodge didn't make me," he says. "It just revealed the truth. About me. About you. About us."

Harper backs away, her hands trembling, her breath coming in short, sharp gasps. The room feels smaller now, the air pressing down on her. The symbols on the wall seem to pulse more brightly, their glow casting eerie shadows that flicker and writhe like living things.

"I won't let you do this," she says, her voice shaking but resolute. "I won't let you... feed it."

Michael's smile fades, his expression hardening. "You don't have a choice," he says simply. "Neither of us do."

~

The lodge nods in approval, my unholy assistants gather, trailing her every move, greedy voyeurs watching their successors demise.

Harper turns and runs, her footsteps echoing through my halls. She can try to escape, but we both know she won't. She belongs here, just as he does. Just as they all do.

The lodge demands more than it gives. And I always gets what I need.

~

Harper staggered down the hall, her breath ragged, her pulse pounding in her ears making it harder to think. She wasn't sure where she was going—only that she had to get away from Michael, from the blade in his hand, from the symbols that pulsed with a sinister glow.

Her feet carried her instinctively to the attic, where Rebecca's box still lay open on the dusty floorboards. The letters, the photographs—they were all still there, relics of a life that had been devoured by the lodge. Harper dropped to her knees, her fingers trembling as she reached for the box, stuffing everything back inside before closing the lid. Gripping the box tightly, and on trembling legs, she ran back downstairs.

If the lodge fed on these things—on memories, on pain—then maybe, just maybe, she could starve it.

She found the matches in the kitchen, tucked away in a drawer with yellowing recipes and forgotten utensils. Grabbing a bottle of cooking oil, she hurried back. The fireplace in the great room was dormant, the marble surround cold to the touch, but Harper worked quickly, stacking the artifacts in a pile on the hearth. Racing to her car, she fumbled in her suitcase and retrieved Michael's journal and added it to the pyre, then the letters from Rebecca's box. She then poured a trail of oil from the fireplace, across the rug and over the couch, cushions and wooden furniture and when it was empty tossed it to the floor.

"You won't win," she whispered, her voice shaking as she struck a match.

The moment the flame touched the pile, the lodge reacted. The walls groaned and buckled, their wooden frames bending inward as if the house was breathing, its lungs constricting in pain. Shadows erupted from the corners, twisting and swirling like smoke. They moved toward her, reaching out with inky tendrils that wrapped around her ankles and wrists.

Harper screamed, stumbling backward as the flames roared to life, consuming the artifacts with unnatural speed. The letters blackened and curled, the black hair singed, the bottle melted, the leather cover of the journal bubbled. The rug caught alight blazing a trail towards and up the couch and then the flames did the rest. Harper watched as Michael's journal and the relics of past misery disintegrated into a shower of embers.

And the lodge screamed.

It was a sound unlike anything Harper had ever heard—high-pitched and fevered, worse than nails on a chalkboard, more like metal being torn apart. It reverberated through the walls, shaking the floor beneath her feet, and she clamped her hands over her ears, tears streaming down her face. The shadows lashed out in fury, their fingers slicing through the air like blades, and Harper scrambled away, her back hitting the far wall.

In the dining room, Michael dropped the knife, clutching his head as the sound filled his ears. He fell to his knees, his vision swimming, and the world around him seemed to shift and warp. The walls melted like wax, revealing a kaleidoscope of memories that surged toward him in a flood.

He was ten years old, sitting at the dinner table while his parents argued. His father slammed a fist on the table, his mother's voice rising in desperation, and Michael stared at his plate, willing himself to disappear. The memory twisted, shifting into his teenage years, the first time he had stood in front of a classroom and the burden of everyone's expectations. The faces of his students blurred, their eyes dark and accusing, and Michael stumbled back, gasping for air.

"Stop it!" he shouted, his voice cracking. "Stop!"

But the visions didn't stop. They came faster, more vivid, each one a vivid fragment of the life he had tried so hard to control. The night he and Harper had fought in the apartment, the way she had assaulted him, her eyes blazing with anger. The look of betrayal on her face when she had discovered his journal and letters. The sound of her voice, trembling and raw, as she told him she didn't know if she could trust him anymore.

The shadows closed in around him, their whispers low and mocking. "*This is who you are,*" they said. "*This is what you've always been.*"

In the great room, Harper wasn't faring any better. The flames on the hearth had begun to sputter, their light flickering as the shadows tightened around her. She felt them seeping into her skin, into her mind, dredging up memories she had fought to bury.

She was seven years old, hiding in the closet while her parents screamed at each other in the kitchen. The smell of alcohol and burnt toast filled the air, and she hugged her knees to her chest, biting her lip to keep from crying. The memory shifted, and she was standing in front of her editor, her hands trembling as he slid her article back across the desk.

"This isn't good enough," he had said, his tone cold and dismissive. "You're not good enough."

The words echoed in her mind, morphing into Michael's voice. "*I was just trying to help you,*" he had said. "*You're so paranoid, Harper. It's all in your head.*"

"No," she whispered, her voice cracking. "No, it's not."

The shadows surged, wrapping around her like a vice, and she screamed as another memory flooded her vision. The night Michael had looked at her with that cold, detached expression, the way he had dismissed her fears, her pain. The way he had twisted the truth, made her question herself, until she didn't know what was real anymore.

"*You were never good enough,*" the shadows whispered. "*You were never enough.*"

The lodge's scream rose to a crescendo, the sound reverberating through its walls like a living, breathing thing. The floor buckled beneath Harper, throwing her forward, and she clung to the edge of the hearth, her nails scraping against the stone. The flames roared back to life and the shadows retreated, their edges fraying and dissolving into the air.

Harper gasped for breath, her body trembling, her mind reeling from the onslaught of memories. The room was silent now, the lodge's presence muted but still lingering, like a predator watching from the shadows. She turned her head slowly, her eyes locking on Michael as he stumbled into the room.

His face was pale, his eyes wide with terror, and for a moment, they simply stared at each other, their breaths ragged and uneven. The lodge had shown them both its truth, its hunger, its unrelenting grip.

"We can't stay here," Harper said finally, her voice barely above a whisper. "We have to leave. Now."

Michael didn't respond. He simply looked at her, his expression unreadable, and Harper felt a cold knot of dread twist in her stomach. She wasn't sure who she was looking at anymore—Michael, or what the lodge had made him.

37

A FAMILY AFFAIR

The lodge is quiet, but it's not the kind of quiet that brings peace. It's the quiet of anticipation, of something watching, waiting.

The air smells like smoke. Faint at first, just a hint of something burned, meat, flesh. I push that thought away, but it grows like the stench, stronger the further I go. I stop in the middle of the hall, my heart pounding, and glance behind me. Nothing. Just shadows, shifting and stretching along the walls, but I know better than to trust them.

"Michael?" I call out, though my voice feels small, swallowed by the lodge.

There's no answer. Just the smoke, growing thicker, moving through the air in ghostly tendrils. I can almost taste it now, acrid and bitter, stinging the back of my throat. I press a hand to my chest, trying to steady my breathing, and that's when I hear it.

A voice. Low and gravelly.

"Harper."

My body goes cold. It's a voice I haven't heard in years, a

voice I thought I'd buried along with everything it represented. My father.

I turn slowly, the shadows around me shifting as if they're alive, and there he is. At least, I think it's him. The figure standing at the end of the hall is unrecognizable, a grotesque caricature of the man I once knew. His body is charred black, the flesh peeling away in ribbons to reveal the glistening muscle and bone beneath. His arms hang limply at his sides, his fingers twisting inward like burned twigs. His face... oh God, his face. The skin is melted, sagging and cracked, and where his eyes should be, there's nothing but empty sockets, dark and hollow.

"Dad?" I whisper, my voice trembling.

He doesn't respond right away. He just stands there, swaying slightly, the smoke rising from his body in thin streams. And then he moves, taking a step forward, his foot dragging across the floor with a sickening scrape.

"You shouldn't be here," he rasps, his voice layered with the sound of wood splitting, fire crackling. "This place... it's not for you."

I take a step back, my hands shaking. "You're not real," I say, more to myself than to him. "This isn't real."

His head tilts, the motion jerky and unnatural, like a puppet on strings. "Real enough," he says. "Real enough to remind you of who you are. What you are."

The hallway feels longer now, stretching endlessly in both directions. The air is so thick with smoke I can barely see, and the heat radiating from his body makes my skin prickle. I want to run, to turn and bolt in the opposite direction, but my feet won't move. I'm rooted to the spot, frozen by the sight of him.

"You're making the same mistakes I did," he says, his voice growing louder, harsher. "Holding on to people who break you. Letting them ruin you."

"No," I say, shaking my head. "That's not true."

"Isn't it?" he snarls, taking another step forward. Pieces of him fall away as he moves—chunks of charred flesh, ash crumbling from his arms, his ribs exposed and glistening. "You stayed with Michael. You let him control you, manipulate you. Just like I let her."

"Stop it," I snap, my voice cracking. "You don't know what you're talking about."

His laughter is a low, guttural sound, the kind of laugh that makes your stomach twist. "Oh, I know, Harper," he says. "I know exactly what you've done. Exactly what you've let him do to you."

"I didn't—" My words catch in my throat, and I press a hand to my mouth, trying to hold back the sob threatening to escape. "I didn't have a choice."

"There's always a choice," he spits, his voice dripping with venom. "You just didn't want to make it. You were too afraid to be alone. Too afraid to lose him."

I close my eyes, shaking my head, but the images come anyway. Memories I've tried to bury, resurfacing with brutal clarity. The fights with Michael, the way he would twist my words, make me doubt myself. The nights I stayed awake, staring at the ceiling, wondering if I was the one who was broken. The way he looked at me, like I was something to be fixed, something to be controlled.

"You think you're different from me?" my father says, his voice sharp and cutting. "You think you're better? You're not. You're just like her. Your mother. She was wicked, too."

"Don't," I whisper, my voice barely audible. "Don't say that."

"Just like her. Wicked and warped," he says again, and his body begins to shake, smoke pouring from the cracks in his skin. "She said I was weak. Desperate. Hopeless. You are the worst of both of us."

The words hit me like a physical blow, and I stagger back, my hands clutching at the walls for support. Tears blur my vision, but I can still see him, his hollow eyes fixed on me, his mouth twisted into a cruel grin.

"You'll never escape," he says, his voice rising to a roar. "Not him. Not this place. Not yourself."

The heat intensifies, the smoke swirling around me like a living thing, and I can't breathe. My chest feels tight, my lungs burning, and the walls begin to close in, the shadows pressing against me. I collapse to my knees, gasping for air, and when I look up, he's gone.

The hallway is empty, the smoke dissipating, but his words linger, etched into my mind like a brand. I press a hand to my chest, my fingers trembling, and force myself to take a deep breath. But it doesn't help. The lodge is alive around me, its walls pulsing, its whispers crawling into my ears.

I am not free. I will never be free.

38

THE SILHOUETTE

I feel him before I see him. The air grows colder, biting against my skin, and the shadows in the corners seem to deepen, pooling like spilled ink. My hands are still trembling from the encounter with my father—or whatever it was that the lodge conjured to torment me. The echoes of his words linger, acidic and cruel, tunneling into my mind. But now, there's something else. Another presence, looming and ominous.

It's him.

I turn, and there he is, standing at the far end of the hallway. At first, I almost don't recognize him. His silhouette is familiar—tall, broad-shouldered, the way Michael used to be—but as he steps into the dim light, the distortion becomes clear. His skin is sallow, stretched too tightly over his bones, and his eyes are sunken, ringed with darkness. There's a wildness in his gaze, something feral and unhinged, and his mouth twists into a sneer that makes my stomach churn.

"Harper," he says, his voice low and uneven, a mixture of malice and mockery. "There you are."

I take a step back, my heart hammering in my chest. "You're not real," I say, my voice trembling. "You can't be real."

He laughs, but there's no humor in it. The sound is sharp and grating, like glass shattering. "Oh, I'm real enough," he says, his head tilting as he studies me. "Real enough to see you for what you are. A liar. A traitor."

"Stop it," I snap, but my voice lacks conviction. I can feel the lodge's influence wrapping around me, twisting my perception, making me doubt everything. "You're not Michael. You're just... another trick. Another game."

"Is that what you think?" he asks, his voice rising, his tone laced with venom. "That I'm just some figment of your imagination? Some shadow for the lodge to play with? No, Harper. I'm here because of *you*."

He takes a step forward, and I retreat instinctively, my back hitting the wall. His movements are jerky and unnatural, like a marionette being pulled by invisible strings. The hallway feels smaller now, the walls pressing in, the air thick with his presence.

"You couldn't leave well enough alone, could you?" he snarls, his voice echoing unnaturally. "You just had to keep digging, keep fighting. You couldn't see what was right in front of you. This place... this lodge... it understands me. It sees me."

"You're insane," I say, my voice shaking. "The lodge has twisted you, Michael. It's—"

"It's *you* who's twisted!" he roars, his voice reverberating through the hallway. His hands clench into fists, his knuckles white, and for a moment, I think he might lunge at me. "You were always like this. Always trying to tear me down, to destroy me. Even now, you can't stand that I've found something that makes sense. Something that *works*."

"It's using you!" I shout, the words spilling out in a rush. "Don't you see that? The lodge doesn't care about you, Michael. It's feeding on you, on us. It's—"

"SHUT UP!" he screams, his voice cracking with fury. His

face contorts, his features twisting into something monstrous, and for a moment, I see the shadow of the lodge in him. It's in his eyes, in the way he moves, in the venom dripping from his words.

The hallway seems to warp around us, the edges blurring, the shadows stretching and shifting like living things. Michael steps closer, his presence overwhelming, and I can't move. I'm frozen, pinned by his gaze, by the strength of his rage.

"You don't understand," he says, his voice quieter now, but no less menacing. "You never understood. All your questions, your doubts, your accusations... they were never about me. They were about you. About your need to control, to manipulate."

"That's not true," I whisper, but the words feel hollow even as I say them.

"It is," he hisses, his face inches from mine. "You wanted me to be something I'm not. You wanted me to fit into your perfect little world, to follow your rules, to play your games. But this place... it showed me the truth. It showed me who I really am."

His hand moves suddenly, slamming against the wall beside my head, and I flinch, my breath hitching. His eyes bore into mine, wild and unrelenting, and I feel the sting of his words.

"You tried to destroy me," he says, his voice barely above a whisper. "But you can't. Not here. Not now."

The shadows around us surge, and I feel them brushing against my skin, cold and invasive. The lodge is alive, feeding on his anger, on my fear, and I know that if I don't do something, it will consume us both.

"Michael, you're mixing things up. Those are the things you did to me," I say, forcing my voice to steady. "This isn't you. You have to fight it. You have to—"

"Fight what?" he interrupts, his lips forming a sneer. "There's nothing to fight, Harper. This is who I am. This is who I've always been. You just couldn't see it."

I shake my head, tears stinging my eyes. "No," I whisper. "No, you're wrong. This place has poisoned you. It's taken everything we were and twisted it into something dark, something wrong."

He laughs again, the sound hollow and bitter. "Maybe it has," he says. "But at least now I understand. At least now I see."

The shadows tighten, pressing the space around me into a bone crushing vice. And still, Michael doesn't move away, his twisted smile locked on my face, the man I once loved warped beyond recognition.

The world tilts. I barely feel my feet moving as Michael grabs my arm, his grip vice-like and cold as iron. His strength seems endless now, an extension of the lodge itself. Before I know it, I'm being pulled down a narrow staircase, the air growing damp. The basement. The moment I step into its shadows, the temperature plummets, and an iceberg presses on my chest, crushing the air out of me.

He shoves me forward, and I stumble, catching myself against a cold, stone wall. The basement is even darker than I remembered, the faint light from the single, flickering bulb above doing little to cut through the dismal gloom. The walls seem to breathe, cracks in the stone pulsing like veins. Shadows twist and writhe along the floor, alive, watching.

Michael paces in front of me, his movements erratic and unhinged. His eyes dart around the room, as if he's listening to something I can't hear, his lips contorted into a cruel smile. "Do you feel it, Harper?" he says, his voice trembling with manic energy. "Do you feel how alive it is down here? How it throbs, with *power*?"

I press my back against the wall, trying to steady my breathing. "Michael, listen to me—"

"NO!" he snaps, rounding on me with a fury that makes me flinch. "You don't get to speak. Not anymore. You don't *understand*. You never did."

He steps closer, looming over me, his breath coming in short, sharp gasps. "The lodge chose me," he says, his voice quieter now, almost reverent. "It saw me for who I really am. Not the man you tried to control. Not the 'husband' you thought you could mold into some pathetic version of your own expectations. No, Harper. The lodge sees everything. It saw my *potential.*"

"You're wrong," I say, my voice shaking. "It's using you, Michael. It's feeding off of you."

He laughs, a hollow, bitter sound that echoes off the stone walls. "You're still clinging to that, aren't you? Still trying to make this about me. About *us.* But it's not, Harper. This is bigger than you, bigger than me. The lodge is eternal. It has always been here, waiting. And now it's *mine.* I am its keeper."

"Keeper?" I repeat, my mind racing. I glance around the room, searching for anything I can use to escape, but all I see are shadows, endless and omnipresent. "Michael, you sound insane."

"Do I?" he snarls, his voice rising again. "Do I sound insane, or do I sound *free?*"

I force myself to look at him, to hold his gaze even as my instincts scream at me to look away. His face is gaunt, his skin pale and stretched thin, and his eyes burn with a feverish intensity. But behind the manic energy, I catch a flicker of something else. Doubt. It's there, buried beneath the bravado, but it's there.

"Michael," I say softly, my tone shifting. "If the lodge chose you... if it really trusts you... then why are you so afraid?"

His expression falters for the briefest of moments, his mouth opening and closing as if searching for a response. "I'm not afraid," he says, but his voice wavers.

"Yes, you are," I press, taking a cautious step forward. "You're afraid because you know it's not true. Because you know the lodge doesn't care about you. It's just using you, the same way it's used everyone before you."

"Shut up," he mutters, his hands clenching into fists. He takes a step back, and I can see the cracks forming, the unraveling beginning.

"You've seen it, haven't you?" I continue, my voice steady now. "The others. The people who came before us. Rebecca. The couples who left nothing behind but ash and despair. You know what happened to them. You know it will happen to you, too."

"SHUT UP!" he screams, his voice echoing through the basement. The shadows surge around us and I feel their cold tendrils brushing against my skin. But Michael isn't looking at me anymore. His gaze is fixed on the floor, his breathing shallow and erratic.

I take another step back, careful not to draw his attention, and my fingers brush against something cold and metallic. A lock. My heart skips a beat as I feel the outline of the door behind me, the latch firmly in place. I glance down, my hands trembling, and see the faint glint of a small, rusted lock holding the door shut.

Michael is still pacing, muttering under his breath, his hands running through his hair. I take the opportunity to crouch down, my fingers fumbling with the lock. It's old and corroded, but it doesn't seem sturdy. If I can just—

"What are you doing?" His voice cuts through the air like a knife, and I freeze, my breath catching in my throat. He turns to me, his eyes blazing, and for a moment, I think he's going to lunge at me.

"I'm sorry," I say quickly, feigning weakness. I let my shoulders slump, my voice breaking as I add, "I don't want to fight anymore, Michael. I just... I don't know what to do."

He hesitates, his gaze narrowing as he studies me. I can see the conflict in his expression, the war between his anger and his need for control. "You don't get to decide what happens next," he says finally, his voice cold and detached. "The lodge will decide. It always does."

As he turns away, I seize the moment. My fingers tighten around the lock, and with a desperate twist, it gives way, the rusted metal snapping with a soft crack. I push the door open, slipping through the narrow gap and into the cold, damp tunnel beyond.

Michael's roar of rage echoes behind me, but I don't look back. I run, my feet pounding against the stone floor, the shadows chasing me, the air thick with the lodge's wrath. I don't know where the tunnel leads, but it doesn't matter. All that matters is that I'm not trapped anymore.

39

THE SHOWDOWN

The tunnel, some kind of service route under the house led to a set of stone steps, emerging through a beacon of light from the outside world. Harper scrambled up them, slipping on snow, ice and moss, banging her shins, making her yelp but once at the top she gulped in clean air, gasping for breath on her hands and knees. As she attempted to reorientate herself, she glanced down the steps and into the tunnel. Instinct told her they were there, just beyond, the shadows unable to leave the foundations of the lodge, trapped there for all eternity.

Above her, the lodge groaned with a terrible sound, a deep, reverberating moan that echoed through its collapsing walls. It was breathing its last, each exhale pulling the world inside tighter and darker. The windows no longer framed the snow-dusted forest outside; they had transformed into vast, endless voids, black and yawning, swallowing all light.

Michael!

He was still inside, whatever he was, but she couldn't leave what remained of him in there. She's made that mistake before and wouldn't repeat it. She'd lost her family through fear and he, no matter how flawed, was all she had left.

Staggering to her feet, Harper summoned the energy to run, skirting the walls of the house that were riddled with cracks, like skin, dry, lined and crumbling, disintegrating slowly.

No way was she going back in the lodge so after pounding up the steps she pulled open the door and stood on the periphery, looking into the great room. From there she called his name.

"Michael, Michael come to the door, please, you need to leave." The floor beneath her feet shifted, tilted and buckled so she took a step back. Her scraped palms burned as she gripped the doorframe. Then she heard him.

"Harper! You can't run from this. You can't run from me!"

She stood firm and watched on as the once-grand room became a chaotic maelstrom of swirling shadows and groaning timbers. The chandelier above swung wildly, its crystals clinking together in a maddening cacophony, and the floorboards undulated. Harper's gaze darted to the staircase, the fireplace, the looming void where part of the floor had once been. The lodge, its walls, were warping and folding in on themselves like the closing jaws of a predator.

Michael entered the room moments later, his face twisted with fury and desperation. His torn shirt hung off his shoulders, his hair disheveled, and his eyes glowed with a feverish intensity that sent a chill down Harper's spine. He looked completely consumed, no longer tethered to reality.

He wasn't looking at her anymore. His gaze was fixed downward, lost in some internal battle. She seized the moment, moving closer to the edge, the pull of the abyss so strong it nearly took her balance.

"Michael," please, come to the door... they can't get you out here... you have to do as I say Michael, quickly, time's running out."

He looked up, his face contorted with fury and doubt. "See, you're doing it again, telling me what to do, he hissed, but his voice wavered. He took another step toward her, his wild eyes fixed on hers.

"I'm sorry you feel like that but if you come with me I promise to be better," Harper said softly, holding his gaze. "We can try to work things out."

His face twisted with rage, and he lunged at her. Harper sidestepped at the last moment, her heart racing as Michael's momentum carried him forward. He stumbled, his foot catching on the edge of the chasm, and for a brief, terrible moment, he hung there, his arms flailing, his eyes wide with panic. It was as though in that second he realized who he was, what was happening.

"Harper!" he shouted, his voice raw with fear. "Help me!"

She hesitated, her breath catching in her throat. For a moment, she thought about stepping into the room and reaching out, about pulling him back. But then she saw the shadows rising from the pit, their tendrils reaching for him, wrapping around his legs, his arms, his neck. Michael's gaze met hers, and in his eyes, she saw the man he used to be—the man she had loved—and the thing he had become.

"I'm sorry," she whispered.

The shadows surged, pulling him down, and Michael's scream echoed through the hall as he disappeared into the darkness. Harper staggered back, her chest heaving, her mind reeling as she ran into the snow. The lodge roared, its walls buckling, its foundation shaking, as if it were collapsing in on itself.

Once she reached her car she turned and listened to the sound of the lodge's destruction as it filled her ears—a cacophony of splintering wood, shattering glass, and otherworldly screams before it gave one final, deafening groan. She stumbled forward, collapsing to her knees, and watched the building implode. The walls folded inward, the roof caving, the shadows consuming everything. And then, it was gone.

All that remained was a smoking crater, the snow around it scorched black. Harper knelt there, her body trembling, her mind numb. The lodge was gone. Michael was gone. And yet, as she stared into the void where it had once stood, she couldn't shake the feeling that it wasn't over.

It would never be over.

40

THE HOSPITAL

Harper awoke to the blinding fluorescent lights and the sharp scent of antiseptic. Her first instinct was to jerk upright, but her body felt heavy, her limbs leaden against the stiff hospital sheets. She blinked, her vision swimming with unfamiliar shapes—the dull beige walls, a monitor beeping steadily at her side, the faint outline of a nurse bustling near the doorway.

Her mind felt fragmented, like shards of glass scattered across her memory. She closed her eyes, trying to piece the fragments together. The snow. The lodge. The shadows. Michael. The name lingered in her thoughts, twisting her insides with a sharp pang. But where was she now? How had she gotten here?

The nurse turned, noticing her movement, and walked briskly to her side. "You're awake," she said, her voice warm but professional. "Take it easy, sweetheart. You've been through quite an ordeal."

Harper struggled to form words, her throat dry and raw. "Where... where am I?"

"You're at St. Peter's Medical Center," the nurse explained, adjusting the IV drip attached to Harper's arm. "You were found in the woods a few days ago, not far from the old Ravenscreek Lodge. Do you remember anything?"

Harper stared at her, the words struggling to form a coherent path in her mind. "The lodge..." she croaked, her voice barely audible. "It collapsed. Michael... he... he's gone."

The nurse gave her a soft, pitying smile, patting her arm. "You've been through a lot, dear. The doctors think the hypothermia might've caused some hallucinations. You were wandering alone in the snow, severely dehydrated and frostbitten. You're lucky someone found you when they did."

Harper's heart raced as she tried to sit up, ignoring the way her muscles screamed in protest. "No," she said, her voice cracking. "It wasn't hallucinations. The lodge... it was alive. It—"

"Easy now," the nurse interrupted, gently pressing Harper back onto the bed. "You've been delirious since you were brought in. The doctors will explain everything once you've had some rest."

Harper's breathing quickened, her chest rising and falling in uneven gasps. Her memories of the lodge were vivid, too vivid to dismiss as mere delusions. She couldn't believe it had been a product of her mind.

As if sensing her distress, the nurse smoothed the edge of the blanket over Harper's chest. "I'll let the doctor know you're awake. He'll be able to answer any questions you have." With that, she disappeared from the room, leaving Harper alone with the rhythmic beep of the monitor and the muffled sounds of hospital life just beyond the door.

Harper turned her head, staring at the window. The sun was shining, the light warm and golden, but it felt wrong. Too clean. Too normal. It didn't match the chaos etched into her memory. She could still feel the lodge's presence, lurking somewhere in the back of her mind, like a splinter she couldn't remove.

The door creaked open, and a man in a white coat entered,

clipboard in hand. His face was kind but unreadable, his eyes scanning her as if she were another puzzle to solve. "Good morning, Harper," he said, pulling up a chair beside her bed. "I'm Dr. Lawson. I've been overseeing your care."

Harper said nothing, watching him with wary eyes as he flipped through her chart. After a moment, he looked up and offered a reassuring smile. "You gave us quite a scare. From what we've gathered, you were found about five miles from Ravenscreek Lodge, wandering in the woods. Hypothermia can cause severe disorientation and, in some cases, hallucinations. It's not uncommon to see or hear things that aren't there."

"I wasn't hallucinating," Harper said, her voice firmer now. "I know what I saw. The lodge... it was alive. It wasn't just a building—it was something else. And I burnt it down with Michael inside. He wouldn't leave even when I begged him."

Dr. Lawson nodded, his expression calm and patient, but Harper could see the skepticism in his eyes. "It's natural to feel that way after a traumatic experience. Our minds have a way of filling in the blanks when we're under extreme stress. The lodge is an ominous place, I've seen it once or twice while I've been hiking. It likely played tricks on your perception, especially in such extreme conditions."

Harper clenched her fists beneath the blanket. "Michael, did they find him, his body will be in the ruins?" she said, her voice shaking. "We went there together. And now he's gone. The lodge... it took him."

Dr. Lawson tilted his head, his pen poised over his clipboard. "There was no sign of anyone else when you were found," he said gently. "The search team combed the area thoroughly. They only found you."

Harper felt her stomach drop, her mind reeling. How could that be? Michael had been there. She had seen him, touched him, fought with him. The lodge had consumed him—it couldn't all have been a figment of her imagination.

"I'm not crazy," she said, more to herself than to the doctor. "I know what happened. I know what I saw."

"No one is saying you're crazy, Harper," Dr. Lawson said, his tone measured. "But it's important to acknowledge how trauma and physical exhaustion can distort our memories. It doesn't mean what you felt wasn't real to you—it just means your mind may have interpreted things in a way that kept you alive."

Harper stared at him, her chest tight with frustration and fear. She wanted to scream, to demand that he believe her, but the words caught in her throat. She felt trapped, not by the hospital bed or the IV in her arm, but by the stain of her own memories. If no one believed her, did it mean it hadn't happened? Or did it mean she was truly alone in what she had experienced?

Dr. Lawson stood, smoothing the front of his coat. "Get some rest," he said kindly. "Your body needs time to recover. If you'd like, we can talk again tomorrow. Sometimes it helps to revisit these things with a clear mind."

He left the room, the door clicking shut softly behind him. Harper turned her head back to the window, watching the sunlight dance across the glass. It felt foreign, like it belonged to another world entirely. She closed her eyes, the beeping of the monitor lulling her into a restless haze.

But in the quiet moments between breaths, she thought she heard it—the faintest whisper, low and distant, calling her name.

41

THE RECOVERY

My room is small, barely large enough for the bed, a chair in the corner, and the tray table that stands at an awkward angle over my lap. There's a plastic jug of water with a disposable cup resting on top of it, both untouched. A monitor next to my bed beeps steadily, its green light flashing in rhythm with my pulse. The sound is strangely comforting, though it also feels invasive, as if the machine knows more about me than I do.

I glance toward the window. Outside, the world looks serene—cars passing by in the distance, trees swaying in the winter wind—but it feels like I'm watching through a screen, disconnected and detached. I turn away from the window, my gaze falling on the IV tube taped to my arm, cool liquid dripping steadily into my veins. It's the only anchor I have to the reality I'm supposed to accept. The doctors say I was found wandering in the woods, hypothermic, frostbitten, and delirious. They call me lucky, as if luck had anything to do with it.

I shift in bed, the thin hospital gown scratching against my skin. Every muscle aches with a dull throb that refuses to be ignored, but the physical pain is easier to bear than the gnawing unease in my chest. My mind feels fractured, like a puzzle that's been forced together in all the wrong ways. Every time I try to piece it back together, the edges don't fit, and I'm left staring at gaps I can't explain.

The door creaks open, and a woman enters. She's in her mid-forties, with dark hair pulled into a low bun and glasses perched on the bridge of her nose. She wears the standard white coat, a stethoscope looped around her neck. Her ID badge reads Dr. Andrea Carlson.

"Good afternoon, Harper," she says, her voice calm and measured. She carries a clipboard, but her eyes are focused on me, studying me with the kind of professional detachment I've come to expect. She pulls the chair closer to my bed and sits down, her movements deliberate, as though she's trying not to startle me.

I don't respond. My throat feels tight, the words trapped somewhere I can't reach.

Dr. Carlson leans forward slightly, resting her clipboard on her lap. "You've been through a lot," she says. "I can't imagine how disorienting this must be for you. But I'd like to talk, if you're up for it."

I stare at her, trying to gauge her sincerity. Her expression is kind, but there's a clinical edge to her tone, a subtle reminder that to her, I'm a case file. A problem to be solved.

"I don't know what you want me to say," I murmur finally, my voice hoarse. "I've already told the nurses everything."

"I understand," she replies. "But I'd like to hear it from you directly. You were found near the ruins of Ravenscreek Lodge. Can you tell me what you were doing there?"

I hesitate, my hands gripping the edge of the blanket. The memories are vivid, too vivid to ignore, but saying them out loud feels dangerous, like giving them too much power. Still, I can't stop myself. The words spill out in a rush, my voice trembling.

"We were staying there, my husband and I. Michael. The

lodge... it wasn't just a building. It was alive. It did things—impossible things. It twisted everything. Michael, me, our memories. It... it took him."

Dr. Carlson doesn't interrupt. She nods occasionally, her pen moving across the clipboard, but her face remains neutral. When I finish, she sets the clipboard aside and leans forward, her hands clasped.

"Harper," she begins carefully, "I understand how real this must feel to you. Trauma and physical stress, especially in extreme conditions like hypothermia, can create vivid hallucinations. The mind tries to make sense of what it's experiencing, even when there's no logical explanation. It's not uncommon for people to see or hear things that aren't there."

Her words hit me like a slap, and my chest tightens. "I wasn't hallucinating," I snap, the anger in my voice surprising even me. "I know what I saw. The lodge was alive. It wasn't just in my head."

Dr. Carlson doesn't flinch. "I believe you believe that" she says gently. "But we must consider the possibility that what you experienced was your mind's way of coping with trauma. You and your husband went to the lodge to work on your marriage, correct? That's a lot of emotional baggage to carry, especially in a remote, isolated environment."

I feel the tears welling up before I can stop them, my frustration spilling over. "It wasn't an overstuffed suitcase," I whisper. "It was real. The walls moved. The shadows... they were alive. And Michael—he... he was consumed by it."

Dr. Carlson tilts her head, her expression softening. "Michael disappeared before you left the lodge the first time and despite intensive searches he has never been found. His belongings were returned to you by the owner of the lodge. You went back to the lodge and Michael wasn't with you when you were found. The search team didn't find any evidence of another person at the property."

Her words hang in the air. I want to argue, to scream, but the truth is, I don't have an answer. How could they not find him? How could they not see what I saw?

"I'm not crazy," I say finally, my voice breaking. "I know what happened."

Dr. Carlson stands, her movements deliberate. She picks up the clipboard and looks down at me, her expression unreadable. "I don't think you're crazy, Harper. But I do think you're in pain and in the absence of closure where finding your husband is concerned, you are experiencing grief and confusion. And sometimes, when we're in pain, our minds create things to help us process it. That doesn't make the pain any less real."

She steps toward the door, pausing with her hand on the handle. "We'll continue this conversation when you're ready. For now, try to rest."

The door closes softly behind her, and I'm alone again. The beeping of the monitor feels louder now, each pulse a reminder of how trapped I am—in this hospital bed, in my own mind. I turn my head to the window, the sunlight blinding and relentless.

Was the lodge real? Or was it just a projection of everything Michael and I brought with us—our toxicity, our failures, our fear? I don't know. I don't think I'll ever know. But in the numbing loneliness of this room, I swear I can still feel it. The way it burrowed into my mind, my soul. The lodge is gone, but it hasn't let go. Not entirely. It lingers, just out of sight.

And sometimes, when the machines quiet and the nurses are gone, I hear it.

A whisper.

Calling my name.

42

HOME AGAIN

Princeton is supposed to be a fresh start. That's what I tell myself each time I step out onto the familiar streets, willing the routine of my old life to wrap around me like a comforting blanket. The air is crisp with the beginnings of spring, students rushing by, their laughter echoing against brick buildings. I walk among them, clutching a coffee from the corner shop, hoping that the mundanity of it all will ground me. But it doesn't. It feels hollow, like a poorly rehearsed play where the actors forgot their lines.

My apartment, once a place of comfort, now feels like a stranger's home. The creaks in the floorboards seem louder, more deliberate, and every shadow feels like it's watching me. I've rearranged the furniture three times in the past week, trying to reclaim a sense of control, but it doesn't help. Nothing helps.

The police visited yesterday. Detective Lasky, a stocky man with kind but wary eyes, sat across from me at the small kitchen table. He had a notebook in hand, but I could tell he wasn't writing much down. He was humoring me.

"We've combed the area around Ravenscreek Lodge," he said, his voice careful, as though speaking too loudly might break me. "There's nothing there. Just forest. No ruins, no signs of a structure ever having been set alight."

I stared at him, my coffee growing cold between my hands. "That's impossible," I said, my voice steadier than I felt. "I was there. I saw it collapse."

He nodded, as though he'd heard this before. "We found the spot where you were discovered, Harper. The house is as it always is. But there's no sign of a fire. Are you sure—"

"I'm sure," I snapped, cutting him off. "I know what I saw. What we experienced."

Lasky sighed, leaning back in his chair. "Look, I don't doubt that you believe what you're saying. But sometimes, when people go through extreme trauma, their minds—"

"Don't," I said sharply, my hands trembling around the mug. "Don't tell me it was all in my head. I know what happened."

He gave me a long, measured look, his expression softening into something like pity. "There's no sign of Michael either," he said quietly. "No one matching his description has turned up, and we haven't been able to find any trace of him. I'm sorry."

I barely heard him after that. His voice faded into the background, no competition against the pounding in my head. No trace of Michael. No trace of the ruins. It's as if they never existed, as if the past few months of my life were nothing more than a fever dream. But I know better.

After Lasky left, I sat at the table for hours, staring at the spot where his notebook had rested. My mind replayed his words over and over, each one a knife twisting deeper. No ruins? How could it be intact? I can still feel the lodge, its presence lingering in my chest like a shadow that refuses to be dislodged.

I've tried to focus on rebuilding. Therapy twice a week, like clockwork. My therapist, Dr. Meyers, is kind but cautious, her questions always dancing around the edges of what she really wants to ask.

"How have you been sleeping?" she asked during our last session, her pen poised over a notepad.

"Fine," I lied.

The truth is, I wake up every night at 3:03, the echoes of a woman's voice, I know it's Rebecca's, ringing in my ears. The nightmares are relentless—Michael's face twisted with rage, the lodge's walls closing in, Rebecca's hollow eyes staring through me. I've stopped trying to interpret them. They're not symbols or metaphors; they're memories, fragments of a reality no one else will believe.

"Have you considered reaching out to friends or family for support?" Dr. Meyers continued, her tone gentle.

"I'm fine on my own," I replied, my voice clipped. The thought of explaining any of this to one more person is unbearable. Michael's family hate me anyway and I know they think I've harmed him in some way. They look at me the way Detective Lasky did—with that mix of pity and disbelief that makes my stomach churn.

Dr. Meyers nodded, scribbling something in her notebook. I wanted to grab it from her hands, to see what she was writing, but I didn't. Instead, I stared at the clock on the wall, watching the second hand tick forward, wishing the session would end.

At home, I try to keep myself busy. I've started cleaning obsessively, scrubbing every surface until my hands ache, as if I can erase the invisible residue the lodge left behind. But no matter how much I clean, I can't shake the feeling that it's still here, seeping into the walls, hiding in the corners of my apartment.

Yesterday, I found my keys on the windowsill. I didn't put them there. I know I didn't. And then there are the mirrors. I've covered most of them with sheets, but the few I left uncovered taunt me. My reflection doesn't always match. Sometimes it lags, just for a moment, and I feel like I'm staring at someone else.

Last night, the whispers started again. I was lying in bed, staring at the ceiling, when I heard it—a soft, insistent murmur just beyond the edge of hearing. My name. Over and over, in a voice that was both familiar and alien. I squeezed my eyes shut, pulling the blanket over my head, but the sound didn't stop.

When I finally fell asleep, the nightmares came again. Rebecca, standing in the ruins of the lodge, her face gaunt and pale, her voice a low, guttural whisper. "The lodge is not done with you yet," she said, her words echoing in the void around us.

I woke with a start, my chest heaving, the taste of ash in my mouth. I sat up, my hands clutching the sheets, and stared at the window. The clock on the nightstand read 3:03.

I don't know how to move forward. I don't know how to rebuild a life when every shadow feels like it's watching me, when every creak of the floorboards sends my heart racing. The lodge may be gone, but it's not over.

I can feel it.

And sometimes, late at night, when the world is silent and the darkness presses in, I hear it.

A whisper.

Calling me back.

43

THE PACKAGE

The package sat on my doorstep like a silent accusation. It wasn't large, just an unassuming brown box sealed with ordinary packing tape, but its presence filled me with dread the moment I saw it. The air outside was brisk, the faint smell of damp leaves lingering from the rain that had passed in the early hours of the morning. Princeton's streets were quiet, muffled by the overcast sky, but inside me, a storm churned. My name—Harper Dwyer—was printed in neat block letters on the top, the ink slightly smudged as though handled with damp fingers. There was no return address.

I carried it inside with shaking hands as I closed the door behind me. I placed the box on the kitchen table, the polished wood scarred with faint scratches that had begun to appear, and no amount of beeswax could remove. It felt like a ritual I didn't want to perform, the box sitting there like a dark omen.

I sat down, staring at it, my stomach twisted in knots. I didn't want to open it. Every instinct screamed at me to throw it away, to toss it into the dumpster at the back of the building and walk away. But I couldn't. The compulsion was too strong, a whisper at the back of my mind urging me forward.

The apartment felt unnervingly quiet as I reached for the tape, the sound of it peeling away sharp and jarring in the stillness. My fingers fumbled, the anxiety making them clumsy, and I had to take a deep breath to steady myself. When the box flaps finally parted, I froze.

Inside, wrapped in plain brown paper, was Michael's journal.

My pulse quickened as I pulled it out, the weight of it heavy in my hands. The familiar leather cover was scuffed and cracked; the edges charred as though it had been dragged from the fire that consumed the lodge. The scent of ash lingered faintly on it, mingling with the faint smell of mildew. It shouldn't have been here. I'd seen the lodge collapse. I'd watched it burn, seen the flames rise and consume everything. This journal was supposed to be gone, destroyed along with Michael and the shadows that had taken him.

But here it was, impossibly intact, as real as the air I was breathing. My hands trembled as I ran my fingers over the cover, the cold leather sending a shiver through me. It felt alive, pulsing faintly beneath my touch like the heartbeat of something unseen. I wanted to drop it; to throw it across the room and pretend I'd never seen it, but I couldn't. The journal had a gravity to it, a pull I couldn't resist.

I opened it with trembling hands, the brittle pages crackling faintly as they separated. The familiar handwriting greeted me—Michael's sharp, precise script filling the early entries. I skimmed the first few pages, the words stirring painful memories of his descent into obsession. His belief that the lodge had chosen him. His theories about its power, its influence. His growing paranoia. It was all there, unchanged, just as I remembered.

But as I flipped further, the writing changed. My breath caught in my throat as I saw it—my handwriting. My own scrawled letters filling the pages, frantic and erratic, as though written in a frenzy. The words repeated over and over, their meaning sinking into my chest like lead.

I have to go back. The lodge isn't done. There's more to be done.

Finish what was started.

It calls to me.

The phrases blurred together as I read, the words swimming on the page as my vision blurred. My heart pounded so hard I could hear it in my ears, my breath coming in shallow, uneven gasps. This wasn't possible. I didn't write this. I couldn't have.

Could I?

I pushed the journal away, shoving it across the table as though it might leap at me. My chair scraped loudly against the floor as I stumbled to my feet, the motion sending a jolt of nausea through me. My hands clutched the edge of the sink as I splashed cold water on my face, the shock of it grounding me momentarily.

The kitchen felt wrong. The familiar vibration of the refrigerator sounded distorted, the faint ticking of the clock on the wall too loud, too sharp. The shadows in the corners seemed to shift and writhe, moving just enough to catch my eye but disappearing the moment I turned to look. My reflection in the window above the sink stared back at me, pale and wide-eyed, the image warped slightly by the uneven glass.

I tried to steady my breathing, but the words in the journal wouldn't leave me. The way they filled the pages, relentless and insistent. The handwriting was mine—I couldn't deny that. Every curve of the letters was painfully familiar. But I didn't remember writing them. My mind raced, grasping for answers that wouldn't come. Was it possible? Could I have written them in some fugue state, the lodge's influence still clinging to me even now?

I turned back to the journal, my legs weak as I sank back into the chair. It sat there, its presence almost taunting, daring me to open it again. I flipped to the newer entries, the ones I couldn't explain, searching for some clue, some thread that might unravel the nightmare.

Toward the back, there was a single line scrawled in the center of an otherwise blank page. The handwriting wasn't mine. It was Michael's.

You can't run from what's inside you.

The words hit me like a blow, the room spinning as nausea rose in my throat. My hands shook so violently that the journal slipped from my grasp, landing on the floor with a dull thud. I stared at it, unable to move, my mind racing with a thousand questions that had no answers. Michael was dead. The lodge was gone. So how was this here? How was any of this possible?

That night, I sat in the living room, the journal on the coffee table in front of me like a cursed artifact. The apartment felt colder than usual, the radiator's steady heat doing little to dispel the chill that seeped into my bones.

When the numbers on the clock flicked to 3:03, I heard it again—the faint, insistent whisper of my name.

"Harper."

It came from nowhere and everywhere at once. I turned to the journal, its leather cover gleaming faintly in the dim light, and for the briefest moment, I thought I saw it move. The whispers grew louder, more urgent, as though they were coming from within the pages themselves.

44

THE SEARCH

The journal was my guide. It sat open on the desk, an unwanted gift that refused to let me rest. Its pages, filled with Michael's meticulous observations and my own scrawled, unexplainable handwriting, called to me with a pull I couldn't ignore. The police had found nothing—no records, no ruins, no trace that the lodge or Michael had ever existed. Their words echoed in my mind as I stared at the journal:

"Maybe it was all in your head, Harper."

But I knew better. The lodge had erased itself, its existence swallowed by the void it created. It didn't want to be found. But the journal was proof. A crack in the facade. A thread left dangling for reasons I didn't yet understand.

Rebecca's name was the only lead I had. Her letter had hinted at truths about the lodge's hunger, its manipulations, and I clung to the hope that her life might hold answers to my own unraveling. If the police couldn't find the lodge, it was because they didn't know where to look. They didn't know how to follow its whispers.

But I did.

The first clue came late one evening as I poured over the

journal, the apartment shrouded by the cloak of dusk, save for the ticking of the clock on the wall. My laptop open beside me, the screen a blur of search results and scanned documents. I'd scoured every mention of Ravenscreek Lodge in online forums, local archives, and obscure books about New England folklore. Most of it was useless—just ghost stories and speculation—but buried among the noise was a single post from nearly twenty years ago.

The poster had written about a strange story they'd heard from their grandmother, who claimed to have known a woman who went missing in the woods near a mysterious lodge. The woman's name was Rebecca Langston. My pulse quickened as I read further, but the details were frustratingly vague. The poster had long since abandoned the forum, their account inactive for years.

But one detail stood out: a mention of Rebecca's hometown, Pine Hollow. A small, forgotten place not far from the lodge's supposed location. It was a starting point.

The police hadn't found Pine Hollow in their search because they hadn't known where to look. The lodge existed outside conventional reality, its reach extending beyond the physical world. The land it claimed was more than just woods and snow —it was a realm of its own making, hidden from those who weren't ensnared by its grip.

But I had been ensnared. I still was.

I drove to Pine Hollow the next day, the road winding through dense, skeletal woods that seemed to stretch endlessly in all directions. The map app on my phone struggled to pinpoint the location, the GPS flickering in and out as if the town itself resisted being found. By the time I arrived, the sun was sinking low on the horizon, casting long shadows over the quaint but desolate streets.

The town was small, the kind of place where time seemed to

have stopped decades ago. The buildings were worn and weathered, their signs faded, and their windows clouded with dust. I parked near the town square, where a single grocery store and a post office stood side by side, and made my way to the local library, which was more of a converted house than a proper institution.

Its shelves were packed with local records, old newspapers, and handwritten accounts from townspeople long since gone. I spent hours combing through the archives, my fingers stained with dust and ink, until I found what I was looking for: an obituary for Rebecca Langston, dated March 4, 1951.

The obituary was sparse, mentioning her as a beloved schoolteacher who had lived a quiet life in Pine Hollow before her untimely passing. There was no mention of her disappearance or her connection to the lodge. But it listed her surviving family members, including her niece: Evelyn Grant.

I scribbled Evelyn's name and last known address into my notebook, my hands trembling with a mix of excitement and dread. This was it. A real person, a living connection to Rebecca and her story. But as I read over the obituary again, a strange detail caught my eye. The obituary's ink seemed too fresh. The edges of the paper too crisp. It felt new, untouched by time, as if it had been placed there for me to find.

Finding Evelyn wasn't easy. Pine Hollow's records were sparse, and Evelyn's name didn't appear in any recent directories. But I was relentless. I reached out to every online community I could think of, posting anonymously in genealogy groups, folklore forums, and even local Facebook pages for the surrounding area. It was in one of these groups—a forgotten corner of the internet where people traded tales of the paranormal—that I found my next clue.

Someone in the group remembered an Evelyn Grant who had lived near the edge of the forest in Pine Hollow. They described her as a recluse, someone who kept to herself and rarely ventured into town. The address they provided matched the one I'd found in the library's records, though they warned me that Evelyn hadn't been seen in years.

I didn't care. I had to try.

The drive to Evelyn's house was suffused with a growing sense of unease. The GPS on my phone failed completely, the signal cutting out as I turned onto the narrow gravel road that led to her property. The trees grew denser here, their bare branches arching overhead like a cathedral of shadows.

Finally, the house came into view. It was small and weathered, its white paint peeling in long strips, the porch sagging under years of neglect. A single light burned in the front window, casting a faint, flickering glow onto the overgrown yard. My breath caught as I pulled into the driveway.

I sat there while I gathered my strength, staring at the house, my mind racing with what I might find inside. The journal was in my bag, a constant reminder of why I was here. My heartbeat thundered in my ears as I opened the car door, stepping out into the cold evening air. The gravel crunched beneath my boots as I approached the house, the scent of damp wood and decay filling my nostrils.

I raised my hand to knock, hesitating for just a moment. Then, with a deep breath, I let my knuckles rap against the door. The sound echoed in the stillness, and I waited, my heart pounding in my chest.

Somewhere in the woods behind me, I thought I heard a faint whisper—a voice carried on the wind, calling my name. I turned, scanning the shadows, but saw nothing. Just the endless expanse of trees, their skeletal forms swaying gently in the breeze.

When I turned back to the door, the light in the window flickered, and I thought I heard footsteps approaching from inside. I held my breath as I prepared myself for whatever—or whoever—was about to answer.

The door creaked open slowly, revealing a woman in her late sixties, her face shadowed by the dim light of the single bulb hanging in the entryway. Her eyes, sharp and cautious, flicked over me with a guarded intensity that made me hesitate. Her graying hair was pulled back in a loose bun, and she wore a heavy cardigan that looked worn but comforting, like she'd spent years wrapping herself in it for protection.

"Yes?" she asked, her voice low and slightly hoarse, as though she hadn't used it much in recent days. Her tone wasn't unkind, but it carried the nuance of someone who didn't want company.

"Evelyn Grant?" I asked, my voice shaky. "I'm... I'm Harper Dwyer. I've been looking for you."

Her expression darkened immediately, her hand tightening on the edge of the door as though she might slam it shut. "Why?" she asked, her voice clipped.

I hesitated, unsure how to explain. I hear feel the journal calling me from inside my bag, like it was begging me to pull it out, but I resisted. "It's about Rebecca," I said finally. "Your aunt. I've... I've been to Ravenscreek Lodge."

The name landed like a thunderclap. Evelyn's face paled, her grip on the door faltering. For a moment, I thought she might refuse to answer, but then her eyes darted to the darkening woods behind me, as though she feared someone—or something—might be listening. She stepped back, pulling the door open wider.

"Come in," she said quietly, glancing around one last time before closing the door behind me.

The inside of the house was modest but cluttered, every available surface covered in books, papers, and trinkets that looked like they'd been collected over decades. The air was thick with the smell of old wood and faintly stale coffee. Evelyn motioned for me to sit at the small kitchen table, its surface scarred with rings from countless mugs. She poured herself a cup of tea from a pot on the stove, her movements deliberate and slow, before sitting across from me.

"What do you know about Ravenscreek?" she asked finally, her voice barely above a whisper.

I hesitated, unsure how much to reveal. "I stayed there," I admitted. "With my husband. But it wasn't... it wasn't what we thought it would be."

Evelyn's eyes narrowed, her fingers tightening around the handle of her mug. "No one who goes there knows what it really is," she said, her tone bitter. "Not until it's too late."

I leaned forward, the words tumbling out before I could stop them. "Rebecca—your aunt—she left something behind. A letter. It warned about the lodge, about how it... how it feeds on people. I think she knew what it was."

Evelyn's face softened slightly at the mention of Rebecca, but the tension in her shoulders didn't ease. "She didn't just know," she said quietly. "She tried to stop it."

The room felt smaller suddenly, the air thick, as Evelyn's words sank in. "What do you mean?" I asked, my voice barely audible.

Evelyn set her mug down with a soft clink and leaned back in her chair, her gaze fixed on some distant memory. "When Rebecca came back from that place, she wasn't the same. She was... fractured. Haunted. She wouldn't tell us much, just bits and pieces. But she spent months trying to figure out what the lodge really was. She read everything she could get her hands on—local legends, folklore, occult texts. Anything that might give her answers. She even began writing letters to herself, as if she were guarding against the temptation to return."

My skin prickled, knowing I'd seen those very letters with my own eyes but having become used to not being believed, kept it to myself until I'd heard more. "And did she find anything?" I asked, my heart pounding.

Evelyn hesitated, her jaw tightening. "She found enough to know she should've stayed away. The lodge isn't just some haunted house, Harper. It's something much older, much darker. It... it feeds on people. On their pain, their fears, their worst impulses. And it doesn't let go."

Nausea washed over me but the fear of what she might hear outweighed by the need for answers. "Tell me, please. I have to know."

"Fine. But don't say I didn't warn you," she said, her voice hard

Evelyn stood. She paced the room, her hands wringing together as though trying to strangle the words before they could escape her mouth. When she finally spoke, her voice was low and measured, each word weighted with a history I could barely comprehend.

"The lodge wasn't always there," she began, her eyes fixed on the floor. "The land it stands on... it was cursed long before it was built. They say the curse dates to the late 1600s, when a settlement tried to take the land from the local tribes. There was a massacre—blood spilled on the soil; screams buried in the roots of the trees. The survivors said the land became... wrong after that. The animals fled, crops wouldn't grow, and anyone who stayed too long went mad."

My breath caught as I listened, the pieces of the puzzle

slotting together in horrifying clarity. "So why build on it?" I asked, my voice barely above a whisper.

Evelyn stopped pacing, her gaze locking onto mine. "Because some people are drawn to darkness," she said. "In the early 1900s, a man named Elijah Marrow bought the land. He was a recluse, an eccentric with too much money and too many dangerous ideas. He believed that suffering was a kind of energy —something that could be harnessed, manipulated, even controlled."

The room felt colder as she spoke, the shadows in the corners seeming to deepen. "He built the lodge as a kind of experiment," she continued. "A place designed to draw people in, to amplify their pain, their fears, their worst impulses. The lodge feeds on it, Harper. It twists people, turns them into... into something else."

I felt a chill run down my spine, my mind racing with memories of the lodge's shifting walls, its whispers that seemed to crawl inside my head. "And Rebecca?" I asked, my voice trembling. "What happened to her?"

Evelyn's face crumpled, the strength she'd held onto slipping away. "Rebecca was one of the first," she said quietly. "She and her husband went to the lodge in 1950, looking for a retreat. But it wasn't long before things started going wrong. She said the walls moved when she wasn't looking, that the air felt heavy, like it was alive. Her husband... he didn't make it."

"What do you mean?" I asked, dread pooling in my stomach.

"She said the lodge got to him," Evelyn whispered. "It fed on his anger, his guilt, his darkest thoughts. He became violent, paranoid. And one night, he disappeared. Rebecca found his journal weeks later, hidden in the woodshed. It was filled with... symbols, strange writings, things that didn't make sense."

The journal in my bag seemed to drag me down with every

word, its presence a dark reminder of everything I'd lost. "And Rebecca?" I pressed. "How did she escape?"

"She didn't," Evelyn said, her voice breaking. "Not really. She came back, but she was never the same. She tried to warn people, tried to stop them from going there. But no one listened. Then she disappeared too."

Evelyn looked at me then, her eyes filled with a pain that mirrored my own. "You need to let it go, Harper," she said, her voice firm. "The lodge doesn't just feed on you. It *claims* you. If you keep delving, it'll pull you back, and this time, it won't let go."

But her words only solidified my resolve. The lodge had already claimed too much—Michael, my sanity, my life. I couldn't walk away now. Not when the answers were so close. Not when I could feel its pull, stronger than ever.

"I can't," I said, standing. "I have to find a way to stop it hurting more people."

Evelyn's shoulders sagged, a look of deep sorrow crossing her face. "Then I hope you're ready to pay the price," she said quietly.

I felt a chill run down my spine as her words echoed in my mind.

Evelyn moved towards the door and flung it open. Her movements abrupt. "You should leave," she said, her voice sharp. "I shouldn't have let you in."

"What? Why?" I asked, panic rising in my chest.

"Because the lodge doesn't like it when people get too close to the truth," she said, her eyes darting to the window. "And neither do the things that follow it. I've spent years trying to block out what Rebecca told me; I've been plagued by nightmares, terrified they'd come for me and you being here just brings all that back."

Her words chilled me to the bone, but before I could respond, she was ushering me toward the door. “Go home, Harper,” she said, her voice firm. “Forget about Rebecca. Forget about the lodge. If you keep digging, you’ll only make it worse.”

45

RAVENSCREEK

The journal sat in the passenger seat, a silent companion radiating an unbearable heaviness. I had sworn I destroyed it, watched its pages curl into blackened ash in the lodge's fireplace. Yet here it was, unburned, immaculate, waiting for me. It seemed alive, its presence not just physical but suffused with something eternal. Every mile I drove toward the place where I believed the lodge had once stood, I felt its pull growing stronger, like invisible threads wrapping tighter and tighter around my limbs, dragging me forward.

The road stretched ahead, winding along the outskirts of the vast forest, the branches now budding yet they still resembled clawed hands grasping at the slate-gray sky. I remembered the day Michael and I traveled this road. Ignorant and innocent. Heading through a snowstorm into a blizzard of epic proportions, mentally, spiritually and physically.

The air in the car grew colder and I turned the dial, so the heater was blasting at full strength. I pulled my jacket tighter around me, but the cold crawled into my mind, icy fingers dragging out memories I had buried deep, memories I had no wish to revisit.

The first memory hit me like a slap. I was eight years old, running barefoot through the yard of my childhood home, the grass slick with rain. My parents arguing as they always did, their angry words filtering up the stars to my bedroom.

But it didn't end there. A flash of light—no, fire. Flames licking at the edges of the roof as the house burned. My father's silhouette in the doorway, screaming my name, but his voice twisted and wrong. His face was blackened, charred flesh peeling away to reveal the glint of bone beneath. His eyes were empty sockets, and yet I felt them boring into me, accusing.

"You let me burn," his voice whispered now, no longer confined to memory. It slithered through the car. I pressed the gas pedal harder, trying to outrun it.

The journal shifted slightly on the seat beside me, and for a moment, I thought I saw movement in its pages, as though words were crawling across them like insects. I refused to look. I couldn't look.

Instead, my thoughts twisted again, this time pulling me back to the lodge. I saw Michael's face, contorted with rage and fear, his hands trembling as he screamed at me. "This is your fault, Harper! You poisoned us. You poisoned *me!*"

The memory warped. His face began to change, his features stretching unnaturally, his mouth widening into a grotesque grin that split his cheeks. His eyes turned black, oily pools that seemed to swallow the light.

I blinked, and the vision snapped back to the present, but the echoes of his voice lingered, scraping at my mind like nails on glass. I glanced in the rearview mirror and gasped. For a split second, I thought I saw him sitting in the backseat, his twisted grin reflected in the glass. But when I turned, the seat was empty.

The forest outside grew darker, the trees leaning closer to the road as if conspiring to trap me. Shadows darted between them, shapes that defied logic, their movements frantic. At one point, I thought I saw a figure standing just off the road—a tall, gaunt silhouette that didn't move even as my headlights swept over it. Its head tilted slightly as I passed, and I felt its gaze follow me long after it was out of sight.

The road itself began to change, the asphalt cracking and splintering until it resembled the torn surface of a wound. The steering wheel vibrated in my hands as the car jostled over the uneven surface, and I had to fight to keep it steady. The crunch of the tires grew louder, morphing into a low, droning noise that resonated in my skull. It sounded like a voice, deep and distant, speaking words I couldn't quite make out.

I checked the clock on the dashboard, but the numbers had distorted, the digits melting into an incomprehensible jumble. Time didn't seem to exist anymore. I couldn't tell if I'd been driving for hours or minutes. All I knew was that I couldn't stop.

Then I saw it.

The lodge stood before me, as though it had never crumbled into ruin. Its towering silhouette was impossibly intact, standing proudly under the twilight sky. The sharp angles of the roof seemed sharper than ever, and the windows—those dark, reflective voids—gazed back at me, alive with some unknowable presence. My heart stuttered in my chest as I stepped forward.

I knew this place had been destroyed. I *watched* it collapse, the shadows swallowing it whole, leaving nothing but a smoking crater in the earth. And yet, here it was again, whole and undisturbed, as though mocking my memory, daring me to question my sanity.

The door creaked open.

The sound was slow, drawn out, the kind of noise that seemed to scrape against your nerves. Warm light spilled onto the porch. For a moment, the golden glow looked inviting, but then it seemed to darken at the edges, as if tainted by something sinister lurking just beyond the threshold. A figure emerged, and I froze, my breath catching in my throat.

The man who stepped out looked so ordinary, so painfully human, that the sight of him jarred me. He was tall, broad-shouldered, with a weathered face framed by dark hair streaked with silver. His thick sweater and worn jeans gave him the appearance of someone who had lived a simple life in a place far removed from chaos. As if from a different time, a long-gone era. Something about him didn't sit right. His smile, warm and polite, seemed just a fraction too wide, his eyes just a shade too sharp as they locked onto mine.

"Hello there," he said, his voice calm and steady, though a note of confusion lingered at the edges. "Are you lost?"

I couldn't answer. My mouth opened, but no words came out. The journal, now pressed tightly against my chest felt like a burden, its bulk sinking into me like a lead anchor. The man's gaze flickered briefly to the book, his brows furrowing slightly before returning to me.

Behind him, the door swung open wider, and a second figure emerged—a woman, younger than the man but just as unnervingly composed. Her dark hair was tied back neatly, and her buttoned up coat was clean and unwrinkled, and her old-fashioned boots were shiny and new, as though she hadn't stepped out into the world a day in her life. Her eyes, sharp and calculating, darted to me, and I felt her assessing me, her stare piercing through my layers like a scalpel.

"What's going on?" she asked, her tone soft but measured, her body language rigid and controlled. She stepped forward slightly, her hand resting lightly on the man's arm as though to steady him—or herself.

"She has a journal, like mine, do you see," the man said, his voice dropping as if he didn't want me to hear.

"Are you alright?" the woman asked, her eyes narrowing ever so slightly as she studied me and briefly, the journal. Her voice was too gentle, too deliberate, and it only made my panic surge.

"How long have you been here?" I managed to croak, my voice trembling as the words spilled out. "How long have you lived in this house?"

The man tilted his head, his expression puzzled but cautious. "Years," he said slowly, his tone careful. "My wife and I bought this place years ago. Why?"

The words slammed into me like a punch to the gut. "No," I whispered, shaking my head violently. "That's not possible. This place—it burned. It collapsed. I saw it... I saw it destroyed."

The woman's face tightened, her polite expression faltering for just a moment before she schooled it back into place. "I think you might be mistaken," she said carefully, taking a step closer. "This house has been here for decades. Maybe you've confused it with somewhere else?"

"No," I said, louder now, my voice rising as panic clawed at my throat. "I know what I saw. I know this place. I *was here*. It isn't supposed to be standing."

The man raised his hands in a calming gesture, his brow creasing further as he glanced at the woman. "Miss, it's alright. You're clearly upset—"

"Don't patronize me!" I snapped, the words ripping out of me before I could stop them. My chest heaved, my grip on the journal tightening as I took another step forward. "I know what this place is. I know what it does."

The woman's lips pressed into a thin line, her eyes narrowing as she exchanged a glance with the man. "Maybe we should call someone," she murmured, her voice low but audible enough to send a chill through me. "She's clearly distressed."

The man nodded slowly. "Why don't you come inside," he said, his voice soft but firm. "Warm up. We'll call someone who can help."

The thought of stepping inside that place made my stomach twist violently, but the pull of the lodge was stronger than ever. I took a shaky step back, then another, my boots felt like lead. "I have to go," I said, my voice trembling. "I shouldn't be here."

The woman tilted her head, her eyes narrowing further as though she were trying to understand something just out of reach. "Are you sure you don't want to come inside? I'm sure we can help with whatever is troubling you," she asked again, her tone almost gentle now, as though speaking to a child.

"I have to go," I repeated, backing away toward the car. The lodge loomed behind them, dark and foreboding, its windows reflecting the golden glow of the porch light. The man and woman watched me, their expressions unreadable, and for a moment, I thought they might follow me. But they didn't. They just stood there, framed by the light spilling from the door, their stillness unnerving.

I climbed into the car, slamming the door shut with trembling hands. The lodge loomed in the rearview mirror, impossibly large and oppressive, its shadow stretching out across the clearing. My fingers fumbled with the ignition, and the engine roared to life, its growl loud and jarring.

As I reversed, I glanced in the mirror again—and froze.

The man and the woman were still standing on the porch, but their faces were no longer their own. The man's face twisted grotesquely, his features elongating and warping until he looked exactly like one of the images I saw in the old photographs inside the lodge. His sharp, piercing eyes burned into mine through the glass, his mouth stretching into a wide, unnatural grin that revealed too many teeth.

Beside him, the woman's face began to shift, her delicate

features melting and reshaping until she wore another face. Mine. Her lips moved although I couldn't hear her words. Her hollow eyes were filled with something I couldn't comprehend —something ancient, hungry.

I screamed, slamming the gas pedal as the car lurched forward onto the main road. The lodge disappeared as the trees closed in around me, but their faces remained burned into my mind, twisted and wrong, impossible to forget.

The journal sat on the passenger seat, and I swore I saw its cover ripple, as though something inside it had stirred. As I sped away, the pull of the lodge only grew stronger, its presence seeping into my very bones. And in the distance, just beyond the edge of my vision, I thought I heard laughter—echoing through the forest.

46

REFLECTIONS

The desk was a mess of scattered pages, ink-stained fingers, and the rhythmic tapping of furious typing. Harper sat hunched over her laptop, her hair hung limp around her face, unkempt and damp with sweat, as if the words she was pouring onto the page were physically draining her.

The clatter of keys was relentless. Every sentence she typed seemed to drag something out of her—pieces of herself that she couldn't afford to lose. Her memoir was almost complete, the culmination of weeks of obsessive writing, sleepless nights, and haunting visions that wouldn't leave her. The lodge, the journal, Michael, Rebecca—the couple at the door, Evelyn, it was all there, laid bare in black and white. The truth. Her truth.

The lodge, standing pristine despite its destruction. The faces that warped and twisted into reflections of her own. The cursed land, the visions. It was all too surreal.

The police had still found no trace of Michael, no proof of anything she'd claimed. Even she was beginning to question whether her mind had fractured entirely, leaving her adrift in a sea of delusions.

But the reflection. That was real.

Harper's eyes darted to the mirror hanging on the wall across the room. She'd taken to draping a scarf over it during the day, unable to bear the sight of her own face staring back at her. There was something wrong with her reflection—something subtle at first but growing more pronounced with each passing day. It wasn't just the hollow eyes or the pallor of her skin. It was the way the reflection *looked* at her, as though it wasn't a reflection at all, but a separate entity. A shadow of herself, watching, waiting.

Tonight, the scarf lay crumpled on the floor. She'd yanked it down earlier in a fit of frustration, determined to confront whatever it was she saw in the glass. Now, the mirror loomed in the corner, its surface dark and still, reflecting the faint glow of the laptop screen. Her reflection was there, faint but unmistakable, its posture mimicking hers, its face a perfect replica. And yet, it wasn't right.

Harper's typing slowed, her fingers hovering over the keys as she stared at the screen. Her chest rose and fell with shallow, rapid breaths, the tension in her muscles winding tighter with every passing second. She glanced at the mirror again, her heart pounding in her ears. The reflection was still there, unmoving, peering into the room like a voyeur and the way it stared made her skin crawl.

She swallowed hard, her throat dry as sandpaper. "You're not real," she whispered, her voice barely audible over the sound of her own heartbeat. The reflection didn't respond. It simply stared, its eyes dark and unreadable.

With a shaky hand, Harper closed the laptop and stood, her chair scraping against the floor as she pushed it back. She took a hesitant step toward the mirror, then another, her movements slow and deliberate. Her breath came in shallow gasps, her pulse thrumming in her temples.

"Show yourself," she said, her voice trembling but defiant. "If you're real, show me."

The reflection didn't move. It remained perfectly still, its eyes locked onto hers, its expression eerily blank. But as she stepped closer, something shifted. The edges of the mirror rippled like water disturbed by a stone, and the reflection began to change. Harper froze, her blood turning to ice as she watched her own face twist and contort in the glass.

The reflection smiled.

It was a slow, deliberate smile, stretching across its face like a predator baring its teeth. Harper's own lips didn't move, but the reflection grinned wider, its eyes glinting with something dark and malevolent. The corners of its mouth stretched too far, the skin pulling taut as if it might tear. And then it spoke.

"You can't escape me," it said, its voice a perfect echo of her own. "You never could."

Harper stumbled backward, her hand flying to her mouth as a wave of nausea rolled over her. "No," she whispered, shaking her head. "You're not real. You're not real."

The reflection tilted its head, its grin never faltering. "You let the lodge in, and now it's part of you. Forever."

"Shut up," Harper hissed, her voice breaking. "Shut up!"

The reflection's grin widened impossibly, the edges of its face stretching and distorting until it no longer looked human. Its eyes darkened, the irises bleeding into the whites until they were nothing but black pits, endless and hollow. "You think leaving the lodge was enough?" it asked, its voice low and guttural now, no longer resembling hers. "You think you can write it all away?"

Harper's knees buckled, and she sank to the floor. The room felt like it was spinning. She squeezed her eyes shut, willing it all to stop, but the reflection's voice was still there, soft and insistent.

"Finish the story," it whispered. "Write the ending you deserve."

When Harper finally opened her eyes, the reflection was gone.

A scream tore from her throat, raw and primal, as she launched herself at the mirror. The movement was unthinking, driven by a sudden, overwhelming need to mute the voices, the whispers, and to erase the reflection in the mirror, shatter its hold over her. Her clenched fist struck the glass, the sound of shattering shards mingling with her cries. Pain bloomed instantly, sharp and hot, as fragments of the mirror embedded themselves in her knuckles and palms. Blood streaked down her hand, warm and slick, dripping onto the wooden floor in crimson splatters.

The mirror was gone, its frame empty save for icicles of glass clinging to the edges. But in the shards scattered across the floor, she could still see her reflection. Hundreds of tiny Harpers stared back at her, their faces fragmented and warped, but each one smiling that same malevolent smile.

Her chest heaved as she staggered back, cradling her bleeding hand. The room seemed to tilt, the walls took a step closer, the air heavy with the scent of blood. The shards on the floor glinted like eyes in the dim light, and in each one, her reflection's grin seemed to mock her.

"No," Harper whispered, her voice shaking as she backed toward the desk. "No, you're not real. You're not real!" But the reflections remained, their expressions unchanging, their presence antagonistic.

Her gaze fell to one of the larger shards near her feet. The jagged edge gleamed in the lamplight, catching her eye and holding it there. Something inside her shifted, a dark clarity overtaking the panic. She bent down slowly, her fingers trembling as they closed around the shard. It was cold, the edges biting into her already raw skin. She straightened, holding it in front of her like a weapon.

She knew what to do. How to write her own ending.

The laughter started softly, a low, guttural sound that bubbled up from her chest. It didn't feel like her laughter; it felt foreign, alien, as though it had been planted inside her. The sound grew louder, more frenzied, until it echoed through the room, bouncing off the walls and mingling with the whispers that seemed to rise from the mirror shards.

Harper's smile matched the one in the fragments now, her lips stretching into a grin that felt unnatural, almost painful. "You can't have me?" she said, her voice thick with manic glee. "You cannot control me! I will never come back. I have free will and this, is my choice."

With a sudden, violent motion, she drove the shard into her left eye. Pain exploded, a white-hot flash that consumed her senses, but she didn't stop. The laughter poured from her lips, uncontrollable, as she pulled the shard free and stabbed again, this time into her right eye. Blood streamed down her face, hot and sticky, mingling with her tears and pooling at her feet as she dropped to her knees, clutching the bloodied shard in her hand.

The world went dark. In the blackness behind her ruined eyes, as blood pumped and her life force ebbed, she saw the lodge, its silhouette once burned into her mind began to fade.

The whispers too, became faint, as though someone was slowly turning down the volume and a kind of peace settled on Harper, wrapping around her like a cocoon. Harper's laughter turned to sobs, then back to laughter, the sound spiraling into a final rampage of madness before silence fell upon her.

She lay there alone, blind and broken, the shard slipping from her fingers. Her breathing was ragged, each inhale a struggle.

Her final thoughts were of how they'd find her. Whoever

cared enough to look. They'd pity her, of course they would, and theorize that she took her life whilst in the grip of whatever psychosis they had a label for.

But she would die knowing her own truth. She had left this world of her own free will, finally taken control and denied the lodge the one thing it desired, craved, needed. Something precious that belonged only to her.

Her soul.

EPILOGUE

I watch, as I always have, as I always will. They come to me, drawn by something they cannot name, something hidden in the hollow spaces of their lives. I do not need to summon them. The broken ones find me, as they have for decades. They stumble through the snow, seeking solace, seeking peace, and yet all I offer is truth. The kind of truth that shatters them, that strips them down to their marrow, leaving nothing but the raw, quivering remains of what they once were.

Harper was one of my finest. She fought me, oh, how she fought. A worthy adversary and for the first time, I admit defeat.

But she's not my concern now. No, my attention has shifted to the new ones. The man and the woman. They stepped through my doors so innocently, so naively, their arms wrapped around one another as if their love could shield them. I let them believe it, of course. That is how it always begins. A warm hearth, a soft bed, the illusion of safety. They've settled in now, unpacked their bags, laughed over a bottle of wine in the dim glow of the firelight. But the cracks are there, just beneath the surface. I can taste them.

The man, with his restless eyes and weight of

disappointment heavy on his shoulders, tries to mask his discontent. But I see how he clenches his fists when he thinks she isn't looking, how he grinds his teeth in his sleep. His dreams are mine now, and I fill them with whispers, faint but insistent. They tell him of betrayal, of lies he hasn't yet uncovered but is certain must exist. I feed his paranoia, and it grows like a cancer, spreading through his mind until every glance, every word she speaks is suspect.

The woman is quieter, softer in her unraveling. She sits by the window during the day, staring out at the snow, her thoughts drifting to places she'd rather not revisit. Her past is a fertile ground for me, rich with guilt and regret. I bring it all to the surface, showing her the faces of those she's lost, the opportunities she's squandered. At night, when the house is silent, she hears footsteps in the hall, whispers from the walls. She tells herself it's the wind, but I know better. She's already begun to doubt her own mind.

They argue now. Small things at first—the way he leaves his shoes by the door, the way she hums when she's anxious. But the tension builds, each sharp word another crack in the fragile veneer of their relationship. I press on those cracks, widening them, feeding their insecurities until they no longer see each other as they once did. The love they brought with them has begun to curdle, souring under my influence.

The woman tried to leave once. She stood at the front door, her hand on the knob, but I whispered to her. I told her she wouldn't make it. The snow is too deep, the woods too dark, the cold too bitter. And she believed me. She always will.

The man found one of my marks today, carved into the baseboard in the study. He traced it with trembling fingers, his breath hitching as he felt its power. He doesn't understand it yet, but he will. I've planted the seed of obsession in him, and it will grow unchecked. Soon, he'll be carving his own symbols, marking his territory as if it belongs to him. But it doesn't. It belongs to me. They all do.

They're losing themselves now, piece by piece. The man's laughter has taken on a brittle edge, the sound of a mind fraying at the seams. The woman cries in the night, though she doesn't know why. I've begun to show them what they fear most, the things they've buried deep inside themselves. Their reflections no longer match their faces. The man saw his own eyes hollowed out in the bathroom mirror this morning, and the woman swears she heard her mother's voice calling to her from the attic. I give them these gifts, and they unravel beautifully.

But I am not content to simply let them drift apart. I have plans for them. The man will hear her voice when she's not there, calling to him from rooms she's never entered. He'll find notes in her handwriting, cruel things she never wrote, accusations and betrayals that will twist his thoughts until he can no longer bear the sight of her. The woman will find his belongings moved, strange stains on his clothing, objects she's never seen hidden in his drawers. I'll fill her with suspicion, make her question whether the man she loves is capable of things she'd never imagined.

And when their trust is shattered, I'll isolate them further. I'll whisper to him that she's plotting against him, that she's dangerous. I'll show her visions of him standing over her with a knife, his face blank and unfeeling. I'll weave their nightmares into reality, blurring the line between what is imagined and what is real. They'll lash out at one another, each convinced the other is the enemy, until the moment one of them breaks.

Soon, they'll turn on each other. They always do. It's inevitable. I'll make her see him as a monster, and I'll make him see her as a traitor. And when the final blow comes, when one of them breaks the other, I'll be there, wrapping myself around them like a shroud, feeding on their despair, their rage, their anguish. They will belong to me, just as all the others have.

And then, I will wait. Another will come, drawn by the same unnamable force, the same irresistible pull. They always come. The broken ones, the desperate ones, the ones who think they can escape what haunts them. They don't realize that what they're running from isn't behind them. It's ahead, waiting, here within my walls.

Come, pay me a visit sometime.

I will devour everything you are.

And then I will take your soul.

THE END

A NOTE FROM THE PUBLISHER

Thank you for reading! We hope you enjoyed this book. If it left an impression, we'd love for you to share your thoughts in a review on Amazon—your feedback helps other readers discover it too.

At **Black Swan Digital**, we're redefining storytelling with fresh, exciting releases at unbeatable prices. Plus, our community gets **exclusive discounts and early access** to new books. Want in? Join our mailing list here and never miss a great read!

Printed in Great Britain
by Amazon

61492682R00160